Laura Martin writes historical romances with an adventurous undercurrent. When not writing she spends her time working as a doctor in Cambridgeshire, where she lives with her husband. In her spare moments Laura loves to lose herself in a book, and has been known to read from cover to cover in a single day when the story is particularly gripping. She also loves to travel—especially visiting historical sites and far-flung shores.

Also by Laura Martin

Under a Desert Moon
Governess to the Sheikh
A Ring for the Pregnant Debutante
An Unlikely Debutante
An Earl to Save Her Reputation

The Eastway Cousins miniseries

An Earl in Want of a Wife
Heiress on the Run

Discover more at millsandboon.co.uk.

THE VISCOUNT'S RUNAWAY WIFE

Laura Martin

This book is produced from independently certified FSC™ paper
to ensure responsible forest management.

For more information visit www.harpercollins.co.uk/green

Printed and bound in Spain
by CPI, Barcelona

MILLS & BOON

First Published in Great Britain 2018
by Mills & Boon, an imprint of HarperCollins*Publishers*
1 London Bridge Street, London, SE1 9GF

© 2018 Laura Martin

ISBN: 978-0-263-93321-5

For George, my little warrior.

Prologue

Sussex—1814

> *Dear Husband,*
> *I am sorry. Please do not look for me.*
> *Your wife,*
> *Lady Sedgewick*

Chapter One

London—1815

Oliver paused before entering the butcher's shop situated a few streets north of Russell Square. In the past year he'd been to many places a titled gentleman wouldn't normally venture in search of his missing wife, but never in his life had he had cause to go into a butcher's shop before.

Regarding the hanging cuts of meat with curiosity, he pushed open the door, looking up as the bell tinkled, and walked in. A large man wielding an oversized meat cleaver flashed him a smile, indicating he would be with him once he'd finished slicing the half a pig that was hanging over the rear of the counter.

'How can I help you, sir?' the butcher asked as he wiped his bloodied hands on a white rag. 'Got some lovely fresh pork if you're interested.'

Despite the man's words, Oliver could see the hint of mistrust in his eyes—the butcher knew already Oliver wasn't there to buy anything.

'I'm looking for my wife,' he said without any preamble. He'd been in similar situations hundreds of times over the last year and honed his speech to be concise and to the point.

The butcher frowned.

'I spoke to a delivery boy last week who thought he might have seen her in this area, most specifically in your shop.' Taking a miniature portrait from his pocket, he held it out to show the butcher. 'Her name is Lady Sedgewick, although she might be using a different name.'

Oliver watched the man closely and wondered if he saw the tiniest spark of recognition in his eyes.

'Name doesn't sound familiar,' the butcher said, buying himself some time.

'And the woman in the picture?'

'Why are you looking for her?'

Oliver felt his pulse quicken. Just over a year he'd been searching for Lucy, a year of disappointment and dead ends. Every time he thought he might be drawing closer it came to nothing, but perhaps he was finally getting somewhere.

'She's my wife.'

'Lots of reasons a wife might not want to be found by her husband.'

'I mean her no harm,' Oliver said and it was the truth. He'd never wanted to harm Lucy despite everything she'd put him through.

The butcher regarded him for some moments and then nodded as if satisfied.

'Looks a bit like a young woman who comes in once a week from the St Giles's Women's and Children's Foundation. I sell them our offcuts of meat at a reduced price.'

'Where is this Foundation?' Oliver asked, already knowing the answer, but hoping he was wrong.

'St Giles, of course,' the butcher said with a grin. 'Though, you'll need a guide if you want to get in and out of there in one piece.'

'Thank you for your help,' Oliver said, holding out a few coins for the man's trouble. The butcher pocketed them with a nod, then turned back to the pig carcase.

Stepping outside, Oliver took a moment to digest the information he'd just been given. In the year he'd been searching for her he'd imagined the worst, Lucy and their child dead in a ditch somewhere in the country, Lucy having to sell her body on the streets of London, his firstborn son growing up in the filthiest, most dangerous slums, but never had he considered St Giles.

It was a slum, of course, probably the most

notorious slum in London, but no outsiders ever ventured in, not if they wanted to leave again with their lives. He couldn't imagine how Lucy had ended up there, nor could he understand how living in St Giles could be better in any way than living a life of comfort as his wife.

During his years in the army Oliver had never shied away from dangerous skirmishes and he wasn't the sort of officer who stood back and allowed his troops to go into battle first. However, the thought of venturing into St Giles alone sent shivers down his spine. Nevertheless, he strode south. Today would be the day he found his wife and discovered what had happened to his son. Even if it meant navigating the treacherous, warren-like streets of the slum.

Just as he was about to skirt around the back of Montague House, the impressive building that housed the British Museum, he caught sight of a woman hurrying away from him down Montague Street. Her back was to him, but he felt his stomach clench in recognition. She was slender and clad in a brown woollen dress, skirts swishing about heavy and practical boots. The woman's hair was pulled back into a bun that rested at the base of her neck, wispy dark blonde tendrils had escaped and were coiling over her shoulders. It could be the back of a thousand women, perhaps a housekeeper or a shopkeeper's wife, but there was something about the way she carried herself, something about the way she walked.

'Don't be a fool,' he murmured to himself as he felt his feet changing direction. In the months after his wife had disappeared he had fancied he'd seen her everywhere: strolling through Hyde Park, on the other side of a crowded ballroom, even in the face of a serving girl at the local tavern near his country estate. A year ago he'd barely known his wife, he was hardly likely to recognise her from just the back of her head now. It was just because his hopes had been raised by the butcher—that was why he thought he was seeing her here.

Unable to listen to his own reason, Oliver picked up his pace. If he could just get in front of the woman, surreptitiously pause and turn to look at her, he would be able to satisfy himself that it wasn't Lucy without frightening an innocent young woman. Trying not to draw attention to himself, he strode along the pavement, dodging the couples walking arm in arm and the groups of men deep in conversation.

The woman in front of him crossed the street, heading away from the more salubrious area of Russell Square and towards St Giles. His hopes soared and he stepped out on to the road, racing for the pavement opposite. He was only four feet behind her now, almost close enough to reach out and touch her arm.

Contemplating whether to call her name and see if she reacted, Oliver froze as the woman glanced back over her shoulder before crossing another road. At first she didn't see him, instead focusing on the carriage that was meandering down the street, but then the movement from his direction must have caught her eye and she turned a fraction of an inch more. She stiffened, her hands bunching in the coarse wool of her skirts, her mouth opening in a silent exclamation of shock. Though he couldn't see her face clearly, her reaction was enough to tell him he'd finally found her, he'd finally found his wife.

'Lucy,' he growled, lurching forward as she darted from the pavement and into the road. She had picked up her skirts and was running faster than was seemly for a wife of a viscount, but that shouldn't surprise him. 'Stop right there.' He barked the order, just as he would to the men under his command during his time on the Peninsula. Lucy took no notice, instead vaulting over a pile of horse manure and rounding the corner with surprising speed.

In a fair race on a different terrain Oliver would have had no trouble outpacing his wife, but here her smaller size worked to her advantage. She was able to weave through the other pedestrians quickly and by the time they'd reached the outer edge of St Giles's slums Oliver had only gained a few feet.

'Lady Sedgewick,' Oliver bellowed, 'I demand you stop running and face me.'

His words had no impact whatsoever. Oliver slowed a little as he entered the narrower streets. Buildings rose on either side, shadowing the area below from the sun, and although the street ahead of him was deserted save for Lucy's running figure he could feel eyes on him, hidden observers who could mean him no good.

The sensible thing would be to turn back, to retreat to the wider, safer streets and wait for Lucy to emerge. Oliver dismissed the idea straight away; a year he'd been made to wait to confront his wife about her disappearance with their newborn son—he wasn't going to let a bad reputation stop him now.

'I'm coming for you, Lucy,' he shouted as he darted forward, seeing the hem of his wife's skirt swish around the corner, following her trail like a hound with the scent of a fox in his nostrils.

He leapt over a man sprawling drunk in a doorway, muscled through a group of men arguing over a game of dice and ignored the catcalls from women far past their prime, but making a valiant effort to hide the fact beneath a thick layer of powder.

Just as they exited the narrow streets into a courtyard Oliver lunged forward and caught Lucy by the arm.

'Will you stop?' he barked, holding her gently but firmly by the arm. She wriggled, her eyes refusing to meet his, until he pinned her against a wall.

'Is this man bothering you, miss?' A quiet voice came from somewhere behind Oliver. He glanced over his shoulder to see a grubby middle-aged man approaching. Lucy's defender only had about half his teeth and those he did retain were a varying shade of brown. He was dressed in an assortment of dirt-coloured clothes and Oliver could smell the years of ingrained grime. All this he observed in an instant, before his eyes came to rest on the small knife cradled in the man's palm.

Looking back at his wife, he raised an eyebrow. 'Am I bothering you?' he asked.

'Yes,' she spat, wriggling again, fire and passion flaring in her eyes.

'I think you should step away from Miss Caroline.'

'Miss Caroline?' Oliver laughed harshly. 'That's the name you're going by now?'

Out of the corner of his eye he saw the man with the knife step even closer and watched Lucy's face as she contemplated whether to let him attack her husband. Eventually, after too long a pause for Oliver's liking, she sighed.

'Please don't exert yourself on my account, Bert.'

'Are you sure, Miss Caroline? Won't be more than a moment's work to stick him and roll him into the river.'

'Although quite an effort to transport me there,' Oliver murmured. 'The river must be at least fifteen minutes away.'

'That's what the good Lord invented wheelbarrows for.'

'I'm sure that's the exact purpose he had in mind.'

'I'll be just over here—shout if you change your mind,' Bert said, doffing his cap to Lucy.

'What do you want?' Lucy rasped as Bert meandered away.

Oliver blinked in surprise. All the times he'd imagined their reunion he'd pictured her contrite or ashamed or remorseful. He hadn't ever imagined his quiet, dutiful wife to be annoyed and confrontational.

'Do you really need to ask me that?'

She looked at him then, with the large brown eyes he'd remembered even when all her other features had begun to fade in his mind.

'I want to know where my son is and what you've been doing all this time.' He said it harshly, a year of anger and bitterness pushed into one sentence, but he never meant to make Lucy cry. She burst into tears, big racking sobs that pierced a tiny hole in his armour and headed straight for his heart.

Sniffling, Lucy tried to bring herself under control. She hadn't meant to cry, hadn't wanted to show such weakness in front of her husband, but at the mention of their son she'd been unable to hold back the tears. Even though it had been over a year since her son's death, she still couldn't think of him without tears springing to her eyes. He'd been so little, so fragile and in need of her protection, a chunk of her heart had died alongside him.

'David's dead,' she said, knowing this wasn't the way she should break the news of their son's death to her husband, but aware she'd kept it from him for too long already. In truth, she'd meant to write a week or so after David's passing, but she hadn't been able to find the words and a week had turned to a month, which had turned to a year and still she hadn't let Oliver know.

'Dead?' her husband said, letting go of his grip on her arm and stepping away. He nodded once, and then again, as if this was what he'd expected. As Lucy looked at his face she saw it was completely blank, completely unreadable. He looked as though someone had pulled his world out from under his feet and he didn't know how to react.

'I'm sorry,' she said. She meant it, too. She wasn't sorry for running away, but she was sorry for everything that came after. Not letting Oliver know she was safe, not telling him when their son died, not including him in her decision to stay away, to build a new life for herself.

'Come,' Oliver said, his voice gruff. 'I'm taking you home.'

'This is my home.'

He looked around him, frowning as he took in the bedraggled children, skinny and dirty, running through the courtyard. Lucy could still see all the desperation and dirt and disease—she didn't think any number of years spent in the slums would make her immune to it—but now she could also see the people underneath.

'A whole year, Lucy, with not a single word. You owe me this much.'

She opened her mouth to protest but saw the steely determination on his face.

'Come.' He took her by the arm, his fingers gentle but firm, and began to lead her back the way they'd come.

'There's a shortcut to St James's Square,' she said as they walked. She'd often avoided that part of London, always knowing there was a chance Oliver could be in residence at Sedgewick House, but she knew all the routes through St Giles after spending so long living here and knew which ones would take them most directly to the residential square.

Laughing, he shook his head. 'I don't know what other criminals you've got lurking around corners ready to rescue you. We're getting straight out of here.'

'It's not that bad,' Lucy mumbled.

'It's the most deprived area in London.'

She couldn't deny the truth in his words. She'd said as much to the governors of the women's and children's Foundation she helped at during one of their biannual funding meetings. Here, in St Giles, the destitute mixed with criminals and prostitutes and, most heartbreaking of all, the shoeless children who ran wild through the streets, willing to do anything for a hot meal or a few coins.

'I can walk by myself,' she said, wriggling free of the restraining hand on her arm.

'I don't trust you,' Oliver barked. That was fair, she supposed. They hadn't known each other well during their short marriage and her behaviour over the last year hadn't endeared her to her husband.

They marched rather than walked, Lucy having to take two steps to every one of Oliver's long strides, and within two minutes they were leaving the narrow, shadowed streets of St Giles and emerging back on to the main thoroughfare.

Hailing a hackney carriage, Oliver almost stepped out into the path of the horses, but dutifully the coachman pulled to a stop just in front of them.

'St James's Square, number twelve,' Oliver instructed, before bundling her inside and following quickly.

'I…' Lucy began to speak, but Oliver held up an authoritative hand.

'I've waited over a year to hear why you abducted our son and disappeared without a word. We are not going to have this conversation in a carriage.'

'I just…'

'I said no. Whatever it is can wait for twenty minutes.'

Disgruntled, Lucy settled herself back against the padded bench, turning her body away from her husband and looking out the window instead. Ten months she'd lived as Oliver's wife, although for almost nine of those months he had been away at war. She barely knew the man, but that didn't mean she had to tolerate such rudeness.

As they weaved through the streets Lucy recognised most of the landmarks. She'd lived in London for the past year and although she didn't have much reason to set foot in the more elite areas, she had passed through on occasion. She fidgeted as she watched the carriage round the corner into St James's Square, knowing the next few hours were going to be difficult and really she only had herself to blame.

'Come,' Oliver ordered as the carriage stopped in front of a white-painted town house. It was immaculately kept and for a house in the middle of the city huge in size. They could house twenty mothers and children comfortably in the space, maybe more, but instead it was the domain of a single man and a few servants. It seemed such a waste.

The door was opened promptly by a smartly dressed young man with a scar running from eyebrow to chin.

'I trust you had a pleasant afternoon, my lord,'

the young butler said, sparing a look for Lucy, but valiantly trying to hide his curiosity.

'Yes, thank you, Parker. We will be in my study. I don't want to be disturbed.'

'Yes, my lord.'

And with that Oliver had whisked her into his study, closed the door and clicked the lock. Lucy swallowed, eyeing the windows which were all firmly closed. She shouldn't be afraid—for all his faults, her husband was a noble man; he wouldn't hurt her. At least she was reasonably sure he wouldn't.

'Sit,' he instructed, motioning towards two comfortable leather armchairs positioned in front of the unlit fire.

She complied immediately. For all her strong-willed dislike of being told what to do, she recognised now they were completely in her husband's domain. For the next few hours at least she would have to remember he was in charge here.

Watching nervously as Oliver stalked about the room, selecting two glasses and pouring two generous measures of whisky, Lucy was surprised when he set one in front of her. Never in their short marriage had he invited her to join him for a drink, but she supposed then they were occupying more traditional roles of gentleman

and his wife. Now it was clear he had no idea
how to regard her.

'Talk,' he commanded eventually, settling
back into his chair.

Chapter Two

She looked nervous, Oliver thought with grim satisfaction. Drumming her fingers on the fine crystal glass he'd just placed in her hand and shifting her weight in the armchair every few seconds. In truth, Lady Sedgewick looked as though she wanted to be anywhere but here with him.

'What do you want me to say?' she asked, raising her dark eyes to meet his.

He felt a surge of irritation, but tried to conceal it. He'd been raised to be civil even in the most trying of circumstances. And reuniting with his estranged wife could certainly be described as trying.

'I want to know everything,' he said calmly. 'What happened with the birth of our son? Why you left. Why you stayed away. What you've been doing all this time.'

Sighing, Lucy took a gulp of whisky, unable to hide her discomfort as the amber liquid burned her throat.

'I'm sure you've worked most of the details out by now,' she said softly.

'But I want to hear it from you.'

Of course he'd imagined a thousand scenarios in the year he'd been searching for her. An inappropriate lover, a nervous breakdown and, in his more desperate moments, even more unlikely stories involving French spies and a need to serve her country. Despite all his searching, all the time and effort he'd put into finding her the last year, he still didn't know the truth behind why she'd disappeared.

'I got scared,' she said simply. Nothing so extravagant as French spies, then.

'Scared?'

There was a long pause before Lucy continued. As he waited for her to speak, Oliver realised his wife had changed immeasurably in the time she'd been absent. Not that he could pretend he knew her very well when they'd been married. Twice they'd met before they'd said their vows, two awkward meetings where neither had revealed much. And then he'd only lived with Lucy for a month after their wedding before being called back to the Peninsula. All the same, she'd certainly matured in the time they'd spent apart. Gone was the shy, meek debutante and in her place was a poised and almost worldly young woman. It appeared his wife had matured in her absence, in more ways than one.

'We barely knew one another,' Lucy said eventually. That he couldn't deny.

'True.'

'I loved David,' she said quietly. 'I loved him from the first time I felt him kick inside me, maybe even before that. I spent hours dreaming of what he would be like, what he would enjoy and who he would resemble. When he was born…' She trailed off.

Oliver had spoken to the doctor who'd been present at his son's birth. Apparently it had been a difficult labour and for a while it had seemed like their son would not come, but eventually, after many hours, Lucy had given birth.

'He was so beautiful—' her voice was barely more than a whisper '—so perfect in every single way.'

That wasn't how the doctor had put it. *'Characteristic facial features'* had been mentioned a number of times and *'a likelihood of mental difficulties'*.

'The doctor commiserated with me when he looked David over, told me that there was no

reason I couldn't have a healthy child next time.'
There was bitterness in her voice as she recalled
the words.

Lucy glanced up at him and he could see she
was on the verge of tears again, but no matter
how difficult this was for her he had to know
what had happened next.

'I lay there with our son resting on my breast,
cuddled in all warm and safe once the doctor had
gone, and I started to realise that he wouldn't
be the only one judging our son, finding him
wanting.'

'You can't mean…' Oliver said, his eyes widening.

'I didn't know you,' Lucy said quietly, unable
to meet his eye. 'I knew what most men do with
their offspring when they don't view them as
completely healthy—they send them off to be
raised by another family, sometimes even deny
their existence.'

'So you left, before even finding out what my
reaction might be.'

'I couldn't risk it. I couldn't risk you taking
my son away from me.'

'Our son,' Oliver murmured. 'He was my son,
as well.'

'I'm sorry,' she whispered. 'It was cruel of me,

I know that. I knew that at the time, but I had to protect him.'

'You didn't have to protect him from me.'

She regarded him calmly, searching his face as if trying to see if there was truth in his words. Oliver felt a surge of anger. She shouldn't be judging him. He'd done nothing wrong. He hadn't run off with their son without any explanation.

He stood, needing to put some space between them, and busied himself adjusting the clock on the mantelpiece. The seconds ticked past in silence as Oliver struggled to regain control of himself. Outwardly nothing in his expression or stance changed, but inwardly he had felt a tight coil of frustration and anger ready to explode. Now, breathing deeply, he forced himself to remain calm. Nothing would be gained from showing his estranged wife how much she had hurt him, how much her betrayal still affected every aspect of his life.

'Then what happened?' he asked, returning to his seat, motioning for Lucy to continue.

'Does it matter?'

'Yes,' he barked sharply. 'It matters to me. What happened next?'

'I had a little money so I made my way to London. I knew I couldn't seek refuge with anyone I knew. I had to go where no one knew me.'

She was making it sound as though she'd been running from a monster, when in truth he didn't think he'd ever raised his voice towards her or spoken a single word in anger.

'I ended up in St Giles.' Lucy grimaced. 'The first few days were not easy, but then Mary found me. She helps to run a home for women and children and she took us in.'

'David was still alive?' It sounded strange to be saying his son's name after so long of not even knowing what Lucy had called their child. The words almost caught in his throat, but he managed to force them out, gripping the back of his chair for physical support as he said them.

Lucy nodded, pressing her lips together. 'He seemed healthy enough the first couple of weeks, thriving and growing, but then he deteriorated quickly.' Her voice quivered, but she managed to go on. 'I'm told it is quite common in those born with similar conditions to our son to have problems with their hearts and chests. David became unwell and although we saw doctors, they could do nothing. He died when he was three weeks old.'

He watched as she suppressed a sob, swallowing a couple of times and taking a deep breath to compose herself.

'Where is he buried?' Oliver asked bluntly.

Looking up at him with wide eyes, Lucy shook her head before answering.

'He did get a proper burial?' Oliver interrupted, his heart sinking at the thought of his only child being consigned to a pauper's grave.

'I used the last of my money. He's buried in the churchyard of St Giles in the Fields.'

He nodded grimly. Not a peaceful resting place for an innocent young boy, among the plague victims and the executed criminals, but at least he'd had a proper burial.

'You'll take me there this week.'

A spark of indignation flared in his wife's eyes, but he watched as quickly she quashed it and nodded. 'As you wish.'

Visiting his son's grave would be difficult, but he owed it to the child he'd never held in his arms to at least see where he was buried.

Smoothing her skirts down, Lucy stood, placing her almost-full glass on the small table beside her.

'I should be getting back,' she said, inclining her head and taking a step towards the door.

For a long moment Oliver was too stunned to do or say anything. He'd barely begun questioning her, barely scratched the surface of what had become of his wife over the past year. All she'd revealed was the bare bones of the story of how and why she'd fled after the birth of their son. He needed to know so much more.

'Sit down,' he said, catching her arm as she edged past him.

For the first time since he'd cornered her in St Giles, her eyes came up to meet his and Oliver felt a painful flash of memory. He'd barely known Lucy on their wedding day, but when she'd walked down the aisle of the church and turned to face him in front of the altar, he'd felt a hopeful stirring deep inside him. He'd wondered if perhaps their marriage could be about more than convenience, more than producing the heir he so desperately needed and having a wife at home to look after the estate. Quickly he suppressed the memory, setting his mouth into a hard line.

'You're my wife, Lucy. I'm not going to let you just walk out of my life again.'

There was panic in her eyes, the same feral expression as an animal that knows it is cornered.

'You can't just keep me here,' she said softly, as if she knew it wasn't true.

'Twenty minutes,' Oliver said brusquely. 'That's how long you've been in my house. Over a year I've been searching for you.'

'What if I promise not to disappear again?' she said quietly. 'I can give you my address.'

'I don't trust you, Lucy.'

She chewed her lip and Oliver wondered if she had something or someone she wanted to get back for or if she just couldn't bear to be in his company any longer. The idea that she might have a lover was like a dagger to his heart and quickly he had to push the thought away before it did any more damage to his emotions.

Before he could stop himself, he spoke. 'Come,' he said brusquely, 'let me show you to your room. We can continue our discussion at dinner.'

Although they had been married for ten months before Lucy had fled, she hadn't before been to Sedgewick House in London. His main residence was Sedgewick Place, a sprawling country estate in Sussex, and that had been where they'd married and spent the time together before he'd been recalled back to the army. Since she was pregnant by the time he'd left, she had decided to spend the Season in the country rather than travelling up to London, only to have to return to Sussex for her confinement.

With a guiding hand resting in the small of her back, he felt Lucy stiffen, but she allowed him to show her the way out of the room and up the stairs.

'Your bedroom,' Oliver said, opening the door.

He watched her face carefully, noting the widening of her eyes as she realised it was the bedroom of the lady of the house, complete with connecting door to his own room. 'Take some time to get settled in. Dinner is at eight.'

Stepping out, he left her alone, keen to put some distance between them. The revelations of the afternoon had given him a lot to think about. Oliver wasn't the sort of man who made any decisions quickly and he would appreciate having a few hours to himself before he resumed questioning Lucy. One thing was for certain—he wasn't going to let her slip out of his life again and if that meant keeping a close watch on her these next few days, then that was what he'd do.

Sinking down on to the bed, Lucy glanced around the room. It was rather oppressively decorated with dark furniture and busy flowery wallpaper. Quite the change from her room back in St Giles. She had no doubt Oliver's late mother had chosen the decor for the bedroom; it was not a room made for comfort and her mother-in-law had not been one for relaxing.

Quickly she stood, refusing to let the despair she could feel creeping in overtake her. There would be a way out, all she had to do was find it. She sympathised with Oliver, felt dreadful about how she had treated him and understood his desire to know everything that had happened since she'd run away, but she just couldn't stay here. She was needed at the Foundation; people were relying on her—she couldn't just disappear. With a shudder, she wondered what her husband's long-term plan was—surely he couldn't mean for her to stay with him indefinitely. Their lives had changed too much for that to work. Plenty of couples led completely separate lives. There really was no need for them to become entangled once again.

With a glance at the window she shook her head. There was no reason to consider acrobatics when she could easily just walk out the front door. She hadn't heard Oliver turn the key in the lock; she wasn't his prisoner here. All she needed to do was open the door, stroll down the hallway, descend the stairs and slip out the front door. She'd send him a note, of course, perhaps arrange a meeting in a more neutral environment to resolve their remaining issues.

Taking a deep breath, Lucy opened the door and stepped out into the hall.

'Good afternoon, Lady Sedgewick,' a smartly dressed young footman said, giving a formal little bow.

Lucy's eyes narrowed as her heart sank. Oliver

had posted a guard at her door. A guard. Someone to make sure she didn't sneak away. It was insulting and showed her true position in the household: she was a prisoner.

With her cheeks reddening, she conceded that she *had* planned to slip away, but still, how dare her husband send a footman to monitor her movements.

'Is there anything I can get you?'

'Some tea, and water to wash my face.' She hoped he would step away, hurry downstairs and organise the things she had requested, but he didn't move a single inch.

'Of course, Lady Sedgewick. I'll arrange for them immediately.'

Neither of them moved and Lucy raised an imperious eyebrow. She had never been one to talk down to servants, always seen them as the hard-working, genuine people they were, but she wasn't above a bit of play-acting if it meant securing her freedom.

'Immediately,' she said, injecting a sharp note into her voice.

He nodded but still didn't move. Lucy hated any kind of confrontation, but a year living in St Giles had taught her how to look confident even when scared or uncertain.

'Please don't keep me waiting…'

'Peterson, Lady Sedgewick,' the footman supplied with a smile, as if oblivious to the tension between them. 'You'll have your tea and hot water in no time.'

'Thank you,' she murmured, giving in and spinning on her heel, closing the door firmly behind her. No doubt Peterson had strict orders from her husband not to leave his observation post and Oliver was not a man people seemed to disobey lightly.

Sighing, she regarded the room, crossing to the bed to flop down on the floral covers, but hesitated just as her body began to sink down.

They were only on the first floor, barely ten feet from the ground. The window had a generous ledge outside and she was sure she would be able to lower herself down. The remaining drop would only be a few feet. She'd be at risk of a twisted ankle, but nothing more serious, and if she landed correctly she might even get away unscathed. From what she could see there was a garden gate, leading to what she assumed would be a side passage and an easy stroll back to the street.

With a glance at the door, aware that her tea and hot water could arrive at any moment, she dashed to the window and pushed it up. To her relief it was unlocked and, before she could talk herself out of it, she had one leg over the casement and resting on the ledge. The skirts of her practical woollen dress tangled a little around her knees, but one swift tug and she was free, swinging the other leg out the window.

Cautiously she looked down. The garden was deserted, the small patio beneath her devoid of any furniture and the neatly trimmed lawn unbroken by any flower beds. It meant there was nowhere to hide, but if she dropped to the ground she could quickly skirt around the house to the side gate and let herself on to the street.

For a moment she hesitated. Perhaps she did owe it to Oliver to stay, to explain a little more about what had happened this past year. She'd been cruel and selfish to remain distant for so long, but truly what did he think they had to gain by renewing their relationship now? No, she'd escape from here, from the pressure he was putting on her to explain, from the guilt that was threatening to destroy her from the inside. Once she was back on more neutral ground she would consider how best to make amends to her husband, but she couldn't think with his dark eyes boring into her, couldn't reason when he fixed her with that haughty stare.

Before she lost her nerve, Lucy manoeuvred herself first to her hands and knees and then eased her body over the edge of the ledge. As she dangled, her fingers gripping the rough stone, she wondered if she had miscalculated. The drop seemed further than she had first imagined, but knowing there was no way she would be able to pull herself up again, she closed her eyes and let go.

She plummeted for a fraction of a second before coming to a juddering halt. A strong hand gripped her arm, stopping her from falling to the stone patio below. Lucy opened her eyes, looking up into the frowning face of her husband.

'Peterson, in here now,' Oliver shouted, his fingers digging into her flesh as he held her firmly by the wrist.

He said nothing more as the footman joined him at the window and together they hauled her back inside. Lucy stumbled as he set her on her feet and immediately Oliver's arm was around her waist, guiding her to the bed.

Only once they were alone, the door firmly closed behind them, did he open his mouth.

'That was foolish,' he said quietly.

Lucy looked down, unable to meet his eye. It *had* been foolish, but she was desperate.

'I had a man under my command on the Continent, James Havers,' Oliver said, his voice betraying an uncharacteristic amount of emotion.

'He was young, barely twenty when he joined. One day, in the heat of battle, he was trampled by a horse.' Oliver grimaced. 'Our own cavalry. His leg was broken in three places.'

Lucy tried to swallow, but realised her throat was too dry.

'The surgeons tried to set it, but they couldn't. Three days later they amputated, above the knee. Two weeks after that he was dead. The stump had festered.'

Unable to look away Lucy glimpsed a hint of pain in her husband's eyes. She had always thought of him as cold and aloof, but there was no doubt he'd cared for the young man who'd died. She suspected he'd cared for all the men under his command.

'Havers could not help what happened to him. You can,' he said brusquely. 'I do not want to see you putting yourself in such danger again.'

He left, without looking at her again, closing the door softly behind him despite the heat of emotion that had been in his voice.

As she sank to the bed, her whole body shaking at the realisation of what she could have done to herself, Lucy found herself staring at the door Oliver had just left through. She realised she didn't know anything about her husband, at least not anything that wasn't common knowledge among the rest of society, as well.

A few minutes later a pretty young maid bustled into the room, but Lucy barely noticed.

Chapter Three

Oliver stood stiffly by the window, regarding the comings and goings of the street below as he waited for his wife. She was late, but that was hardly unexpected, probably trying to work out a way to swap identities with the maid and escape the house that way.

As the door opened Oliver felt his heart skip a beat in his chest. Gone was the worn, brown woollen dress, gone was the sensible bun and slightly grubby visage, and in their place the Viscountess he remembered.

'Sorry to keep you waiting,' Lucy said, her voice not containing even a hint of remorse.

Oliver had to suppress an unexpected smile. Nearly two years ago he'd asked his mother to find him a suitable bride. With his father and two older brothers dead from a particularly virulent fever, Oliver had unexpectedly inherited the title, land and responsibilities he'd never imagined would be his. Aware his career in the army wasn't normal for a viscount, he'd realised he would need to start fathering some heirs just in case he, too, was taken from earth before his time. Too busy, and often a continent away, to search for himself, he'd asked his mother to make a list of suitable candidates. Lucy had been at the top. His mother had described her as respectable, docile and amiable. Looking at her now, he thought she might look respectable once again, but certainly not docile or amiable.

'Shall we eat?' Oliver asked, holding out his arm.

She hesitated before taking it, but eventually placed her gloved hand on his jacket.

As they walked through to the dining room, Oliver glanced at his estranged wife out of the corner of his eye. She'd always been pretty, in an unassuming way, but when they'd married she'd been young, only nineteen. The girl who'd walked down the aisle had blossomed into a beautiful young woman and Oliver was remembering why he had dreamed about her every night of their separation for the first few months.

'We need to talk about the future,' Lucy said quietly but firmly as she took a spoonful of soup. 'And the past.'

'Why dwell on it?'

He levelled her with a cool stare, only relenting when she hastily diverted her eyes and focused once again on the bowl in front of her.

'We haven't lived as husband and wife for a whole year. It seems silly to take up the pretence again.'

'But we are married, so *not* living as husband and wife would be more unnatural,' Oliver shot back.

'I'm sure we've both moved on with our lives…'

'I haven't,' Oliver said bluntly. 'A year ago you left and an entire year I've been searching for you.'

This at least made Lucy look up and meet his eye. He kept his expression neutral, determined not to let his wife see just how much her abandonment had hurt him.

'I'm sorry,' Lucy said softly and this time Oliver could see she genuinely meant it.

They sat in silence for some minutes, waiting as the next course was served. Then Lucy pushed on.

'What did you tell everyone about me?' she asked, lifting her head to look him in the eye.

'What do you think I said?' he asked.

'I thought perhaps you'd tell everyone I'd died in childbirth.'

'That would have been too easy.'

She nodded. 'So what does everyone think?'

He shrugged. 'Most people don't ask. They whisper in corners about my mysterious wife, wonder if I have you locked in a tower in deepest Sussex or if you are too mad or melancholic to be allowed out into society.'

'And those that do ask?'

'I tell them that you have been unwell.'

'Even after all this time?'

Oliver fixed her with a stony stare. 'I knew I would find you, Lucy, even if it took ten years.'

Her cheeks flushed and she looked hurriedly away.

'We could…' She paused as if summoning up the courage to continue. 'We could get divorced.'

Trying to suppress the snort of laughter, Oliver grimaced. 'Why would we want to do that?'

Divorce was uncommon and scandalous, requiring the husband to make an application to Parliament and for a private act to be passed. It was extremely costly and, if Oliver wasn't very much mistaken, required the husband to prove his wife had been adulterous. He'd only known one person to get divorced in his entire life and the woman's reputation had been completely ruined by the ensuing scandal. The gentleman in question had been left free to remarry, but Oliver had often wondered if the palaver had been worthwhile for the man.

'I know it is unheard of and damages reputations, but it is possible. It would allow you to remarry, get on with your life, start afresh.'

'I don't need to remarry. I already have a wife, Lucy.' He said it sternly.

'You truly mean for us to pick up where we left off a year ago.'

He nodded gravely. 'It will take time. I'm aware of that. The trust between us has been broken and it will need to be built up again, but I am willing to put in the work.'

'And what about me?' Lucy asked quietly.

'I'm not a monster, Lucy,' Oliver said. 'It won't be that terrible living with me as your husband.'

'I didn't mean…' She rallied. 'I have a life, responsibilities.'

'Ah, your Foundation.'

'It's important to me.' She bristled.

'Then I'm sure we can find some acceptable compromise.'

'I don't want a compromise,' she muttered, but Oliver chose to pretend he hadn't heard the mutinous comment.

'We *are* married, Lucy, and we shall be until one of us dies. It is best you accept things are going to change.' The words sounded harsh even to his own ears, but he wasn't about to pander to the whims of a woman who'd abandoned him a year ago and prevented him from ever knowing his firstborn son. 'I am your husband and you are my wife. That's the end of it.'

She studied him for over a minute in silence and Oliver could see his quiet perseverance was getting his point across. They were married, no matter how they felt about one another, and he didn't want to hear any more ridiculous suggestions about divorce or separation. He didn't plan on letting Lucy slip away, even if the next few weeks of adjustment were awkward and uncomfortable.

Lucy's eyes narrowed. It was hard to tell exactly what her husband was thinking. He always spoke in that same calm, infuriating voice, his words carefully considered and chosen. She had to admit she felt a little suspicious. An entire year she'd kept him in the dark as to her whereabouts, her safety, and now he was talking about compromise. Although in the short time they'd spent together after their wedding he had always appeared courteous and kind, if a little distant, Lucy had expected something different when he'd manhandled her into the carriage bound for St James's Square. Perhaps to be locked in a room and physically punished; perhaps to be denied her freedom to walk in the fresh air ever again. Instead he was suggesting they resume their roles as husband and wife, as if nothing much had happened in the intervening time.

'We barely know each other,' Lucy said quietly.

'Luckily we are not alone among married couples of the *ton*—many of them have spent less time together than us.'

She knew it was true. Many marriages were made for reasons of money or titles, with the husband and wife meeting only on important occasions. Theirs had always been a marriage of convenience, allowing Lucy to escape from an overbearing family and Oliver to gain a wife to give him heirs.

She swallowed, trying to suppress the heat in her cheeks despite knowing it was an uncontrollable reaction to what she was about to ask. 'What do you expect of me?'

His eyes met hers and she fancied she saw a flicker of amusement behind the serious façade. Surely he couldn't be enjoying this.

'I expect you to be my wife,' he said, his voice low.

A shiver ran down her spine, not of fear or dread, but anticipation. In the month after their marriage they had been intimate a number of times, as was expected of a husband and wife. Far from the painful, awkward encounters her married friends had whispered about, Lucy had found to her embarrassment she looked forward to the nights Oliver had quietly knocked on her door and slipped into her room.

'We will attend functions together, entertain here and at our home in Sussex, you will oversee the household…' he shrugged '…all the duties of a wife.'

Lucy felt the blush on her cheeks deepen. He wasn't even thinking about intimacy in the bedroom. She lifted her eyes to find he was looking intently at her, not even the hint of a smile present on his lips.

'And the Foundation?' Lucy asked, forcing herself to focus on what was important.

'You may visit, of course. Properly chaperoned.'

'Visit?'

'Yes, advise them on their books, play with the street children, whatever it is you do,' Oliver said with a dismissive wave of his hand.

'We keep dozens of families alive,' Lucy said, the pitch of her voice rising. 'Provide shelter and food and education to those who truly have nowhere else to turn.'

'I'm sure they managed perfectly well before you became involved—they will survive if you take a step back now you have other responsibilities.'

'I won't do it,' she said quietly.

'Won't do what?'

'Attend your parties, organise your household. Not if I can't continue with my work.'

Oliver sighed, rubbing his forehead with the fingertips of one hand as if he had a headache coming on.

'There will be changes to both our lives, Lucy,' he said quietly, his reasonable words and measured tone inflaming her spirit even further. 'We shall have to compromise.' Again he paused before pushing on, holding her gaze as he delivered his next words. 'And if you can't compromise, then I am your husband and you need to remember the *obey* part of your vows.'

She supposed she'd pushed too far, but his words inflamed her anger and reminded her why she'd stayed away for so long.

'They need me,' she said, forcing herself to be reasonable.

'Then you will have to find a way to make them need you less.' He held up his hands in a placating gesture as she pushed her chair away from the table. 'Do not take offence, Lucy. All I mean is the kindest thing to do for any person or organisation is to make it more self-sufficient.'

Forcing herself to calm down, she settled back into her chair. He wasn't saying she couldn't go, not exactly, although it was clear he meant for her to step back from her responsibilities at the Foundation and focus more on those at home. She probably should be thankful. She'd feared he might keep her under lock and key to ensure she didn't disappear again. Perhaps he would send a footman to accompany her for the first few days, but once he realised she wasn't going to run away she doubted her husband would interfere too much in her life. After all, he had his own life to lead. Just over a year they'd been separated; surely he would have built his own life for himself in that time. Friends, a mistress, regular social engagements. He wouldn't want to disrupt his routine too much either, she was sure of it.

Pausing for a second, Lucy glanced again at the composed profile of her husband. Surely he *had* moved on, built a life for himself. He'd told her he'd been searching for her this entire time, but she wasn't quite sure she believed that. It wasn't as though theirs had been a union of love. They'd barely known one another, not enough to inspire that sort of devotion.

'That's settled, then,' Oliver said, laying down

his cutlery. 'I shall arrange for you to have a schedule of our social engagements over the coming weeks and mark in a few suitable dates for you to visit the dressmakers. I brought some of your clothes from Sussex, but it is by no means a full wardrobe.' He paused and Lucy wondered what it must be like to have such an ordered way of thinking. 'We shall refuse all visitors this first week and I shall reintroduce you to society at the Hickams' ball next week.'

Involuntarily Lucy's hand rose to her throat, rubbing the skin of her neck as she tried to control the urge to flee.

'After that, I expect acquaintances will be very curious—we may be inundated with well-wishers for quite a while—but I shall leave it up to you to decide how to deal with them.' He waved his hand dismissively as if not wanting to be concerned with the minutiae of running a household and maintaining a social calendar.

Lucy didn't plan to be at home to visitors; she had much more pressing things to occupy her time than to sit sipping tea with nosy old women.

'At the end of the Season we shall host our own ball, to confirm to the world you are back for good.'

All she could do was nod.

'Good,' Oliver said, as if he had just concluded a business meeting.

They ate dessert in silence, the clinking of the spoons heightening Lucy's feeling of confinement. She wanted to be loose on the streets, free to go wherever she desired, not trapped here with a man who seemed determined to carve her into the perfect society wife.

Oliver stood as Lucy finished eating, offering his arm and escorting her to the hallway.

'I am going to retire for the night,' he said softly.

With a sharp inhale Lucy glanced up at her husband, wondering if he was suggesting she joined him, but there was nothing but his usual, unreadable expression on his face.

'I hope you sleep well,' he said. 'Don't leave in the night.' It was a command more than a request, but Lucy found herself nodding none the less.

He turned and made his way quickly up the stairs, leaving her to stare after him in the flickering candlelight.

Chapter Four

Oliver didn't lift his head as he heard Lucy's soft footfall on the stairs, instead turning the page of the paper and pretending to be engrossed in the news. Out of the corner of his eye he saw her hesitate, then enter the dining room.

'Good morning,' she said.

Carefully he closed the paper, lowered it and looked up.

He grimaced—she was wearing that ugly brown woollen dress again. It made her look more like a milkmaid than a viscountess.

'Good morning.'

He'd have to throw it out, perhaps instruct one of the maids to squirrel it away on the pretence of washing it and then unfortunately misplace it. Eyeing the coarse wool, he reconsidered, throwing it out wasn't drastic enough; he'd have to burn it.

'I'm ready to leave for the Foundation,' Lucy said, the smile tight on her face as if she were having to force herself to be polite. 'You mentioned a chaperon...'

'Yes.'

She looked around, as if waiting for him to summon someone.

'Perhaps you changed your mind...' she suggested hopefully.

'No.' He stood, crossing to her side and offering her his arm. 'I'm ready.'

He felt her stiffen beside him and wished he could see the expression a little more clearly on her face, but a loose strand of dark blonde hair had escaped her bun and obscured some of her features from him.

'You?' she asked, the tremor obvious in her voice.

'Yes, me.'

'Surely a footman...' she suggested.

'No,' he said without any further explanation. He wasn't anywhere near the point where he could trust her not to trick or evade a footman and disappear off into the slums of London.

She opened her mouth to protest, but nothing came out. Oliver smiled in triumph and gently steered her towards the door. He felt the exact moment that she rallied and pre-empted her protest by striding on ahead, only pausing for her to catch up when he reached the carriage.

They spent the entire carriage ride in silence, Lucy's face stony and her indignation at being outmanoeuvred by him rising from her like steam from a kettle. For his part, he was content to sit quietly, pretending to peruse the top sheet of papers he'd brought with him, while surreptitiously regarding his wife out of the corner of his eye.

Even in the offensive woollen dress there was something almost regal about her. She sat with a straight back and lifted chin, a posture that screamed defiance. He couldn't imagine her fitting in the slums of St Giles. She might be able to walk and talk with the locals, but she'd never assimilate. He couldn't quite believe she'd spent the last year living there. Most people didn't choose to live somewhere as deprived as St Giles and not for the first time he wondered what motivated her to live in such squalid conditions when, unlike many of the other residents, she did have other options available.

As the carriage made its way through Charing Cross, slowing to avoid the numerous pedestrians, Oliver stifled a yawn. It had been a long night and he had not got much sleep, finding himself staring at the canopy above his bed much as he had on the days following Lucy's initial disappearance. He was happy to have found her, happy to know she hadn't died of a fever or been stabbed for her purse, but he wasn't so naïve to think these next few months were going to be easy. She didn't want to resume her role as his wife and he knew that meant they would clash in the coming weeks. For his part, he was torn between wanting to spend time with his wife, so they could more easily take up their positions as husband and wife again, and wanting to distance himself from her. He wasn't sure if he would ever be able to forgive her for taking their son away. It wasn't something that a simple apology could solve. He doubted the trust between them could ever be repaired, but he was willing to accept a less-than-perfect marriage.

The carriage rounded a corner, turning north towards St Giles, and Lucy's body momentarily rocked into his. Even through the coarse wool of her dress he could feel the heat of her skin and he had to take a deep breath to compose himself. The last thing that should be in his mind was renewing the physical side of their relationship. First he needed to focus on ensuring she wasn't going to run away at the next available opportunity.

Even so, the distant memory of the nights

they had shared at the beginning of their marriage fought to the surface. Her body writhing beneath his, the soft moans of pleasure, the frantic way she'd clutched his back, urging him on. He hadn't expected such a physical connection and had known at the time Lucy had felt embarrassed by her reaction to him. That all seemed a long time ago, a different life, and he doubted they would ever share such intimacy again.

'We're here,' Lucy said, forcing Oliver back to the present.

Quickly he regained his composure, gathering the papers from his lap before vaulting from the carriage and turning to help his wife down. They'd stopped on the main thoroughfare, the carriage being too large and unwieldly to take into the rabbit-warren streets of the slum, but already Oliver could see his wife growing in confidence, as if she were more comfortable now she was back in the area she considered home.

He could feel eyes on them as they entered the narrow streets, curious but not overly malicious at present. Not for the first time he wondered how his refined wife had thrived in such an environment and once again he had to remind himself that he barely knew the woman beside him. There was clearly much more to her than he'd realised when his mother had proposed her as a marriage candidate.

It would be easy to lose your way in the maze of streets, but the years Oliver had spent in the army meant he had a sharp eye for observation and thought he probably could escape from the slums if he needed to.

'We're here,' Lucy said flatly, her voice without enthusiasm.

They stopped in front of a nondescript door, situated in a brick building with crumbling windows and nestled between a lodging house on one side and a building that leaned dangerously out over the street on the other. To Oliver it looked as though it should be condemned, but as they watched, a young girl threw open a window and hurled a bucket of water into the street below. Definitely lived in, then.

He observed her as Lucy hesitated for just a second, then pushed open the door. They entered into a narrow alley, the bricks on either side dank and dirty, and walked the fifteen feet to a courtyard at the other end.

'Caroline,' a middle-aged woman shouted as they entered the courtyard. She abandoned the scruffy young woman she was talking to and came rushing over. 'I've been so worried.'

Oliver watched with curiosity as the two

women embraced, wondering if this was the woman who ran the Foundation. Mary, Lucy had said her name was.

'I should introduce my husband,' Lucy said, the reluctance evident in her voice.

Mary's eyes widened and Oliver wondered exactly what Lucy had told the older woman when she'd first arrived, desperate and destitute.

'Mary, this is Lord Sedgewick, my husband. Lord Sedgewick, this is Mary Humberton, proprietress of the St Giles's Women's and Children's Foundation.'

'A pleasure to meet you, my lord,' Mary said, rallying splendidly.

Oliver inclined his head in greeting, catching the puzzled glance Mary threw at his wife.

'You are reunited?' Mary asked eventually.

He saw Lucy hesitate for just a moment, and then nod.

'Lucy has been telling me of the work you do here,' he said, filling the awkward silence that was stretching out before them.

'Caro—' Mary started and then corrected herself. 'Lucy has been a godsend. I don't know what we would have done without her this last year.'

'Miss Caroline,' an exuberant voice shouted from one of the windows that overlooked the courtyard. Oliver looked up in time to see the flash of blond hair before the boy disappeared, heavy footfalls announcing his imminent arrival down one of the many staircases.

A door flew open and a boy of seven or eight hurtled into the courtyard, throwing himself into Lucy's arms.

'Old Bert said you'd been kidnapped,' he said, his eyes wide with excitement.

'Not kidnapped, Billy. I just bumped into an old acquaintance.'

Oliver grimaced at the casual way she described him. A husband should be more than an old acquaintance.

'Is this him?' Billy asked, squinting up at Oliver. 'Bert said he had a big knife, more like a sword, and he dragged you off by the hair screaming.'

'Old Bert can exaggerate sometimes,' Lucy said, suppressing the smile on her lips as she looked down at the boy with affection.

'*Exaggerate?*' Billy mumbled with a frown. Then his face suddenly lit up. 'Stretch the truth to make it sound more exciting?' he asked.

'Well done,' Lucy said, ruffling the young boy's hair.

'Did he hurt you?' Billy asked, his voice a loud whisper, a dark glance directed Oliver's way.

Before Lucy could answer, Oliver saw the boy tense and fling himself towards him, fists swinging as he dived at Oliver, teeth gnashing and eyes dark. Catching the young lad easily, he held him at arm's length, trying to remain gentle but at the same time determined not to be bitten. Who knew what diseases a street child carried in his mouth?

'He didn't hurt me, Billy,' Lucy said quickly, stepping forward to pull the young boy away with a surprising show of strength.

Oliver received a dark, distrusting look from Billy, but no further attempts to attack him were forthcoming.

'Get back to your studies, Billy,' Mary admonished gently, 'or you'll fall behind the rest of the class.'

Reluctantly Billy gave Lucy one final hug before racing back up the stairs he'd come down. Within seconds there was a low rumble and a few excited shrieks followed by a dozen curious faces at the window of what must be the schoolroom. Billy had lost no time in informing his classmates about Lucy's return and her mysterious companion.

'Back to your seats,' a deep voice called and slowly the faces trickled away.

'One of the things I'm most proud of,' Mary

said, stepping closer and taking Oliver's arm. 'Our education programme. No child that stays here with us gets out of lessons to read and write. Some of those who stay longer also learn a little mathematics. Probably not enough to allow them to be clerks, but certainly enough to be able to take money behind a bar in an inn, or work out weights and prices in a butcher's shop.'

Oliver had come across all sorts of people in the course of his life. Those who were selfish and thought only of their own profit; those who were determined to pauper themselves in the service of others. Mary was one of the kind ones, he could see, but she was astute, too. She knew exactly what the young children of St Giles needed, and it wasn't lessons in French or Latin, but basic skills aimed at allowing them to navigate through life just a little easier than their parents.

'Come, let me show you around,' Mary said.

'I don't want to inconvenience you.'

'Nonsense. This is purely selfish. I'm hoping if you see the good work we do here you'll want Lucy to remain involved.'

Oliver was safely ensconced in the office. Hopefully his accounts would be absorbing enough to keep him from wandering, Lucy thought.

He'd been remarkably well behaved on his tour of the Foundation, asking Mary insightful questions and greeting the children and adults he met politely. Lucy didn't know what she'd expected, but not this. Perhaps a surly superiority, or a dismissive air about him, but Oliver had been genial and courteous.

'What on earth happened?' Mary asked, pulling Lucy into her private rooms.

Lucy collapsed into one of the low armchairs and let out a heartfelt sigh.

'Somehow he found me, followed me and insisted I went home with him.'

Mary was one of the only people who knew the truth about Lucy's background. Most of the residents, as well as the patrons of the orphanage, believed she was the daughter of some minor country gentleman, probably caught up in a scandal that had brought her low in life. Mary had been the one to find her and David shivering on a street corner just over a year ago and she'd been the one to comfort Lucy when David passed away. She'd helped Lucy grieve, then slowly brought back her purpose in life by giving her a role at the Foundation. In return, Lucy had been honest with the older woman, telling her the details of her background and why she'd fled from her marital home.

'He seems perfectly pleasant on the outside,' Mary mused. 'Has he hurt you?'

With the kind of women they helped at the Foundation they were both well aware of the outwardly charming man who beat his wife roughly behind closed doors.

'He's been gentle,' Lucy admitted. 'Hasn't raised a hand against me, or even his voice.'

She knew Oliver would be well within his rights to lock her in her bedroom, beat her with a stick for her disobedience and force himself on her until she was with child. And, despite hardly knowing the man she was married to, Lucy *did* know he would never hurt her.

'What does he want?'

'To be my husband. And for me to be his wife.'

'Hardly an unreasonable request,' Mary murmured.

Despite the fear of the future Lucy was feeling, she couldn't help but smile. Mary had never held back from saying exactly what she was feeling.

'I thought he would have moved on by now,' Lucy said glumly.

'Do you want him to?'

'Of course. I left. I could hardly wish him to wait for me all this time.'

'But he has. And now you have the chance to be a lady again.'

'I was never made for that life,' Lucy said. It wasn't quite true. The life of a lady was what she'd been born into, what she'd been raised to be. Her entire childhood had been aimed at preparing her for marriage to a respectable gentleman. This life, this vocation she felt at the Foundation, would have been foreign to her younger self, but now she couldn't imagine returning to a pampered life of idleness, having a maid to help her dress, a cook to prepare her meals.

'Perhaps there's a way for your two lives to meet in the middle,' Mary said. 'It seems your husband is content to let you continue at least some of your work here and I dare say you could find a way to enjoy some of the perks of being married to a viscount.'

Of course Mary was right. That would be the ideal solution. It was much like what Oliver had proposed.

'That's what he said,' Lucy grumbled, feeling decidedly put out and not quite knowing why.

'Change, dear,' Mary said, patting her on the hand. 'It's difficult to accept when the decision has been taken from your hands, especially when you've been independent for as long as we have.'

'I don't want to let you down,' Lucy said, then corrected herself. 'I *will not* let you down.'

'I know.' Mary paused as if wondering whether to say any more. 'He's not your father, Lucy. Give him a chance at the very least.'

Lucy's relationship with her father could be described as sour at the best of times. She hadn't contacted him in the year she'd been living in St Giles and would be content to not ever speak to him again. The old man was controlling, but worse than that, he was cruel. Lucy would never forgive him for how he'd treated her younger brother, William, and still blamed him for the young boy's death. At the age of five, when the old man had realised William was *different*, unable to speak, unable to move around by himself, he'd sent him away to live with a succession of families, the last of whom had mistreated him badly. To this day Lucy still mourned her sweet younger brother.

Mary squeezed Lucy affectionately on the arm before bustling out to carry on with the business of the day. For a few minutes Lucy just sat where she was, wondering if she was being unreasonable in how she'd approached this situation with Oliver. Deep down she knew she was the one in the wrong. She'd run away without a proper explanation, she'd neglected to inform her husband that she was still alive, she'd built a new life without bothering to enquire if Oliver was doing the same. She knew all this, but it still was difficult to accept Oliver's proposal that they return to being husband and wife.

Shaking herself from her self-imposed mental slump, Lucy rose and exited Mary's rooms. Today she'd been planning on preparing the accounts for the next governor's meeting in four weeks' time. It wasn't too time-consuming or difficult as she was the one who kept all the Foundation's day-to-day accounts. This biannual meeting took a little preparation, but nothing too arduous.

Making her way back to the office, Lucy felt her heart sink as she saw the empty chair where Oliver had been sitting. His papers were neatly stacked on the desk, telling her he hadn't grown bored and returned home. Instead he was somewhere loose in the Foundation.

Frantically she dashed from the office, racing down the stairs and into the courtyard. If she thought logically, there were only a few places Oliver could be. Most of the upper levels of the sprawling building were made up of small living quarters for the women and children needing shelter. It was only the rooms on the ground floor that were communal. Still, he could be in the dining room, one of the two classrooms, the laundry, the workrooms…

Hearing a soft peal of laughter, Lucy paused and listened for a few seconds before turning in the direction of the dining room. The large room was set out with two long tables for the residents to take a communal lunch together, but presently at eleven in the morning it was deserted, save for two figures hunched over one of the tables.

'*B-o-a-t,*' the young boy sitting squinting at the paper in front of him read.

'And what does that spell?' Oliver asked softly.

'*Boat.*'

'Good. How about this one?'

Lucy shifted and the noise was enough to make Oliver and Freddy, the young boy he was sitting with, look up.

'Miss Caroline,' Freddy shouted, throwing himself from his seat and rushing towards Lucy. 'Billy said you'd been kidnapped.'

Rumours were always quick to spread in the Foundation. No doubt it would take much longer for the truth to circulate. It was nowhere near as sensational.

'No, Freddy, not kidnapped.'

'Mr Oliver is helping me with my spelling,' Freddy said.

Lucy regarded her husband through narrowed eyes. She had no idea what he was playing at, wandering around the Foundation and talking to the inhabitants, but surely it wasn't anything as innocent as just helping Freddy with his spelling.

'That's kind of him,' Lucy said eventually.

'Freddy tells me he wants to be a Bow Street Runner when he grows up.'

Coming from a family of mainly unsuccessful petty criminals, Lucy wasn't sure how realistic this ambition was, but she always encouraged the children to have aspirations.

'I need to be able to read so I can look at clues.'

'Can I borrow Mr Oliver for a moment?' Lucy asked.

Freddy turned back to his spelling and Oliver rose quickly, following her back into the court-yard.

When she was sure they couldn't be over-heard, she whispered, 'What are you doing?'

Her husband frowned. He gestured back to the dining room where he'd left the young boy still puzzling over his spelling.

'What are you *really* doing?'

Oliver regarded her for thirty seconds before speaking and when he did his tone was cool.

'You seem to have a poor opinion of me, Lucy, when I have not given you cause to doubt me. All I want is for *my wife* to return home and once again be my wife. I'm not a monster, I'm not ask-ing anything any reasonable man wouldn't and I have been nothing but patient with you these last twenty-four hours.' He paused, standing completely straight and looking like the army officer he'd been for many years. 'You, on the other hand, have tried to run away, refused to divulge much about your life and now look at me like a monster for helping one of your young charges with his spelling.'

She felt the heat rise in her cheeks. He was right, although she was loath to admit it. She was struggling with their reunion, but not because of how he'd behaved. Perhaps it would have been easier if he'd shouted and thrown things, behaved like the man she had once pictured him to be to ease her conscience.

Opening her mouth, she tried to apologise, but found the words wouldn't come. It was rude and cowardly of her, but she wondered if maybe by not apologising she'd push him away, make him leave her here to the life she'd built.

'What are you so afraid of?' he asked, for the first time a hint of softness in his voice.

It wasn't a question she had the answer to. He looked at her with a mixture of pity and resignation, before turning on his heel and returning to the boy in the dining room. It seemed he wouldn't abandon a promise, even one as small as helping a child with his schoolwork.

Chapter Five

'Blue is certainly your colour,' the dressmaker's assistant twittered as she held a swathe of material up to Lucy's cheek.

'I'm not sure. I don't want anything too ostentatious,' Lucy said.

Out of the corner of his eye Oliver observed the proceedings. Before today he'd never witnessed what happened when a woman wanted to order a new dress. He'd had vague ideas about a quick perusal of material, perhaps picking a style out of a book, and thought that was probably all there was to it. How wrong he'd been.

So far the dressmaker and her assistant had been occupying their drawing room for the past half an hour and they were still discussing colours. It was going to be a long afternoon. Still, he reasoned, at least he'd had the sense to make an appointment for the dressmaker to visit the house rather than finding himself trapped for hours on end in a stuffy shop on Bond Street. He'd done it so they would have less chance of bumping into some gossiping acquaintance, but now he could see the merit of home appointments for so many other reasons.

'What do you think?' Lucy asked, breaking into his thoughts.

He blinked a couple of times, surprised to be addressed by his wife. Despite her thawing to him these last couple of days, she still seemed determined to keep her life and his as separate as possible.

'That colour,' he said, pointing to an abandoned swathe of silk draped carefully over the arm of a chair.

'The coral?'

'It suits you,' he said with a shrug.

'It does bring out the honey shades in your hair,' the dressmaker said.

'And such a warm colour,' the assistant added.

Oliver knew nothing about honey shades or the warmth of a colour, he just knew that when Lucy held up the coral silk against her skin something tightened inside of him.

'I like it,' she said, giving him a small smile.

Pretending to return to the papers in front of him, Oliver had to suppress the confusion blooming inside him. There was something rather enchanting about his wife; he'd felt it when they'd first married. It had been purely arranged as a marriage of convenience. He'd needed a wife to give him an heir and look after his interests at home while he was off fighting on the Peninsula. The details of Lucy's home life had always been a little vague, but he was under the impression she was so keen for marriage to get away from an overbearing family. Given the reasons behind the marriage, he'd never expected to actually start feeling affection for his wife alongside the physical attraction that had bloomed immediately.

That affection and attraction were trying to rear their heads once again and this time it was entirely unwelcome. He couldn't forgive her for how she'd left him, how she'd taken David away from him before he'd even had a chance to look into his son's face. He didn't want to desire his wife—he didn't even want to feel that same affection he'd hoped for in the early days of their marriage. Yet here it was, trying to muscle its way in.

Turning a page to keep up the pretence of working, he regarded his wife for a little longer. As a debutante, Lucy had never been thought of as the diamond of the Season. She'd been out in society for a year before he'd proposed to her with no other suitors, but in his eyes she was beautiful. Slender and lithe from a year of living a simple life, she still had curves in all the places he liked. More than that, though, was how her face lit up when she smiled, how her brow furrowed when she was worried. He loved how expressive her face was, how you could tell so much from a single glance.

'Off the shoulder, do you think?' the dressmaker asked.

For a moment Oliver didn't realise all eyes were turned to him. Carefully he put down his papers and rose, walking over to the three women.

The dressmaker was holding up two sample dresses, one with a tight bodice and low-cut front, the puffy sleeves sitting well off the shoulders. It was a design to draw attention, a dress that exposed a fair amount of skin.

'I'm not sure...' Lucy said and Oliver could see the hesitation in her eyes. Although the dress was lovely, and would no doubt make Lucy look beautiful, it wasn't her style. It was too ostentatious, too scandalous for a woman who was used to wearing a brown woollen sack.

'The other one,' he said.

The second design was still tight in the bodice area, but not so low cut, leaving more to the imagination.

'Good choice, sir.'

As the dressmaker and her assistant stepped away to find their tape measures, Oliver stayed positioned just in front of Lucy. He wanted to reach out, to run a finger over her cheek, feel the softness of her skin, the moistness of her lips. They had barely touched since their reunion, just gloved hand on jacket as he offered her his arm, and already Oliver was yearning for more.

'Time to take your measurements,' the dressmaker said, bustling in between him and his wife.

Reluctantly Oliver moved away. He knew this was his cue to depart and leave the women alone to do the more personal aspect of the fitting, but for a moment he lingered, watching his wife hold out her arms obediently as the tape measure was looped around her back. All the time he'd searched for her he'd told himself it was to find out what had happened to their son and to get his wife back for social occasions and the running of his household. Never had he allowed himself to believe there might be a deeper reason for desiring their reunion.

'Parker,' Oliver called, waiting as his young butler promptly turned and faced him. Despite it being four years since Oliver had been his superior officer in the army, the young man still almost saluted. Oliver saw his arm twitch at his side as he struggled to suppress the movement.

'Yes, sir.'

'Meet me in the dining room.'

The butler grinned, nodding swiftly and hurrying off to prepare the room.

Oliver followed behind. With Lucy still being pushed and prodded by the dressmaker, he was feeling restless and the only solution was to use up some energy.

As Oliver reached the dining room, he saw Parker had recruited two footmen and between them they were moving the dining table and chairs to one side. A couple of the more expensive pieces of furniture had been moved out of the way and an antique vase placed on a high shelf.

Within minutes the centre of the room was clear of any obstacles, a long, wide space big enough for the coming physical workout.

Oliver stretched, pulling each arm to one side, and then opened the large display cabinet at one end of the room. He removed two fencing foils, long and sleek, giving them both an experimental swish.

Parker, the butler, shrugged off his jacket and rolled up his sleeves, revealing a few more scars on his forearms to match the vertical slash down one cheek.

'I hope you've been practising, Parker,' Oliver said as he handed the foil to the butler.

'Never fear, sir, one of these days you'll beat me.'

The younger man was always respectful and deferential in his work as butler, but there was a subtle shift when the jackets came off and foils came out. It was as though they were back in the training camp, still superior officer and soldier, but a comradeship flourished that was peculiar to the army.

'I'll go easy on you, Parker,' Oliver said, getting into position.

They fought, foil clashing against foil with satisfying clinks, moving backwards and forward with lunges and parries. As they clashed Oliver felt some of the tension that had been building inside him the last few days dissipate as it always did with physical combat.

They were fairly evenly matched, with points being traded backwards and forwards as the minutes ticked by. Oliver didn't really care who won. For him it was more about the thrill of the fight, the wonderful way he felt liberated as his body lunged and defended.

'What on earth…?' a small voice said from the doorway as the foils clashed.

Oliver spun around to see Lucy's shocked face in the doorway.

'Forgive us,' he said with a bow. 'Just a little light exercise.'

'Shall I put the room right, sir?' Parker asked, wiping a film of sweat from his forehead.

'Don't let me stop you,' Lucy murmured, backing away, but Oliver had already tossed his foil to the butler and was following Lucy from the room.

He caught up with her on the stairs.

'That's a very peculiar use of the dining room,' she said. He could tell she was itching to ask for an explanation, but held back from fear of getting overly involved or invested in his life.

'Sometimes I find I need to work out a little energy,' Oliver said, offering her his arm.

'And your butler can fence?'

'He can fight,' Oliver corrected. 'He was my sergeant for a while on the Peninsula.'

'And now he's your butler.'

'And now he's my butler.'

Lucy looked at him with curiosity and he wondered if she might ask more. He knew she was interested in people, but so far she had kept her enquiries into his life to a minimum, as if asking about it risked pulling her deeper into it.

'That's very kind of you,' she said. 'Giving him a job. I know many soldiers struggle to find employment after returning from the war.'

It was an awful thing to see when walking the streets of London. Former soldiers who had once fought bravely for their country, abandoned by the very people they'd served. Many of the returning soldiers found their families had moved on and their jobs filled, leaving them without a true place in the world. It was a hundred times worse for those who had been injured, losing an arm or a leg or an eye, unable to find even the most menial of jobs to provide them with food and shelter, and having to resort to begging on the street.

'He's a good man—loyal. I never have to worry about my silverware disappearing with Parker running the household.'

Parker *was* a good man, one of the best, but with his facial scars he would have been turned away by any of the grand households who wanted their footmen and butlers to be aesthetically pleasing, sometimes even more than they wanted them to be efficient at their jobs.

When it became clear she wasn't going to ask

any more he turned the subject back to her dress fitting.

'Will the dress be ready in time for the ball in two days?'

'Mrs Farrar assures me it will be ready even if she has to stay up all night.'

'Good. I don't want anything to upset our plans.' He saw her stiffen at the idea of the ball but couldn't stop himself from adding, 'It is very important we reintroduce you to society as my wife.'

'We wouldn't want the gossips speculating about whom you might have holed up in here,' Lucy murmured.

'This isn't a joke, Lucy.'

'I know. It's my life.'

'Our life. As husband and wife.'

'But my freedom.'

'Freedom?' he asked, letting out a cold laugh. 'I thought you'd grown up in the year we were apart, Lucy. No one is free, we all have responsibilities, all have to do things we don't want to.'

'*You* get to choose how your life ends up,' Lucy said, turning to face him, lifting her chin so she was looking him straight in the eye. 'And how mine does.'

'There you are wrong. No matter what I feel,

we're still married—I'm just as trapped by that as you.'

Her eyes searched his face, as if trying to work out his true feelings.

'You have the power to at least apply for a divorce—only men can do that. You have the power to set me free from this marriage, let me go back to my old life.'

'That's not going to happen, Lucy. We're married and married couples live together and they socialise together. I'm not asking you to chop off a limb or scale a mountain. All I want is for you to fulfil your part of our wedding vows.'

They stared at each other in silence for over a minute before Lucy turned on her heel and stalked away. Oliver waited until he was alone in his study before he sagged. That exchange had not gone as he'd hoped. Every time he clashed with Lucy he wished it ended differently, but she was so distant, so difficult to engage and he could feel the simmering anger beneath his own words. How could she treat him like this when it had been she who'd run away? She who had taken their son? She didn't have the right to remain aloof and angry. Admittedly she'd built a life for herself in the year they'd been separated, but that was none of his concern. He wanted her back here as his wife and if he could, he'd wipe out all trace of the world she'd been living in, but realistically he knew that wasn't an option.

He wondered if she would ever thaw, if she would ever look at him with anything more than distant coolness. Surprisingly he wanted that, even though he doubted he could ever return the feelings. Perhaps they were destined to live their lives as many married couples did, putting on a front for society events and then barely speaking at home. It was what he'd imagined, when he'd first found her, but every so often he wondered if that would be enough or if one day, when his vexation had burnt itself out, whether he would want more than a cold and unfeeling marriage.

Chapter Six

Lucy shifted uncomfortably on the seat, feeling the layers of petticoats clinging to her legs and making her hot despite the cool October air.

'Try to at least pretend you're enjoying the evening,' Oliver said from his position across the carriage.

Lucy felt like screaming. He was so calm, so unfazed by the evening Lucy had been dreading ever since he'd found her again.

Tonight was the night of the Hickams' ball; the night when Oliver would introduce Lucy to his friends and acquaintances as his wife. All week she'd seen this event as the point of no return; once he'd brought her out in public there was no way he'd ever let her slink off into the night as a free woman.

'Remember to smile once or twice.'

Suppressing the urge to deepen her frown,

Lucy contented herself with looking out the window. They were barely moving, the press of carriages thick as they approached the house, and the temptation to get out and run was strong.

'It might not be as bad as you're dreading,' Oliver said more softly, even giving her a brief but reassuring smile.

His words threw her. It was much easier to build her husband up into a heinous villain, but deep down Lucy knew that wasn't the truth. Oliver was asking her to do something she didn't want to, but he wasn't a monster. He'd kept his side of the bargain and allowed her to continue her work at the Foundation. She knew the sensible thing to do would be to keep her husband happy and play the part of the dutiful wife tonight.

Somehow she couldn't follow her own advice. Something inside was driving her to keep pushing, keep fighting. Perhaps it was fear, perhaps it was a certainty that she didn't want to return to the mundane routine of her old life, but whatever it was kept her from doing what she knew was right; plastering a smile on her face and pretending she was happy to be there.

Letting a deep sigh escape, Lucy looked out of the window. They'd inched forward, but still weren't at the front of the long line of carriages.

This felt so different from her Season as a debutante, before she'd ever met Oliver, when her mother had whisked her around London in the hope she would find a suitable husband to marry. Lucy had hated it, not the balls or the socialising, but the constant pressure from her mother to impress a gentleman with a title and a fortune, when Lucy had been young and shy.

That had been part of the reason she'd accepted Oliver's proposal so readily. Of course he was titled and rich, which kept her parents happy, but also marriage to him meant she wouldn't have to endure another Season as a young woman seeking a husband. It wasn't the main reason, which had been escape from her odious father and unhappy home life, but it had certainly been an added incentive.

Their carriage finally reached the steps in front of the house and a footman opened the door.

'Come,' Oliver said as he took her hand to help her from the carriage. He ensured she was steady on her feet before leading her up the steps and into the house.

The press of people was suffocating as they edged through the guests to the ballroom. Lucy had certainly been in more crowded places, but the scent of perfume and the press of layer upon layer of fabric was a different kind of crowded to the jostling mass of people in St Giles.

'Lord and Lady Sedgewick,' a footman announced as they entered the ballroom.

Lucy wondered if she imagined the slight pause in conversation that followed their names. No one looked directly at them, but there were a number of sideways glances directed their way. For a moment she wondered what the gossips had said about her absence from society for the year she'd been away. Then, just as her nerves were getting the better of her, she felt Oliver squeeze her hand.

Straightening her back and lifting her chin, she smiled, surprised at how reassuring she found Oliver's subtle reminder of his presence at her side.

'Sedgewick, what a surprise,' a tall, thin man shouted as he made his way through the crush of people. 'And the elusive Lady Sedgewick.' The man leaned in closer to Lucy and gave her a conspiratorial wink. 'We all thought he'd made you up.'

'You're not meant to actually say that,' Oliver grumbled.

'Seeing as Sedgewick has forgotten his manners, I'm Lord Redmoor.'

'Back away from my wife, Redmoor,' Oliver

growled, but Lucy could see there was affection in his eyes.

'Calm down,' the Earl of Redmoor said, placing a kiss on Lucy's gloved hand and lingering just a little longer than was proper. 'He's just worried you're going to swoon over my superior looks and charming manner. And after all the trouble he's been to trying to find you.'

'Sometimes you say far too much,' Oliver murmured to his friend. Then held up a hand to stop the interruption before correcting himself. 'Always you say far too much.'

This was a new side she was seeing to her husband, a totally unexpected side. Of course he would have friends. He had a whole life she didn't know about. When they'd spent the month together in Sussex after their wedding, he'd been mainly preoccupied with getting the estate business tied up before his return to the Peninsula, but that didn't mean the man was normally a recluse. He might be serious and unsmiling with her, but many men were different when around their peers.

'True, I suppose—by-product of being an earl,' Redmoor said, leaning in to Lucy as if taking her into his confidence. 'No one dare tell us to shut up.'

'Redmoor, I knew you long before you were

an earl and you've always contributed more than your fair share to the conversation.'

It was a stark reminder of how little she knew about Oliver. His life before their marriage was not a subject he readily discussed. She knew the very basics: he was the third son, unexpectedly coming into the title after his father and brothers were struck down with the same illness. She assumed he'd been to Eton or Harrow, and then Cambridge or Oxford, just because that was what most wealthy sons of the nobility seemed to do, but she didn't actually *know* any of these details.

Likewise, his time in the army had remained a mystery. She'd been much more timid when they'd first married, barely more than a girl and with no experience in talking to someone much more worldly. And now... Well, this past week she'd focused more on how to keep herself distant from her husband than finding out what he was like. It made her feel a little shallow and self-centred.

'Very true,' Redmoor conceded. 'Anyway, you two are the talk of the ballroom. I heard four different conversations about you on my way over here.'

Oliver grimaced.

'Don't look like that, old chap. A little gossip

can be quite thrilling. And at least now people know you haven't murdered Lady Sedgewick.'

'They thought that?' Lucy asked, her eyes widening.

'There have been rumours,' Oliver admitted, his voice tight.

'Oh, so many rumours.' Redmoor said, counting off on his fingers, 'He'd murdered you, you were stark raving mad, you'd run off with a footman, and—my all-time favourite—you were a French spy and had returned to your homeland.'

None of the options cast either of them in a positive light.

'We'll be inundated with callers tomorrow,' Oliver said, glancing at Lucy.

'Everyone will be eager to know what the elusive Lady Sedgewick has been doing with herself this past year...' Redmoor paused and for a moment Lucy thought he was going to enquire, but it seemed he thought better of it. 'Enough,' he said with a flourish. 'You should dance with your wife, Sedgewick. Save a dance for me later this evening, eh?'

Lucy inclined her head, watching Lord Redmoor as he darted away through the crowds, head held high as if he were almost untouchable.

'You are good friends?' Lucy enquired.

'We have been since school. Met him at Eton

when we were thirteen.' She'd been right about the school at least. 'Then university together, then we both signed up to the army. Of course we were deployed to different areas, but our paths crossed a number of times. It was good to have a friendly face on the Peninsula.'

'Lord Redmoor was in the army?' Lucy asked, surprised. A future earl was often expected to stay away from dangerous pursuits for the sake of the line of inheritance.

'Like me, he was not the firstborn son. His older brother was married with a child on the way when Redmoor took his commission, but unfortunately the child was stillborn and Redmoor's brother was thrown from a horse a few months later.'

'It must be hard having your whole future changed— the decisions taken out of your hands,' Lucy said.

Oliver looked at her sharply, as if wondering if she were talking about herself, and Lucy tried to dispel the notion with an encouraging smile, but when he spoke next the clipped tone had returned and she knew she'd lost the intimacy with which they'd just spoken.

'Quite, but one must do one's duty.'

'Of course,' she murmured.

'We should dance.'

It wasn't quite the romantic proposal at a ball that she had dreamed of as a young girl, but theirs had never been a romantic relationship, so she inclined her head and allowed Oliver to lead her to the dance floor.

As a young girl she'd learnt all the steps to the popular dances, practising with her governess for hours on end. In the year before her marriage to Oliver, she'd been out in society, attending balls in London with all the other eager young debutantes. For a while she'd smiled at the eligible bachelors, made herself available and agreeable to dance with, but if Lucy was honest it wasn't one of her strengths. Yes, she could execute the steps of a cotillion or quadrille, but she didn't feel the music as some people seemed to. She would have to count the tempo in her head, meaning she wasn't one of the debutantes that could talk and laugh merrily with their partner while they danced. And more than one gentleman had hobbled away from a cotillion with her after she'd accidentally stamped on a foot.

Still, now she wasn't trying to impress anyone. And it wouldn't matter she couldn't dance and converse at the same time. There were some advantages to being a married woman at least.

They took their positions for a waltz and Lucy felt Oliver's firm hand at the small of her back.

As they began to move she was surprised to find he was a good dancer. He swept her around the floor with an easy confidence, not allowing her occasional faltering to throw him off rhythm. She supposed she shouldn't be surprised. Her husband was a physically fit man—she'd seen how well he'd fenced in the strange sparring match with the butler. An unsolicited memory of one of their nights together after their wedding popped into her mind. He'd been talented in the bedroom, too, with an unwavering energy that had kept them tumbling in the sheets hour after hour.

'You're blushing,' Oliver said, his voice matter-of-fact.

'I haven't danced for a while,' Lucy said as he spun her into another twirl. 'I'm out of practice.'

'Not much opportunity to dance with the residents of St Giles?'

'Probably not a useful life skill to focus on.'

He smiled then, just a small twitch of his lips, and Lucy felt herself softening towards him. Underneath his serious façade and his need to act within the laws of propriety at all times, there was more. The way he reassured her before they'd entered the ball, how he'd acted with the young boy Freddy at the Foundation and now this rare flash of humour. She'd been quick to assume there could be nothing but acrimony between them, but perhaps she'd been wrong, perhaps he was a man she could find a deeper connection with. Not love, of course—that was the content of fairy tales and nothing more—but maybe something more than the awkward cohabitation relationship they had at the moment.

'This is our first dance,' he said, leaning in a little closer. 'Can you believe that? Married two years and this is the first time we've danced together.'

Lucy thought back, surely it couldn't be true, but he was right. They had met outside the London Season, his mother scouting for a demure and respectable wife for her son. Lucy had been on the shortlist and their contact before the marriage had been arranged had been limited to two short strolls around the garden of his Sussex estate. He'd obviously found this sufficient to judge Lucy would make him an adequate wife and, for her part, she couldn't wait to escape her oppressive family home and the grief that still plagued her after her brother's death. There had been no dancing, no courtship, no romance.

She felt the warmth of his hand through the silk of her dress and cautiously looked up into his eyes. He was gazing down at her, his expression softer than it normally was when she irked him, which was almost constantly, and for a moment she wondered if he felt something more towards her than just duty. It was the way his eyes had darkened, his lips softened. Lucy knew she was probably being fanciful, but for just a second she felt as though she glimpsed a deeper, hidden part of him, a part of him that wasn't a tight-laced viscount but instead just a man.

'Thank you for the dance,' he said, bending over her hand as the music finished.

Lucy found her words were stuck in her throat, her mouth too dry to utter anything more than a squeak, so docilely she allowed him to escort her from the dance floor.

'Shall we take some air,' her husband asked, 'before I throw you to the wolves?'

He motioned over his shoulder to the clusters of middle-aged women and their daughters all straining to get a glimpse of the woman society had been speculating about this past year.

'What do you think of your first ball as Lady Sedgewick?' Oliver asked as they strolled along the terrace. It was short; even walking slowly it barely took them thirty seconds to reach the stone balustrade at the end, but with dozens of candles lighting the outside space, it was a pretty place to take some air.

'It's not as bad as I feared,' Lucy said, surprising herself with her honesty.

Up until this point her strategy had been to hold Oliver at a distance, answering any queries about her life, past or present, as generically as possible. She supposed she was afraid of giving him any assistance in achieving his aim: turning her back into a society wife and pulling her away from her important work at the Foundation.

'We never did any of this, did we?' He motioned to the ballroom. 'The balls, the socialising. I just married you and then left you.'

'We didn't exactly have the time.'

'I'm sorry about that. I should have stayed for longer.'

She'd wanted him to. Despite the circumstances of their marriage, despite not knowing him on their wedding day, the optimistic young girl Lucy had been had *wanted* to be a good wife to her husband. She'd wanted to ride out and visit the far corners of his estate with him, to welcome him home after a long day with a glass of his favourite drink. And for a month she'd been that perfect wife. But then he'd left and she'd found out she was pregnant and all her priorities changed.

'It was your duty,' she said, but without any reproach.

'It was, but still not the ideal way to begin a marriage.'

'Not much about our marriage has been ideal,' Lucy agreed.

'I almost came back to you,' Oliver said, his voice catching, 'Just before our boat left Portsmouth I thought about abandoning my men and returning home to you. I often think how things might have been different if I had.'

Strange, Lucy thought. They'd barely known one another. She couldn't imagine Oliver even considering abandoning his duty for anything as inconsequential as a wife.

'You'd have been shot for desertion.'

Oliver laughed, 'Probably.'

The thought was strangely disturbing. Although she was resisting the idea of their lives being intertwined once again, she didn't like the idea of him not existing, not being out there *somewhere*.

'We should go and face the gossips,' Oliver said, taking her gloved hand and placing it into the crook of his arm. 'Before you freeze.'

It was cool for an autumn evening, but the sky clear and even a few stars visible in the darkness.

'Do we have to?'

He paused, turning his face to hers. For a moment she saw a flicker of something in his eyes and found herself moistening her lips in anticipation. Then the moment had passed and she was left wondering exactly what went on behind her husband's stony visage.

Oliver surveyed the ballroom, letting his eyes swivel this way and that, but in reality only focusing on where his wife stood in the middle of a gaggle of women.

'How's married life?' Redmoor asked, appearing at his side.

Oliver grimaced. 'She hates me.'

'Not true, I'm sure.'

'She thinks I'm ruining her life.'

'Strange girl. Most women would jump at a second chance to take up the role of Viscountess.'

'Lucy isn't most women.'

'Does she know how you feel about her?' Redmoor asked.

'I don't feel anything towards her.'

Redmoor laughed, an infuriating laugh that hinted at some deeper understanding.

'Anger, perhaps, and certainly betrayal.' Oliver pushed on, ignoring his friend's unbelieving expression. 'I find her unbearable to be around sometimes.'

'That'll pass.'

'I'm not sure.'

He had mellowed to his wife over the past week, the burning anger and feelings of betrayal simmering down to a more controllable level. Oliver doubted he would ever forgive Lucy for taking away his opportunity to ever see their son, but at least now it wasn't the only thing he thought of when he looked at her.

'She hasn't tried to run away again?' Redmoor asked.

Grimacing as he remembered the ridiculous escape attempt out of the first-floor window, he shook his head. At the very least Lucy seemed content to stay at Sedgewick House until they came to some agreement about the future. He knew in her mind that involved persuading him to move on with his life and allowing her to move on with hers, but that was never going to happen. He took his marriage vows seriously and Lucy was his wife despite everything they'd been through in the past year.

'No,' he said.

'Well, that's a good start. Perhaps you should do something romantic, spend some time together as a couple.'

'Redmoor,' Oliver said firmly, 'I am not in love with my wife.'

'Whatever you say, my friend,' Redmoor said in a tone that clearly stated he didn't believe Oliver.

'I want her to turn up to society events, run

my households, perhaps one day give me children. That is all.'

'I'm not saying anything,' Redmoor said, raising his hands up in mock-defeat.

Oliver nodded, starting to turn away to look across the ballroom.

'Although…' Redmoor continued, '…not many men would spend a whole year of their lives searching for a woman they didn't care for.'

'It was the right thing to do,' Oliver said stiffly.

He *did* care about Lucy, of course he did. They were married and that meant he had certain responsibilities, to keep her safe and comfortable, but he didn't love her. That would be ridiculous. He barely knew the woman. They'd spent a pleasant but brief month together when they'd first married and then nothing more. Theirs had been an arranged marriage, beneficial to both parties, with no expectations of love involved whatsoever.

It was true he had felt peculiarly hurt by her desertion and not just in terms of the loss of his son. He'd wanted Lucy, his wife, back and that feeling hadn't subsided over the year of his search.

'Anyway, it hardly matters how I feel about her—she's barely communicating with me.'

'Still worried you're going to stop her from helping the orphans?'

'Destitute women and children,' Oliver corrected absently. 'I don't know what more I can do on that front,' he said. 'I've not stopped her from going to that place whenever she wants and I've assured her a hundred times I don't want to take it away from her. I just need a little co-operation from her side.'

'Give her time,' Redmoor said sagely, 'it's only been a week.' He leaned in closer, 'And maybe remind her of the benefits of marriage.' He winked salaciously, like a streetwalker enticing a client, and then left Oliver to his thoughts.

His feelings about resuming that part of their relationship were mixed, the memories of the nights they'd spent closeted in their bedroom were still fresh despite the time lapse. Lucy had enjoyed his attentions, that much would have been hard for her to hide, even though she'd been embarrassed by her response to him. For his part, he hadn't expected such a physical connection with his wife. When they'd come together on their wedding night it should have been awkward, two virtual strangers sharing a bedroom, but it had been more than anything Oliver had ever expected. The thought of tumbling into bed with Lucy again did hold a certain appeal, but he wondered if he could ever feel that same connection with his wife after all she'd done to betray his trust.

Glancing over to where Lucy had been, he frowned. He couldn't see her anywhere. In the coral silk dress she was difficult to miss, but as his eyes scanned the ballroom he knew immediately that she wasn't there. His heart sinking, he began pushing through the crowds. There was a possibility she had momentarily nipped out to the ladies' retiring room or perhaps to get some air, but his instinct told him that this wasn't the case. For some reason or another she'd left, alone and unchaperoned.

Parting the crowds, Oliver made his way swiftly into the hall, stepping out the front door into the cool air of the night and racing down the steps just in time to see a flash of coral silk disappearing in between some of the parked carriages. Part of him hoped she was making her way to his carriage, at least that would be a safe way of abandoning him at the ball where they were meant to make their first debut as a couple.

Quickly he raced after her, aware of the eyes watching him as he weaved through the carriages. For a moment he thought he'd lost her and felt an awful plummeting of his heart, but then out of the corner of his eye he saw that flash of coral silk again.

Emerging from the rows of parked carriages, he saw her walking calmly down the street away from the Hickams' house. She wasn't hurrying, just walking with her head down in a purposeful manner.

'Lucy,' he called out when he was certain he was close enough if she decided to run.

She stopped, turning with surprise in her eyes.

'Oliver,' she said, her voice a little shaky, but her demeanour otherwise not betraying any guilt for leaving the ball without him.

'What are you doing?' he asked.

'Going home.'

'Why?'

She sighed. 'I knew this ball was not a good idea.'

'What happened?' he asked, trying to keep the annoyance from his voice. Perhaps he was being too hasty in judging her, perhaps something terrible had happened or some nasty debutante had made a heinous comment.

'Nothing happened,' she said.

'You can't just leave,' Oliver ground out, feeling his temper flare at the nonchalant way she was behaving. 'And certainly not without telling me.'

'I'm leaving,' she said quietly. 'There, you've been informed.'

'What is wrong with you?' Oliver asked, hearing the disbelief in his voice. 'You're the one that left, you're the one that ran away. I've done nothing but try to accommodate you this last week and you can't even treat me with basic respect.'

'You abducted me off the street, pulled me from my home and have imposed your rule ever since,' Lucy countered, her voice rising.

'I will not have this discussion with you in the middle of the street.'

He reached out for her arm, thinking to guide her to their carriage, but she pulled away from him.

'Don't be a fool,' he said quietly. 'People are watching. And you can't walk all the way home on your own.'

'I don't care if people are watching,' Lucy countered.

'Well, I do. You might have decided to turn your back on this life, but these are my friends, the people I socialise with. Think of someone else but yourself for once and spare me further embarrassment. You've caused enough already.'

He saw the defiance flare in her eyes and for a moment he thought she would defy him and stalk off down the street, but as the seconds dragged out he saw her sag a little and nod curtly.

Quickly he escorted her to his carriage, helping her up before she could change her mind.

They sat in silence and that suited Oliver just fine. He was angry, more than angry. She could have run into all sorts of harm wandering off on her own through London at this time of night. It was reckless and stupid, and he couldn't understand what had been so terrible she would have put herself at risk like that.

Noting her tense posture and her resolute gaze fixed out of the window of the carriage, Oliver settled into his seat. There was no point discussing this tonight; both their tempers were too high. Tomorrow hopefully he could be more rational and perhaps she would deign to explain her behaviour to him.

Chapter Seven

Lucy skulked in her room, glancing at the door every few minutes, trying to decide whether to dash downstairs and find some breakfast. She was famished—the maid who normally brought the morning cup of tea and slices of toast and jam hadn't materialised this morning and so far she hadn't plucked up the courage to go downstairs and face Oliver.

It was courage that she needed. Last night she'd acted badly—appallingly, in fact. She had agreed to attend the ball and then just walked out without giving him the courtesy of letting him know she was leaving. It had been rude, inexcusably so, especially when he had done nothing to deserve such treatment. As always Oliver had been a perfect gentleman and she nothing more than a spoiled child.

Sighing, she reached for the door. *It's better*

to face your mistakes, she'd always tell the children at the Foundation and now she would have to take her own advice.

The house was surprisingly quiet, with not even the faraway bustle of a maid and no footman standing ready in the hallway. Cautiously she descended the stairs and peeked into the dining room. Breakfast was laid out as usual, with no sign of Oliver. Guiltily she sent a quick prayer of thanks heavenwards and rushed in to fill her grumbling stomach. Perhaps she wouldn't have to face Oliver yet anyway.

'The tea will be cold,' a low voice said from behind her.

She swivelled, regaining her composure enough not to let out a squeal of shock at her husband's figure in the doorway.

'I will ring for some more,' Lucy said, trying to keep her voice even and calm.

'I've given the servants the morning off.'

'All of them?'

'All of them.'

She swallowed, wondering what he needed the house entirely empty for.

'But I can fetch you a fresh pot of tea,' he said.

Blinking in surprise at the offer, Lucy started to refuse, but Oliver was already out of the door and out of sight before she could stop him. After she'd recovered from her shock, she glanced once again at the covered breakfast things, trying to quiet her grumbling tummy, and then with a sigh set off after her husband. She couldn't allow him to crash around in the kitchen just to make her fresh tea.

'You really don't need to,' Lucy said as she dashed down the stairs to the warm kitchen.

Her ever-efficient husband already had filled the kettle and was in the process of carrying it back to the stove to heat the water.

'We need to talk,' Oliver said. 'And I always find this sort of discussion done best on a full stomach, with a steaming cup of tea in your hands.' His tone sounded ominous and Lucy felt a bubble of panic at the back of her throat.

Unable to hold his gaze, Lucy glanced around the kitchen, aware she hadn't been down here in the week she'd been staying at Sedgewick House. She hadn't met many of the servants, hadn't tried to integrate herself into the day-to-day life of the household in any way at all.

Expertly Oliver laid out all that would be needed for the tea in a neat line while he waited for the water to heat.

'You don't find many gentlemen familiar with their kitchen,' Lucy said quietly, fascinated by the systematic way he'd set everything out.

'Seven years in the army,' Oliver said grimly. 'It prepares you for all situations. Even the necessity for a gentleman to make his own tea, or—God forbid—cook a simple meal or two.'

'You can cook?'

Oliver grimaced. 'Finest goat stew this side of Gibraltar, but perhaps not to your taste.'

She raised her eyebrows in question.

'I find it is a dish best served to a stomach growling with hunger, so you eat it so quickly you don't notice the taste.'

Carefully he made the tea before placing two cups on a tray with the steaming teapot and a little jug of milk.

'Shall we return to the dining room?' he asked.

Reluctantly Lucy agreed. It was cosy down here in the kitchen and somehow it made the conversation they needed to have seem that little bit less daunting, but she knew it was no place for the master of the house to conduct his business. Especially the business of reprimanding his wife.

'We need to talk,' Oliver said only once he had poured out the two cups of tea and waited for Lucy to start on her breakfast.

The toast suddenly seeming dry in her mouth, Lucy swallowed a couple of times, trying to clear the obstruction before realising it was nerves making her feel as if her oesophagus was nar-rowing.

'I'm sorry,' she blurted out, needing to get in her apology before he went any further.

In the short time she'd known her husband she hadn't often seen him surprised. It always appeared as if he were prepared for any eventu-ality, another by-product of nearly a decade in the army, she supposed.

'You're sorry?' he asked, as if hardly daring to believe what he was hearing.

'I should have made more of an effort.'

'What happened at the ball?' he asked. 'Did someone say something to you?'

It would have been better if they had.

She shook her head, unable to lie to him. 'No, everyone was curious but polite. They made vague enquiries about where I'd been this past year, but didn't ask anything outright.'

'Then what happened?'

Lucy sighed, it was difficult to explain, but she owed it to him to try. 'I was standing there in the middle of a gaggle of young women and they were twittering on about the best material for a day dress and how that differed from an evening dress, and all I could think was how lit-tle any of it mattered. All that expense, all that opulence, and for what?' She dared not look at her husband as she carried on with her rant. 'Just so a group of rich people could impress another group of rich people.'

'So you just decided to leave?'

'I felt as though I were suffocating—I had to get out.'

'Because they were talking about ball gowns?' Oliver asked, his expression unreadable.

'I'm sorry I left, especially without telling you. It was not the right thing to do. I didn't think about how you might worry for my safety. I just needed to get away.'

For over a year she hadn't had to consider anyone but herself when it came to her immediate needs. It would take a bit of adjustment to factor in another person.

'You shouldn't have left,' Oliver said, 'not without me. You could have been hurt, walking the streets of London unchaperoned.'

He said it so reasonably that Lucy found the blood flooding to her face, her cheeks burning with the shame of how she'd handled the situation.

'Why are you being so reasonable?' she asked.

'What is the point in reacting in any other way?'

'Most people can't help it. Most husbands

would shout at me for causing such embarrassment, not sit here and discuss my reasons calmly.'

'Would you prefer it if I shouted?'

She glanced at him sharply, wondering if he was joking, but there wasn't even a hint of a smile on his face. Completely unreadable, that was her husband, especially when it came to emotions.

'I'm sorry,' she repeated, 'I treated you poorly. You deserved more than how I acted at the ball.'

'At least we are in agreement on that point,' Oliver said and this time there was just the tiniest hint of a smile on his lips. 'So let's talk about the future.'

Taking a deep breath, Lucy nodded. 'I will endeavour to do better,' she said. Last night as she'd lain awake in bed she'd realised that she was treating Oliver badly. He was her husband, there was nothing to be done about that, and it was looking as though they would spend the rest of their lives entwined in one another's life. This thought had scared her; over the last year she'd come to appreciate the freedom to make her own decisions, to be in control of her own fate, and now she was back living with someone who had the legal right to every last bit of her. It had petrified her and as such she hadn't waited to see what sort of a man Oliver was, instead assuming the worst.

She'd been convinced he would take away everything that had come to matter to her—the Foundation, her new friends, the freedom to walk about London and go where she pleased. When she stopped to think about it, it wasn't true. All he had asked was she once again be his wife, but he'd never said she couldn't continue with the things she loved at the same time.

'I've been selfish,' she said quietly, glancing up into his serious face. 'I was scared you would take everything I've built this last year away from me and so I treated you hostilely. It was silly of me and I'm sorry.'

'It is an adjustment, trying to be a married couple after so long apart. Especially when we barely knew one another in the first place,' Oliver said.

'I thought you were asking the world of me, but now I can see your request is reasonable.'

'So you will begin to act like Lady Sedgewick?' Oliver asked.

'I will. I'll accept visitors for tea, I'll attend dinner parties and balls, and smile at all the inane chatter.' She paused, deciding on a meek and mild approach for her next request. 'But may I continue my work at the Foundation?'

Oliver sighed and for a moment she thought he were going to refuse. With her heart hammering in her chest, she began to voice a protest before he'd even spoken, but he held a hand up to silence her.

'I've never tried to stop you,' he said. 'And as long as it pleases you to do so you can continue working at the Foundation.'

Surprising herself as much as him, Lucy leapt from her chair and flung her arms around her husband's neck. Stiffly he patted her on the back as one might a distant relative. Lucy realised once again they'd barely touched in the past week, certainly nothing more than a gloved hand upon a jacketed sleeve. A far cry from the surprising intimacy of the first month of their marriage.

'Thank you,' she murmured as she stepped away, knowing most husbands would not have been anywhere near as understanding or generous and having to reassess her opinion of Oliver in her mind.

Chapter Eight

Glancing at his wife's profile, Oliver tried to get a handle on the turmoil of emotions raging inside him. Things had been much calmer, much more pleasant at home since they'd had their little conversation about the future. Lucy had relaxed a little more around him, begun acting more like her true self rather than a nervous house guest. It was a slow progress, but progress all the same. Oliver was nothing if not patient.

For his part, he had let go of some of the resentment he felt towards her. If he was honest, he still hadn't forgiven her for taking David away and for giving him an entire year of worry and uncertainty. He probably never would. But he did realise that if they were going to have a future together, he needed to try his hardest to move on, or at the very least let Lucy think he had.

'Are you sure you want to do this?' Lucy

asked, her face pale as she looked at him from across the carriage.

He nodded wordlessly, worried his voice might betray the depth of emotion he was feeling if he spoke.

She was taking him to visit their son's grave for the first time. He'd known where it was for over a week, after he'd prised that information from her on the day of their reunion, but this was the first time he would set foot in the actual graveyard.

Three times that week he'd walked to the boundary wall of the graveyard—once he'd even made it as far as the gate into the church—but never had he been able to step inside. Today Lucy had mentioned she was going to visit the grave of their son, as she did every week, and had tentatively invited him to join her.

They stepped out of the carriage, Oliver drawing his collar up against the downpour that soaked him within seconds before the coachman jumped down and offered them an umbrella. Holding it out so Lucy would be covered, Oliver shivered as the droplets of rain began coursing down his neck.

'Come under,' Lucy said, pulling on his arm until they were huddled together underneath the umbrella. Her warm body pressed up against his arm and immediately he felt better. This wasn't something you wanted to be doing alone.

Avoiding the worst of the puddles and mud, they made their way around the side of the church, into the graveyard. Even in the muted daylight, Oliver could see the tombstones nearest the church were old and worn, some of them crumbling or split in two while others had suffered from exposure to the elements, and the inscriptions unreadable.

'This way,' Lucy said as she led him down the stone path. Further away from the church the graves were much more recent and there were a few mounds of earth with crude wooden crosses marking the spots of burials within the last six months.

They carefully picked their way through a row of graves before stopping in front of a simple tombstone with just one line of writing.

'David Oliver Greenhall' it read, and as Oliver let his eyes focus on the words, he felt a deep ache in his heart. This was his son, his boy, the child that could have been so many things. He might not ever have got to hold him, to look into his eyes, but that didn't mean he hadn't loved him.

Beside him Lucy crouched down, seeming not to notice as her skirt soaked up the muddy water lying around the grave. She laid a hand on the stone and closed her eyes, speaking softly so Oliver could barely hear the words. At first he thought she was saying a prayer, but as snippets of phrases floated up to him he realised she was just talking to their son. Oliver listened as she told him about their reunion and how she had brought his father to visit his grave.

Eventually she stood up and Oliver could see the tears streaming down her face. Instinctively he reached out and wiped them away with his thumb, pulling Lucy close to him and embracing her as the sobs racked her body.

'I'm sorry,' she said, 'I don't normally get this emotional. Would you like a few minutes alone with him?'

Oliver nodded, handing Lucy the umbrella and waiting until she had stepped away before crouching down himself. It seemed strange to talk to a stone and at first no words would come.

'David,' he said hesitantly, 'it's your father.' He felt ridiculous saying the words. He'd never got to be the boy's father. Lucy had disappeared with their son before he could even hold him in his arms.

'You haven't once left my thoughts this past year. I wish I could have done more for you. I wish I could have done something for you.' He paused, swallowing a couple of times as he tried to suppress the image of him holding a tiny baby. It was one he'd dreamed of a hundred times, one that had never got to become a reality. 'I hope wherever you are, you're now at peace. Know that you'll always be in my heart.'

He reached out and laid a hand on the tombstone, closing his eyes for a few seconds as the image of how he'd always imagined his son flashed in his mind. Slowly he stood, taking a moment to steady himself, before turning to face Lucy.

She waited for him to step back, then bustled to the grave, pulling out a couple of weeds and brushing a muddy smear off the tombstone. When she was satisfied all was straight, she rejoined Oliver.

'I'd like to build a memorial on the estate for David,' Oliver said quietly as they walked back towards the church, the rain heavier now and hammering down on the umbrella, almost obscuring his words. 'I thought about trying to get permission to move his body, but I think that would be cruel. Nevertheless, I would like some form of remembrance near the rest of my deceased relatives and ancestors on the estate.'

'You'd like David to be remembered as your firstborn?' Lucy asked, her eyes widening.

'Of course. I was thinking a small memorial next to where my parents and brothers are buried, so he's surrounded by family.'

He saw her bite her lip before taking a few deep breaths and realised Lucy was trying hard not to cry.

'That's a very nice thing to do,' she said eventually.

'He was my son,' Oliver said simply.

Sedgewick Place was where David should be laid to rest, but that couldn't be helped now. The very least Oliver could do was build a memorial among the rest of the Greenhall family, somewhere he and Lucy could visit while staying in Sussex so far away from the resting place of their little boy.

They walked from the graveyard, pausing by the carriage. Lucy seemed reluctant to give up his arm and Oliver wasn't going to be the one to shrug her off.

'Perhaps you could walk me to the Foundation,' she suggested. 'If you don't mind being out in this weather.'

'Not at all.'

It was the first time she'd requested his company voluntarily and Oliver felt a flicker of warmth inside him. Today was difficult—visiting his son's grave for the first time was always going to be painful. He'd expected his resentment of Lucy to flare, for the feelings of betrayal to rise up, but instead he was just glad she was there with him, there to share his pain.

They walked, skirting around puddles and jumping back from the splash of carriages as they flung water from their wheels on to the pavement. For a while Lucy remained silent, although just having her presence voluntarily on his arm was enough for Oliver.

'Tell me,' he said eventually, 'how you came to be so involved at the Foundation.'

He half-expected her to withdraw into herself again, but instead she treated him to a cautious smile.

'At first, when Mary found me and David, we were just normal residents. She brought us to the Foundation, gave us food and a small room, and promised to help me look for a job once David was a few weeks older.'

Oliver nodded, seeing the sadness in his wife's eyes just as he did whenever she mentioned their son.

'When he passed away she was the one who helped me organise the burial and she told me I'd have a home at the Foundation for however long I needed it. For weeks I did little more than cry and mourn, but Mary made sure I ate a little and slowly she encouraged me out of my room to mix with some of the other residents.' Lucy smiled fondly as she remembered the kindness shown to her by the older woman. 'A few months after David died, Mary came in all in a flap about her accounts. There was a governor's meeting and she couldn't get the figures to balance properly.'

'You always were good at the accounts,' Oliver murmured, anticipating where the story was leading.

'I suppose I was. I offered to take a look at them for her—it seemed the least I could do after she'd been so kind to me. I had them sorted and in order in a few hours, much to Mary's amazement.' She shrugged. 'They weren't much different to household accounts, but just on a larger scale.'

'I can see how you became indispensable.'

'I had been planning on finding a job somewhere, but Mary asked if I wished to stay. In return for doing the accounts and various pieces of administration, I'd get my room and food, and a small weekly wage.'

'A good deal for both of you.'

'Exactly. And that's how it started, but as time went on and I got to know the work Mary was doing and the residents in the Foundation, I wanted to get more involved. I still do the accounts and most of the paperwork, but I also teach a few lessons and oversee the programme we run to get women into work.'

'It is rare to see such passion for one's work,' Oliver said.

It was true, not many people enjoyed their jobs like Lucy seemed to. For her it was a vocation, a calling. He'd felt the same way about the army at first. He'd believed in the cause, in the idea of liberating the repressed, but after years of his friends and comrades being killed and injured he'd become more jaded. Marrying Lucy and wanting to be at home with her and his new child had been the final reason to give up his commission in a long line of reasons. And ever since, he'd felt a little directionless. He envied Lucy her passion. Although he was proud of his family estate, running it didn't give him the same thrill Lucy's work seemed to provide her.

'And you never thought to move away from the Foundation? Find a residence elsewhere?'

Lucy shrugged, but he noticed his words had cut deeper than he had anticipated. He wondered if staying in such a place as St Giles was her idea of penance. Penance for losing their son, penance for not being able to do more for him. It would make sense; there was really no reason for Lucy to stay in the slums, even if she worked at the

Foundation every day. Something else other than convenience was keeping her there.

They turned into the narrower streets, stepping carefully through the muck on the pavements, trying to avoid the worst of it. This was the fourth time Oliver had been to the Foundation now and he was beginning to find the route familiar. Today there was hardly anyone outside, and the few people that hurried past had upturned collars and downcast faces against the rain.

'Your money,' a low voice demanded as they rounded a corner.

Beside him, Oliver felt Lucy stiffen, but she didn't show any other sign of panic. He cursed— he'd become complacent, forgotten what sort of place this was. Strolling arm in arm with Lucy had made him forget they had entered one of the most deprived areas of London.

He watched as Lucy dipped her head and searched the thief's face, frowning slightly through the pouring rain.

'Give me your money and no one has to get hurt,' the man said, flashing a knife from the sleeve of his coat.

'Do I know you?' Lucy asked.

'No questions. Just your money.'

Oliver narrowed his eyes. He could probably disarm the thief if he acted quickly, a swift blow to the throat was usually enough to stop any assailant, especially if you could take them by surprise. The thief wouldn't expect a finely dressed couple to fight back. If he'd been on his own that was exactly what Oliver would have done, but he had Lucy's safety to think of now.

Carefully he dug a hand into his jacket, loath to give over anything to this criminal, but not willing to put Lucy at risk.

'What are you doing?' Lucy rasped at him, pulling his arm from his jacket. 'If we give him money, it'll just encourage this behaviour.'

'You make it sound like a child refusing to eat their vegetables. I'm not sure thievery is so easily discouraged.'

'I understand you might be going through a difficult time,' Lucy said, turning back to the man in front of them, 'but this is not the answer. There are people who can help you get back on your feet.'

'Assuming he wants to reform,' Oliver muttered. The crazy woman was going to get herself killed.

'Your money,' the man demanded, his voice a little more shrill than before. Oliver knew soon he would become irrational.

'There is a very good charity—they have their headquarters down New Compton Street—they can help with a warm meal and a place to stay if you need it. And work, too.'

'Your money,' the man demanded again, his voice almost hysterical.

'Please excuse my wife,' Oliver said, pushing Lucy to safety behind him. 'She's got too much compassion.'

Lightning quick Oliver struck out with his arm, the side of his palm jerking into the thief's throat. The man gurgled and gasped, sinking down the wall as he clutched at his neck.

'Oliver, really,' Lucy admonished, 'you could have hurt him.'

Giving her a withering glance, he stepped over the man's legs, pulling Lucy behind him, ignoring her protests as he marched her quickly through the streets. Only once they were inside the walls of the Foundation did he let her stop to catch her breath.

'You didn't need to hit him.'

'I could have tried talking him to death, but that didn't seem to be working that well for you.'

She opened her mouth and closed it again.

'Violence is never the answer.'

'When a man threatens my wife with a knife, violence is always the answer.'

He saw her expression soften and knew he was forgiven.

'Thank you for getting us out of that situation,' she said.

'What situation?' Mary asked as she bustled into the office.

'A man just tried to rob us,' Lucy explained.

'I hope you didn't give him anything.'

So this was where Lucy got her cavalier attitude to knife-wielding thieves from.

'Lord Sedgewick hit him in the throat.'

Mary laughed, a short sharp bark of a laugh that Oliver found he quite liked despite its ear-splitting qualities.

'Good work—not that I don't have sympathy for the poor chaps, living in squalid conditions with no hope of employment—but we can't help everyone.'

'I must be getting to the children,' Lucy said.

Today was the day she took one of the classes, Oliver had learnt, an obligation she was not in any hurry to give up.

'Shall I meet you back at home?'

He shook his head, thinking of the man with the knife and knowing he would find it difficult to let Lucy wander through these streets on her own ever again.

True to his word, Oliver had waited for her throughout the afternoon at the Foundation. She knew he'd been worried about her safety after the encounter with the would-be thief on their walk. She didn't dare tell him the number of times she'd been robbed in the past year. Normally it was just pickpockets, little hands that sneaked in and found your purse before you knew anything was happening, but a couple of times before she had been threatened with a knife by one of the more desperate souls who passed through the slums. Of course she exercised common sense and tried not to walk alone through the most dangerous areas, especially after dark, but St Giles was familiar to her, a home of sorts, and sometimes she did forget the potential dangers lurking around dark corners.

Over the months, she had thought about moving away from the Foundation on a number of occasions. Although St Giles was where she needed to be for her work, it didn't mean she had to live there. Even Mary, the most devoted to the women and children, had a small residence in a more salubrious part of London and spent half her nights there.

For Lucy it was about connection. In St Giles she felt closest to her son. It was where he was buried, where he'd spent most of the few weeks of his short life. If she was completely honest, there was also an element of thinking she had to do penance for failing to protect him better. Not many people chose to live in St Giles out of choice and Lucy knew her decision to stay there so long hadn't been entirely rational, but in a way it had been her home for just over a year.

'Shall we go home?' Oliver asked as she pulled on her cloak, still damp from the rain earlier in the day.

'I wondered if you wanted to spend a little time out and about?' His face clouded with suspicion and Lucy had to suppress a laugh. 'Don't worry—I'm not going to get you handing out leaflets to the women of London.'

After her behaviour at the Hickams' ball she had resolved to make an effort with her husband. That meant actually talking to him, getting to know him and allowing herself to see he wasn't the cold man she had first supposed. Tonight was her olive branch, a suggestion to spend time together for the sole purpose of just being together.

'What do you propose?'

'A little light entertainment,' Lucy said.

To her delight Oliver agreed, although he insisted on taking a carriage as soon as they were able to hail one as they reached the main thoroughfare.

'Where are we going?' he asked as she hopped

up behind him after giving instructions to the coachman.

'It's a surprise. I promise you an evening of entertainment unlike anything you've ever witnessed before.'

He grimaced, no doubt picturing all manner of sins.

'Is it somewhere fit for a viscountess?' he asked.

Lucy bristled before casting him a sidelong glance and realising he was joking. Joking in that very serious, difficult-to-interpret way of his, but joking all the same.

'Surely it can't be scandalous if I bring my husband,' Lucy said.

'I can just see the headlines: *Lord and Lady Sedgewick seen entering notorious gambling den.*'

'It's not a gambling den.'

'*Lord Sedgewick takes his wife to obscene theatre performance.*'

'They would blame it on your corrupting influence of course. *I've* been shut away in Sussex for a year.'

This time he laughed, a proper eye-crinkling, spontaneous laugh that seemed to come from deep inside him. She hadn't seen him laugh like that before and instantly she wanted to hear it again.

'I wouldn't be so sure the gossips think you're the innocent party in our strange relationship—many see me as the suave and dashing wronged husband, dedicated to a wife who's either mad or melancholic.'

'I suppose my behaviour at the Hickams' ball didn't help,' Lucy said with a sigh.

'But all the young women are now swooning over me, talking about how I must be the finest of husbands to put up with your behaviour.'

'And where have you been to hear the opinions of swooning young women?' Lucy asked.

'Here and there…' he sighed dramatically '…I just can't seem to get away from them.'

'I'll have to step up my role as protective wife,' she murmured and, although Oliver laughed, she was only half-joking.

What a difference a couple of days could make. Just a week ago she'd been doing anything she could to persuade Oliver to end their marriage, to allow them to go their separate ways and live independent lives. Now, only a few days later, she felt a mild pang of jealousy as he spoke of other women, even though their entire conversation had been in jest.

Throwing a sidelong look in his direction,

Lucy regarded her husband. He was tall and lean, with dark hair and dark eyes. His expression was normally serious, but when he smiled he was a devastatingly handsome man. She could see other women being interested in him romantically and that was before one took his social standing and substantial fortune into account.

Trying not to overanalyse her feelings, Lucy sat back and watched their progress through the streets of London.

Before long they'd crossed the river and the carriage had slowed in the narrower streets of Southwark.

'Southwark,' Oliver said with a grimace. 'This can't be good.'

'Don't try to tell me you don't frequent Southwark when the fancy takes you,' Lucy said, watching as he leaned forward to peer out of the window.

'Maybe as a young man, but I've found my tastes have changed as I've got older.'

She couldn't really imagine him as young and carefree, just another twenty-year-old making his way in the world, enjoying a break from his studies with all the delights Southwark had to offer. By the time she'd met him he was already in his late twenties and hardened by years spent in the army.

'This way,' Lucy said as the carriage drew to a halt and they stepped down. She took him by the hand and led him across the street to a gaudily painted set of double doors.

Lucy had been to the Charleston Rose twice before, both times with Mary. Today she took out a couple of coins, paid the small entrance fee and waited while a woman clad in a very tight dress guided them to a table.

'I'm trying to work out why you've been here before,' Oliver said, a frown on his face as he perused the room. The tables were half-full, mainly consisting of single or groups of men, varying in age of barely adult to old and decrepit. Sashaying between the tables were women, some young, some past their prime, all dressed in brightly coloured dresses with tight bodices that left little to the imagination. In one corner an elderly man played a jaunty tune on the piano as other patrons continued to enter and take their seats.

'Don't worry—I've never worked here,' Lucy said. It was meant as a joke, but she saw his face darken and realised she'd pushed too far. 'One of the young women we took in to the Foundation a little over six months ago is the star of the show. She's done very well for herself and I like to keep in contact whenever I can.'

With that explanation Oliver relaxed a little and went back to regarding the other audience members. There were one or two women perched on the hard chairs, but it was predominantly a male audience.

A few minutes later, the curtain lifted and seven women walked on to the stage, their heels clattering across the wood, and the pianist quickly changed the music he was playing and picked up the tempo. Six were dressed identically, with white skirts fat with petticoats ready to be flung around and red-and-white bodices. The seventh, a pretty young thing called Millie, stood front and centre, dressed in a deep maroon, her hair loose and cascading down her back.

The show started. Millie sang while the other girls danced behind her, fast numbers with lots of risqué glimpses of stockinged calves and bare thighs. When Mary had first brought her here last year, Lucy had been enthralled; her sheltered upbringing hadn't prepared her for this sort of spectacle. Even the time she'd spent living in St Giles hadn't broadened her horizons as much as she'd first thought. It had seemed inconceivable for a young woman to mesmerise so many men, to use her voice and her body to enthral and entertain.

'She's very good,' Oliver murmured in a gap between songs. 'Lovely voice.'

Most of the men in the room had their eyes fixed on Millie, despite the ever-increasingly scandalous dancing of the women behind her. There was something enthralling about her, something special you couldn't put into words, but was there all the same.

After half an hour and an energetic finale, Millie took a curtsy to raucous applause and whistling and trooped off the stage with the dancers.

'What did you think?' Lucy asked.

'I never imagined I would be sitting in a place like this in Southwark with my wife,' he said slowly.

'But did you enjoy it?'

'I did.'

That reserved admission was enough to keep a smile on Lucy's face as Millie came hurrying over to greet them.

'Caroline,' she gushed, kissing Lucy on the cheek, 'I've missed you.'

Curious eyes turned to Oliver.

'My husband,' Lucy said.

'You're married? Congratulations. When did that happen?'

Lucy hesitated and felt herself stiffen in anticipation as Oliver stepped forward.

'It's a pleasure to meet you, Miss…'

'Millie, everyone calls me Millie.'

'It's a pleasure to meet you Millie. You gave an enthralling performance tonight.'

Millie blushed a little, then gave a pretty curtsy.

'My wife tells me you know one another from the Foundation.'

'Caroline was the reason I had the courage to come and audition for the job here. Without her I don't know where I'd be now.'

'Excuse me, miss, can I buy you a drink?' a young man said, fumbling over his words to the delight of his cackling friends at the table behind him.

'Go,' Lucy urged, knowing socialising with her fans was as much part of the job as singing and dancing.

'We'll catch up soon,' Millie promised as she turned away, smiling sweetly at her admirer.

Lucy allowed Oliver to guide her outside, but stopped him before he had chance to hail a carriage.

'Let's walk for a while,' she said, slipping her hand into his arm.

The evening was clear and cool, but the moonlight gave a pleasant glow to the streets as they walked.

'It seems your friend is happy in what she does,' Oliver said as they walked.

'I think she is. She loves singing, loves being up there on stage.'

'And what comes after?' Oliver asked quietly.

Lucy knew there was more to Millie's job than just singing and enjoying the odd drink with an admirer. She needed patrons, men who provided her with that little bit of additional income that allowed her to survive. It was the cruel way of the world, that someone as talented as Millie still had to degrade herself if she wanted food on the table.

'It's not ideal, of course, but I'm amazed what conditions people will thrive in when they've come from worse situations.'

'Lucy,' Oliver said, his voice with an uncharacteristic amount of emotion, 'did you ever have to…?' He trailed off, unable to finish the question.

'No,' she said simply.

'Good.'

'I was one of the lucky ones. Mary found me before I became desperate.'

He nodded, eyes fixed ahead.

'Let's talk of something else.'

Arm in arm they strolled along the cobbled streets. It wasn't a romantic spot; Southwark had a reputation as the borough of vice and crime, but Lucy felt peculiarly content walking with her husband along the moonlit street.

Skirting the impressive building of the cathedral, they climbed the stairs, Oliver lifting her bodily over the prostrate form of a drunk lying sprawled across two steps. Up on the bridge they paused, leaning on the wrought-iron barrier, looking down into the river.

'Tonight we sampled the entertainment from your world. Tomorrow shall we try some from mine?' Oliver asked.

He probably meant an opera—the favourite entertainment of the *ton*. A place where fewer people seemed focused on the stage than on being seen.

'That would be lovely,' she said graciously. Opera had never been her favourite choice of evening entertainment, but he had agreed to her excursion. The least she could do was agree to his.

'Thank you for a most interesting evening,' he said, turning towards her.

His eyes were dark in the moonlight and, as he straightened and took a step towards her, Lucy had an overwhelming desire to kiss her husband.

She felt her body sway towards him before she could grasp any sort of control and to her horror she felt her lips part in anticipation.

As a new bride she had enjoyed the physical part of her relationship with her new husband, but they'd last kissed well over a year ago. He was barely more than a stranger. She shouldn't be throwing herself at him. Only a few days ago she was doing everything in her power to get him to let her live her life completely separate from him.

'Lucy,' Oliver said, lifting a finger to brush a strand of hair behind her ear. It was an intimate gesture, one that made her want to melt into his arms and never come up for air.

Quickly, before he could see the naked desire in her eyes, she stepped away. A friendly, mutually respectful relationship was one thing—she had found these last few days she could tolerate and even enjoy a platonic marriage to Oliver—but she could not allow it to become anything more than that.

Shivering, but not from the cold, she reminded herself of the pain she'd felt when she'd lost her son. She couldn't ever risk heartbreak like that again and the only way to ensure that was to avoid being intimate with her husband. No matter how much her body was drawing her towards him.

Chapter Nine

He'd sensed something; Oliver was sure of it. A gentle sway of her body towards him, a softening of her lips. For a moment he would have sworn she wanted to be kissed, but he'd hesitated, worried about scaring her away, and then the moment had been gone.

When analysing that moment, Oliver realised with surprise that he'd wanted it, too. He'd wanted to kiss his wife, wanted to pull her into his arms and renew the intimacy they'd once shared.

With a shake of his head he dismissed the idea. The progress they'd made on their relationship in the past week had been nothing short of extraordinary. He shouldn't complicate matters with thoughts of a more intimate relationship. Still, sitting here in his study, he couldn't help but mull over the previous evening, when he knew he should be reading through the letters his steward had sent up from Sussex.

A loud crash from the kitchen followed by muted shouts got him on his feet. Normally he didn't interfere with the running of the house. He had a very capable butler and cook here in London, and a housekeeper who ran his country estate like a military operation back in Sussex. Nevertheless, when the shouting didn't abate he headed for the back stairs down to the kitchens.

He was surprised to find Lucy had beat him and was working on calming the normally stoical cook down, patting her gently on the arm and guiding her to the long bench that ran along one side of the table.

'He'll have to go,' Mrs Finch said, waving a trembling finger in the direction of a boy Oliver recognised.

'I didn't do nothing wrong,' he protested. 'You said I could eat the leftovers. You shouldn't have said that if it wasn't the truth.'

'Freddy, why don't you sit down and we can talk in a moment?' Lucy said.

He was tempted to leave them to it. Lucy seemed to have matters under control, but he was curious as to how she would mediate between the cook and the young boy. And he was curious as to why Freddy from the St Giles's Women's and Children's Foundation was standing in his kitchen causing his normally calm cook to shake with anger.

'He ate a whole ham,' Mrs Finch said, shaking her head. 'It clearly wasn't a leftover.'

'Shouldn't have been left on the side, then,' Freddy grumbled.

'And the insubordination—he's hardly got the attributes to work in a great house.'

'Mrs Finch,' Lucy said, her voice low and soothing, 'Freddy has had a difficult life and sometimes the things we take for granted—such as food on the table—he hasn't always had. He's young and enthusiastic, and he might not have the polish that most of the lads in service do, but I know you've been running this household for a long time and I hoped if anyone could take him under their wing and show him how to act in a good household such as this it would be you.'

The cook looked a little mollified and Oliver had to suppress a smile. He could see how a year of working with a host of different people had made Lucy into quite the negotiator.

'Be patient with him and I'm sure soon he will be more of a help than a hindrance.'

'He needs to stop eating so much,' Mrs Finch grumbled, but Oliver could see his wife had won the cook over.

'When he realises there will always be food available, that he won't go for days without eating again, then I'm sure he will not feel the need to eat whatever is in sight. Until then, Lord Sedgewick and I are happy for him to have an extra helping here and there.'

Oliver nodded in support as Mrs Finch glanced in his direction.

'Will you give him a chance?' she asked.

'Yes, my lady.'

'Thank you, Mrs Finch. I won't forget this.'

Turning to Freddy, Lucy smiled kindly. 'Be a good lad and do what Mrs Finch tells you,' she said encouragingly.

Oliver slipped from the kitchen, climbed back up the stairs and waited for Lucy. She jumped in surprise as he stepped out into her path as she reached the top of the stairs.

'Since when is Freddy a member of our staff?' Oliver asked.

Lucy bit her lip and looked a little sheepish.

'I thought Mrs Finch could use a hand in the kitchens and Freddy is a good boy. He just needs someone to believe in him to get him started in life.'

'Am I going to find any more of your waifs and strays around the house?' Oliver asked. In truth, he didn't mind, as long as none of her protégés started pilfering the silver.

He could tell there was at least one more by the way her cheeks flooded with colour.

'I might have asked a young woman called Florence to be my lady's maid,' Lucy said.

'I'm sure she has great experience of dressing hair and looking after clothes,' Oliver said drily.

'She's a quick learner.'

'In the meantime, can I expect you to adopt a simple style?' he asked and before he could stop himself he was thinking of Lucy in nothing but a thin shift, her hair loose and falling down her back. Involuntarily he reached out, curling a stray strand of dark blonde hair around his fingers.

Even this simple contact was enough to send a jolt through his body and quickly he was suffused with an overwhelming desire for his wife.

'I'm sure I can manage to be adequately turned out,' Lucy said, oblivious to his discomfort.

'Mmm…' Oliver didn't trust himself to speak. He wondered how she would react if he just bent his head and kissed her. Surely one kiss couldn't ruin their fragile relationship.

'I will prove it to you tonight,' Lucy said, setting her shoulders back as if preparing to go into battle.

'I'm sure,' Oliver murmured, hardly hearing

her words, instead wondering what the skin at the base of her neck tasted like. It looked so soft, so inviting. Once he'd kissed her there—the memory of it was burned into his mind—but what he wouldn't give to brush his lips over her sensitive skin again.

'And if I look the part of a viscountess tonight, Florence can stay?' Lucy pushed for an answer.

'Florence?' Oliver asked, his mind trailing a long way behind the conversation, too preoccupied with thoughts of Lucy pressed up against him.

'My maid.'

'What about her?'

'Are you quite all right?' Lucy asked, peering at him strangely.

'Yes,' Oliver said, managing to pull himself together. He was a man of thirty-one, not some green boy, and this was his wife. Perhaps, he thought, there was no harm in reminding Lucy of some of the pleasures of marriage.

Lucy adjusted her hair in the mirror and turned to one side, then the other, checking everything was in place. Despite what she'd said to Oliver, Florence was an appalling lady's maid, but it was hardly surprising when she'd been dragged up by an alcoholic mother in one slum of London and beaten near to death by a gin-drinking husband in another. What the young woman lacked in skill or refinement she made up for in enthusiasm and Lucy was sure, *one day*, she'd make a fine lady's maid.

Smoothing her dress, she pulled on the white satin gloves Oliver had given her soon after their marriage with her new initials—*L.S.* for Lucy Sedgewick—embroidered on the lower edge and the Sedgewick crest beneath them. Satisfied she looked presentable, she thanked Florence for her help and made her way downstairs.

Oliver was waiting, punctual as ever, with her thick cloak in one hand ready to help her on with it.

'Surely it's not that cold outside,' Lucy said, thinking they were only going to be sitting in the carriage and walking to the theatre.

'You'll be glad of it later in the evening,' Oliver said, placing it over her shoulders.

'Where are we going?' Lucy asked, wondering if her assumption about the opera had been wrong.

'Wait and see.'

They took the carriage, heading away from central London as Lucy peered out of the window and wondered what Oliver could have planned.

He was tight-lipped, unwilling to reveal their destination until they arrived.

Settling back into her seat, Lucy watched her husband. There was something different about him tonight. He looked determined and purposeful, which he always did, but tonight these attributes seemed amplified. She wondered what his purpose was and shivered at the thought it could be something to do with her.

'Come,' Oliver said as he helped her down from the carriage.

Lucy had to contain a squeal of pleasure as she realised where they were. Far from spending the evening cooped up in a theatre or opera house, instead Oliver had surprised her by bringing her to the Ranelagh Pleasure Gardens.

'Have you been here before?' Oliver asked.

Lucy shook her head. She'd always wanted to visit, had asked her mother more than once during her Season in London if they could spend the afternoon there, but her mother had never agreed. Their main reason to come to London was to find Lucy a husband and strolling around a pleasure garden was probably not the best use of her time.

'You can see more of the gardens during the day,' Oliver said as they paid their entry fee and walked through the gates. 'But I think there's something rather magical about visiting in the evening.'

As they walked in, the path lit up by dozens of lanterns perched on walls and resting on the ground, Lucy gasped.

'It's beautiful,' she said, squeezing Oliver's arm.

'We never got to do much as a couple before,' he said quietly. 'I want to make up for that now. This is one of my favourite places in London and I wanted to share it with you.'

Feeling a swell of warmth towards her husband. she smiled up at him. It was almost impossible to remember why she had been so reluctant to reunite with him. She knew he was still hurting from how she had abandoned him, but these past few days he had been really trying to put that behind them.

'Come this way,' Oliver said, leading her off the main path and down a well-lit set of stairs. They passed a few other couples on the way, but when they reached the bottom the gardens seemed quieter, as if they had the magical place to themselves.

Carefully Oliver guided her down ever-darkening paths until they reached a small fountain, illuminated by lanterns and splashing away in the darkness.

'The stories say if you throw a coin into the fountain it will grant you one wish,' he said, reaching into a pocket and pulling out two shiny coins.

Wordlessly Lucy took her coin and closed her eyes, squeezing them tight as she formulated a wish in her mind. Then she tossed the coin into the fountain, watching as it splashed and caused ripples to break out on the surface of the water. A moment later Oliver did the same.

'What did you wish for?' he asked, stepping closer and wrapping an arm around her waist. Lucy stiffened instinctively at the contact, but relaxed after a second, allowing her body to sink into his.

'Surely that would spoil the wish.'

'I'm not superstitious. I can tell you mine if you prefer.'

Suddenly Lucy had a deep desire to know what her husband had wished for. She had wished for the same thing she prayed for every evening— that her boy was at peace and no longer suffering as he had been in life.

'What did you wish for?' Lucy asked, knowing deep down it would be dangerous to ask, but not able to stop herself all the same.

'I wished for a kiss,' Oliver murmured.

She had plenty of time to stop him as he bent

his neck slowly, covering her lips with his own as if they had all the time in the world. Even though she knew she shouldn't kiss him, that it went against her need to stay distant from Oliver, she didn't do a single thing to stop him and as his lips met hers she pulled him in closer.

Little jolts of pleasure coursed through her body and Lucy felt as though she were awakening for the first time in over a year. The spot where his hand met the skin of her cheek felt as though it were on fire and all Lucy could think of was keeping this moment going for ever.

'So lovely,' he murmured, kissing the angle of her jaw, her neck, her throat, before returning to the softness of her lips.

Right then, in that moment, Lucy couldn't think of anything more appealing than giving in to every primal desire that was rampaging through her body. She wanted to lie down under him, rediscover the pleasure they had shared at the beginning of their marriage, spend hour upon hour in bed until she knew his body as well as her own.

Reality came crashing back down as suddenly as the first flash of lightning in a summer storm.

'Stop,' she said, planting her hands on his chest and pushing him away.

'Stop?' he asked, his voice deep and confused.

'We can't do this.'

'Of course we can, Lucy. We're married. It's natural.'

In a way he was right—most married couples didn't practise a completely celibate relationship. Still, theirs wasn't the most usual of unions.

'I can't do this,' Lucy said, then corrected herself. 'I won't do this.'

'What's this all about?'

'Please, Oliver, just take me home.'

He looked at her for thirty seconds without speaking and for a moment she thought he would press the issue, but instead he offered her his arm and briskly led her back the way they'd come, walking so quickly she almost had to run to keep up.

Chapter Ten

Oliver glared at an approaching acquaintance, unaware quite how unwelcoming his visage was until the woman and her daughter scuttled away, glancing back over their shoulders with alarmed expressions on their faces.

'Good job there are no children here tonight,' Redmoor murmured as he slipped into the space beside Oliver. 'You'd scare them half to death with that expression.'

Oliver grunted, for once not feeling in the mood for Redmoor's witty remarks. He had insisted they come to the Fletchers' ball despite Oliver's foul mood and now Lucy was completely avoiding him, making everything worse.

'No progress in sowing the seeds of marital harmony?' Redmoor asked.

'No.' It wasn't strictly true. They'd made a lot of progress. Two days ago he'd been satisfied that

Lucy wasn't about to slip away in the middle of the night any more. They'd found an easy truce, a compromise of a relationship that meant they were civil and even friendly towards one another, but now Oliver wanted more.

'Is she here?' Redmoor asked, scanning the room.

'Dancing with our host, Lord Fletcher.'

'Poor girl.' Lord Fletcher had a reputation for being a little overfamiliar with his female guests and no doubt Lucy was being treated to a long accounting of his family history and lineage, admittedly one of the finest in the country, but still not a thrilling subject for the dance floor.

Oliver had no inclination to save her, though, despite knowing what a foul time she would be having. Ever since the previous night, she'd either avoided him or ignored him. Walking around with a troubled look on her face that showed she was fighting some sort of inner turmoil, but refusing to tell him what it was.

Oliver believed the world would be simpler if people just spoke their minds a little more often. In Lucy's case, he would be able to respond to her fears much better if she would just tell him what they were. Instead he was left guessing whether she was avoiding him because she hadn't enjoyed the kiss, if she found him repulsive or if she'd vowed never to be intimate with a man again after the trauma of their son's death.

'She's avoiding me.'

'Barely two weeks into your reunion and already she's avoiding you. What did you do?'

Oliver shrugged—in truth, he had no idea. At the time she'd seemed to enjoy their kiss. Her body had responded to him, her lips had invited him in and then it was as if she had regained conscious control of herself and regretted their moment of intimacy immediately.

'You'll get through to her eventually,' Redmoor said, his voice low and reassuring. 'You're just impatient because you've been waiting so long for this moment.'

'I have not been…' Oliver started speaking, then stopped himself as he saw Redmoor's grin. His old friend was baiting him.

'No one searches for an entire year for a woman they do not care about,' Redmoor said, repeating his comment from the other night.

'Of course I care about her—she's my responsibility.'

She was so much more than that. The turmoil of his emotions the past couple of days was difficult to deal with. He wanted to gather Lucy in his arms and make her promise she would never run away again, then make love to her over and over again. But at the same time he still couldn't trust her, still wondered every morning if she would turn up to breakfast, still found himself holding back out of fear she would crush some part of him.

'I'm going to rescue my wife,' he said, watching as the dance ended and Lucy was escorted off the dance floor by Lord Fletcher.

'May I steal my wife for the next dance?' Oliver asked as he stepped in beside Lucy.

The look of relief on her face was immediate, replaced after a few seconds by one of startled wariness. Momentarily at least she'd forgotten she was avoiding him.

'Charming young lady,' Fletcher said, planting a sloppy kiss on her palm, 'I don't know why you kept her hidden away for so long, Sedgewick. It's a crime to the rest of society.'

'I wanted her all to myself,' Oliver murmured, whisking Lucy away.

'Thank you,' she said as they took their places on the dance floor for a waltz. Two dances, that was all they'd ever shared in life and both had been waltzes. Not that Oliver minded—he liked the slower tempo, the need to hold one's partner close. And it gave much more opportunity for whispered conversations.

Oliver pulled her in closer to him, purposefully narrowing the gap between them to the smallest possible while still maintaining at least the semblance of propriety.

'You need to start talking to me,' he whispered in her ear as he spun her on the first note.

'I do talk to you.'

'About things that matter.'

She remained silent.

'I'm not a monster, Lucy. I want to know when things are upsetting you. I may be able to help.'

'Nothing is upsetting me.'

'You've been avoiding me all day.'

'I've been busy.'

He fell silent, whisking her across the dance floor with ease as he tried to think of another approach.

'I think we should start sharing a bedroom,' he said bluntly. He was ready when Lucy stumbled, missing the step and then another, and he caught her deftly, lifting her slightly before setting her back on her feet. 'We've been married for nearly two years. I can only see benefits to the arrangement.'

'Surely our current arrangement is working perfectly fine.'

'I don't want *perfectly fine*, Lucy,' Oliver growled.

'It's too soon,' she protested.

'Then when? A month? A year? A decade?'

'Yes.'

'Yes to what?'

'I don't know,' Lucy said, visibly flustered. She clearly hadn't been expecting him to press her on the issue; he'd been so reserved until now. 'We should have this conversation in private.'

'Good idea,' Oliver said, whisking her off the dance floor, hearing the murmur of surprise from the other dancers and spectators, but hardly caring.

'Everyone is looking at us,' Lucy said, pulling back as he tugged her by the hand through the crowd.

'Let them look.'

He exited the ballroom, ignoring the curious stares from a group of middle-aged women in the hall, and started testing doors.

'Oliver, we can't do this,' Lucy said, glancing back over her shoulder.

'Of course we can. We're married. There's no scandal in a man being alone with his wife at a ball.'

She opened her mouth as if to protest, but at that moment he found an unlocked door and pulled her into a darkened room.

Lucy swallowed as she heard the click of the lock. She wasn't afraid of Oliver, not that he'd physically hurt her, but she was a little scared of being alone with him. Last night had shown she couldn't trust herself to behave sensibly around him.

She'd never seen him like this before. Until now he'd treated her gently, emotionally as well as physically, content to let her come to him in her own time, but now she was reminded of the man in his study searching for answers on the first day of their reunion.

'Sit,' he said and she found herself obeying, sinking into a plush sofa before her mind had even fully registered the command.

He sat next to her, so close she could smell his scent, that mixture of soap and something sweeter. It was intoxicating to have his body so close to hers and already she felt what little resolve she had slipping.

'Last night,' he said, leaning in so their faces were almost touching, 'I very much enjoyed our kiss by the fountain. I think you did, too.'

She nodded once before catching herself.

'I thought so. I remember how you used to moan underneath me when we were first married. It was the same yesterday.'

Feeling her cheeks burning, Lucy was glad of the near total darkness. Her response to him physically wasn't at all ladylike. Although what happened in the bedroom of married couples was a taboo subject for well-brought-up young ladies, she knew most women did not enjoy it as much as she'd found herself doing. There were always whispers of enduring the deed, of lying back and waiting for it to be over, but her experience had been much, much different.

'I enjoyed kissing you—you enjoyed kissing me. We are married, husband and wife, so there is no moral reason we cannot be intimate, but instantly you regretted it. Enlighten me as to why?'

'I don't know what you're talking about,' Lucy said, knowing this wishy-washy answer wouldn't be enough to pacify her husband.

'So if I was to kiss you again you wouldn't pull away?'

The primal, instinctive part of her swelled with anticipation, needing to feel his lips on hers again.

'Give me one good reason why I shouldn't kiss you,' Oliver said, his voice low.

Lucy knew there were many reasons, arguments she'd thought out in depth in her mind, but right now she couldn't think of a single one of them. Her mind was completely blank.

'We shouldn't,' she said, but even to her own ears she sounded unconvincing.

'One good reason,' Oliver murmured as he leaned forward, 'and I'll stop.'

She shuddered as his lips met hers, his body heavy above her own. Already she was half-reclined on the sofa and as he kissed her she felt her body sinking further into the soft upholstery.

The last of her reason and common sense fled as he trailed his fingers through her hair and cupped the back of her neck, sending shivers down her spine.

For the entire duration of their separation Lucy had been devoid of physical contact and it wasn't until Oliver had kissed her last night that she'd realised how much she'd missed it.

Lucy wrapped her arms around Oliver's muscular back, running her hands over the fabric of his jacket and wishing it was skin. She felt him shift slightly and then his lips were tracing a path down her neck on to the exposed skin of her chest. He pushed the neckline of her dress lower, fighting against the ties and the fabric, until she felt the cool air on her breasts, then she could think of nothing else as his mouth captured a nipple and she let out a guttural groan.

Lucy felt her hips thrust up towards him, moving rhythmically even though there were layers of clothing separating them. He murmured her name and just as she was about to beg him for more she felt his hand on her thigh.

Higher and higher his fingers moved, so leisurely Lucy felt like screaming, then he was caressing the very tops of her thighs, making her want to press her legs together and urge him to continue to her most private place.

Just as his fingers dipped inside her Lucy stiffened, and suddenly all reason came flooding back as quickly as it had fled.

'Stop,' she said, pushing him off her.

Oliver rolled, but his quick reflexes saved him from tumbling to the floor.

'What is it, Lucy?' he asked and to her surprise his voice didn't sound frustrated or annoyed, just concerned.

'I can't do this.'

'Why not?'

'I just can't. Please, Oliver.'

'I'm not going to force you. Good Lord, what sort of man do you think I am? I just want to understand.'

'You can't understand.'

'Try me.'

She hesitated, wondering how to put into words the deep hole David's death had left in her. Her fear of surrendering to her desires, to resuming a full and physical relationship with her husband only to find herself pregnant again. She didn't know if any other children she and Oliver might have would be healthy or not, but she couldn't risk the small chance of another child being born, only to die a few weeks later. Her already fragile heart would completely shatter and this time she wasn't sure she would ever be able to piece it together again.

'I don't want to become pregnant again,' she said quietly.

'Because of David.'

She nodded. 'And…' She trailed off, shaking her head. She wasn't ready to reveal that part of herself yet. Oliver knew about David, had in so many ways shared that loss with her, but he didn't know anything about her brother and the way her family had treated him throughout his short life. Now wasn't the right time to tell him, not when they were both so vulnerable. Perhaps one day she would feel comfortable enough to reveal the challenges her brother had faced each and every day, but it wasn't today. Even though she knew William and his short and difficult life were as much to blame for not wanting to try to bring another child into this world as was her grief over David.

'And what?' he asked.

She shook her head, repeating, 'I don't want to become pregnant again.'

Oliver sank on to the sofa beside her, but didn't make any attempt to touch her again. She felt the gulf widening between them as the silence stretched out for over a minute.

'You don't want to have any more children?' he asked eventually. 'Or you don't want to have any more with me?'

'I can't love another child like I did David only to lose them,' she said.

'Why do you think you'd lose them?'

She shrugged, trying to hide her vulnerability with the movement.

'The doctor said there was no reason we couldn't have a healthy child next time,' Oliver said, pushing her.

'What do the doctors know about these matters?' Lucy asked. 'They can't predict whether a child will be born healthy or not. Hundreds upon hundreds of babies are born with physical or mental problems.'

'But there's no suggestion we would be at any higher risk of having another child like David,' Oliver persisted.

'There are other conditions, as well,' Lucy said quietly.

She thought of her brother, that dear, sweet

boy, marred by his difficult birth and discarded by their father. Oliver didn't even know William had ever existed, not many people did. It was a family secret her father had fought hard to keep. He'd been adamant it would affect their standing in society if it became widely known his wife had given birth to an *imbecile*. Lucy flinched at even the thought of the word. She'd hated it when her father had used it—William was many things, but he was not an imbecile. He struggled to speak, he struggled to move and he didn't have full control of his bodily functions, but there was a quiet intelligence behind his eyes that fought to be seen.

'We can't live our lives in fear,' Oliver said. 'Yes, something terrible may happen, but that is true of any situation. I may get struck by a carriage when crossing the street, you may be thrown from a horse when out riding, but that doesn't mean we avoid going outside.'

'This is different. We can protect ourselves from this easily, too.'

'By not having a full marriage? By leading a celibate life for the next thirty years?'

'Yes.' She couldn't look at him as she spoke. It was a lot to ask of anyone.

'No, Lucy. I'm not willing to accept that.'

'You'll force me?' she asked defiantly.

'Good Lord, you do have a low opinion of me, don't you?'

She felt embarrassed immediately. She'd lashed out, cruelly, and Oliver didn't deserve it. There was no scenario where Oliver would force himself on her and the only reason she'd suggested he would was to hurt him, to push him away.

'I'm sorry,' she said quietly. 'That was unkind.'

She risked a glance up at him and saw the hard set of his jaw in the muted light. Oliver was a problem-solver and now she was the problem. No doubt he would work tirelessly to come up with a solution to their problem, but she doubted he would find one.

'There are…' he paused as if trying to choose the correct words carefully '…*methods* that people use to reduce the chance of a pregnancy.'

Lucy's eyes widened involuntarily. Of course she knew of such practices; working at the Foundation had been an education in many ways.

'They're not reliable,' she said quickly.

'Maybe not one method on its own, but if we combined two or three…'

She felt the lure of temptation and almost found herself agreeing straight out.

'I don't want there to be any chance.'

'Let me at least look into it,' Oliver said.

Hesitating for a moment, Lucy weighed up the options. She wouldn't agree to anything unless it was virtually foolproof and she doubted anything Oliver would come up with would be that effective. If she agreed, she was purely buying herself some time.

'Fine, look into it,' Lucy said. 'But I'm not promising anything.'

The kiss he planted on her lips shocked her so much she barely had time to react and he had pulled away before she could even think about protesting.

Chapter Eleven

Lucy opened the door to the office at the Foundation to see Oliver and Mary jump apart guiltily. A frown forming on her face, she raised her eyebrows in question.

'Good morning,' Mary said, a little too cheerily.

'What are you doing here?' Lucy asked her husband bluntly. He'd been gone before her this morning and she'd found herself both disappointed and relieved. After their kiss and following truce the night before, she had slept uneasily and still didn't quite know how she felt about Oliver's intentions to find some way for them to become intimate without any resulting pregnancies.

'A little bit of business,' he said vaguely.

'Business—what business?'

'Why don't I fetch you a cup of tea, dear?' Mary said, sidling towards the door.

Normally the older woman was adept at dealing with confrontation, but right now she looked as though she'd rather be anywhere else but here.

'Stay,' Lucy said, taking a step to the side and effectively blocking the only exit from the room. 'I want to know what you were discussing.'

'I needed Mary's help with something,' Oliver said, giving a little cough of embarrassment before he spoke.

Lucy felt her cheeks flooding with heat. Surely he hadn't asked Mary, her closest friend and the woman she respected most in the world, about their intimacy dilemma?

He must have seen the expression on her face so quickly pressed on.

'We need to take a little trip,' he said, looking her squarely in the eye. 'And I know how important the work you do for the Foundation is.'

'We'd be lost without you,' Mary agreed.

She had a horrible feeling she wasn't going to like the next words.

'To try to compensate for taking you away for a few days, perhaps a week or two, I thought I would offer some other form of support to the Foundation to help things keep ticking over while you're absent.'

'Other support?'

'Money,' he said bluntly.

'You're paying Mary off?'

'Nothing like that, my dear,' Mary rushed to interject.

'It's just a little donation so you can rest assured that the Foundation won't struggle in your absence.'

'We can hire a teacher to cover the classes you normally take,' Mary said, an optimistic smile on her face.

'And the accounts?'

'You can bring them with you,' Oliver said. 'No point being idle throughout the journey.'

'There would be some money left over,' Mary added. 'Enough to make repairs on the worst of the rooms.'

'Would you excuse us for a moment, Mary? I'd like to have a word with my husband.'

The older woman scurried out of the room in relief.

'What do you think you're doing?' Lucy hissed. 'You can't just come here and bribe Mary to let me go.'

'You're always so melodramatic.' Oliver sighed.

'And you're trying to control me, exactly what you promised you would never do.'

'I have merely tried to smooth the way for you taking a break for two weeks. I didn't want Mary to feel the strain of your absence.'

It all sounded so reasonable when he said it, but the anger was roaring inside Lucy and there was no way to dampen it now.

'You haven't even mentioned this trip to me. Does it even exist? Or is it just a way to prise me away from the Foundation? To make Mary see money is more useful than me?' Her voice was rising now, but Lucy couldn't rein it in, no matter who might be listening outside.

'It is a trip you are not going to like,' Oliver said with a sigh, 'so I thought I would organise the details first. That way you would have less time to dwell on our destination.'

'Where do you want me to go?'

'Brighton.'

'No.'

'Lucy, I know it won't necessarily be a pleasant trip, but I made a promise to your father.'

'Then you go. I'm staying here.'

'That's not an option. I promised him when I found you I'd bring you to visit, and I'm not going to break a promise.'

'I'm not going.'

'The Foundation will be fine without you for a couple of weeks, then you can just take up where you left off when you get back.'

'But there will be a new teacher for my classes…' she reminded him.

'Which can only be a good thing. More teachers mean a better education for the children.'

'Don't pretend there is a selfless motive here, Oliver,' she said. 'You could have donated money at any point. Instead you do it now when you need something in return.'

'I don't *need* anything, Lucy,' he said calmly, his eyes turning hard and his mouth forming a thin line. 'You're my wife, remember. I could forbid you from ever coming to this place again. I'm not going to, because I know how much it means to you, but I could. The donation is to make it easier for you to leave for a couple of weeks. It has no bearing on your involvement here in the future.'

'I'm still not going to Brighton,' she said.

'We leave tomorrow. I'll instruct your maid to pack your bags.'

He leaned in and kissed her gently on the cheek before she could pull away.

'I'm not going,' she called after him as he left.

Sinking down into a wooden chair, Lucy rested her head in her hands. She'd dealt with so much this past year. How was it she couldn't seem to deal with her own husband?

'Are you unwell?' Mary asked from the doorway a couple of minutes later.

'What did he say, Mary?' Lucy asked. 'Is this

really just about a trip away or is it the start of prising me away from here for good?'

'You worry too much, my dear,' Mary said, coming into the room and patting her hand. 'He's a good man, and it is clear he cares for you.'

Lucy snorted and Mary gave her an admonishing look.

'Just because he doesn't kowtow to your wishes doesn't mean he doesn't care for you.'

'He's trying to organise my life.'

'With this donation he's trying to make up for taking you away from something you love. I don't think he has an ulterior motive. He just wants to ease your guilt about leaving us in the only way he can.'

'That's a very trusting way to look at it.'

'Not all people are bad. And I think your husband truly cares for you.'

Lucy thought of the way he looked at her, the escorts to the Foundation, how he took time out of his schedule to accommodate hers. Just as she was softening a little towards him she rallied. It didn't make up for his attempting to take her to Brighton to visit her father.

'He wants me to visit my father,' she said miserably.

'Does he know how sour your relationship is?'

Lucy shrugged. She hadn't divulged much

about her family when they were first married so she supposed he only knew the public face of the De Pointe family.

'Perhaps you should tell him. You can't expect him to anticipate your needs and wants if you never communicate with him.'

It was true, as little as she wanted to admit her friend was right.

'I can't tell him about William,' she said, feeling the tears rush to her eyes as she thought of her brother.

'Why not?'

'I just can't.'

She'd kept her brother secret for so long it wouldn't feel right talking about him, even now.

'Well, then, go along with his plan, let him see how cruel your father is for himself and then it's likely you'll never have to visit again.'

'Why do you have to be so level-headed?' Lucy grumbled.

'I like him,' Mary said after a moment.

'My father? You've never met him.'

'Your husband. He's different from most of the titled ladies and gentlemen I've met.'

In her work fundraising for the Foundation, Mary had encountered much of the *ton*. Although they had a few steadfast patrons who were generous and kind, most of the upper classes were too self-interested to get involved with a charity like theirs.

'I think it's because he wasn't raised expecting to inherit the title.'

'Could be, or it could just be him. You should give him a chance to show you what marriage to him could be like.'

'You're sounding more and more like his advocate,' Lucy grumbled.

'I just want you to be happy, my dear, and I think if you let him your husband could make you happy.'

She thought of the uncontrollable desire she'd felt for him on the occasions they'd kissed and the easy companionship they shared when she let herself relax around him. Perhaps Mary was right, but she just didn't seem to be able to lower her defences when Oliver was around. It might be habit, a way to protect herself from further heartbreak, but she just couldn't seem to let him closer.

'Go on this trip, enjoy your husband's company and let him see why you don't wish to ever see your father again. Your place here will always be waiting for you. I need all the help I can get.'

'Thank you, Mary,' Lucy said, getting up and embracing the older woman. 'I'm sorry I said what I did.'

She regretted accusing Mary of accepting a bribe from Oliver—once again she'd spoken rashly in anger. It was a trait she couldn't seem to break.

Chapter Twelve

Oliver tapped his fingers on the carriage seat and felt the thumping of his heart in his chest. After spending so many years in the army hardly anything fazed him, but today he was nervous. Lucy was still barely talking to him after catching him giving Mary the donation and he couldn't quite work out if she was angry because of implication that the money could replace her or angry with him for arranging a trip to see her father.

In truth, the last place he wanted to go tomorrow was Brighton. He had met Lucy's father on three occasions: the first to ask for her hand in marriage, the second on their wedding day and the third a few months after she had disappeared. He'd travelled to Brighton to see if her family had heard from her and found the old man to be rude and condescending, but worst of all barely worried about the safety of his daughter. The older man had, however, kept his word to write every three months with any news or rumours he'd heard that might have helped Oliver in his search. In return, Oliver felt obliged to fulfil his end of the agreement and take Lucy to visit her father now he had found her.

As well as keeping a promise, the trip had another purpose. Lucy had hardly mentioned her family throughout their short marriage and he had a strange instinct that there was something she was hiding from him. He didn't know if it was anything that might impact on their relationship, or her reluctance to have any more children, but if there was even the slightest chance it might he wanted to be fully informed. Oliver was a great believer in gathering as much information as possible before attempting a final assault.

Still, Lucy's bizarre family and their trip to Brighton would wait until tomorrow. This afternoon he had a more important mission to complete.

'Where are we going?' Lucy asked. They were the first words she'd uttered to him since he'd picked her up at the end of her working day. She'd held out for an admirably long time, throughout their walk through St Giles, the carriage ride through central London and only now they were approaching the East End did her curiosity cause her to break her silence.

'It is probably easier if I explain when we get there,' Oliver said, knowing he was only postponing the inevitable.

Lucy fell silent, looking out of the window again as they pulled up outside a smart house with a private side entrance, one that wasn't overlooked by the road or any neighbours.

'Come,' Oliver said, taking her hand and helping her down, wondering all the time if he was making a mistake.

It was late afternoon, the sun still up and the street busy, so he led her quickly to the side entrance before knocking on the door.

A well-dressed middle-aged lady opened the door and smiled warmly.

'Lord Sedgewick, I presume this is your wife?'

Lucy shot him a questioning glance, but he just motioned for her to follow the woman inside.

They made their way through to a comfortable sitting room, with plush furnishings and dim lamps, the curtains pulled closed despite the abundance of sunlight outside the windows.

'Can I get you some refreshments?'

Lucy shook her head, but Oliver quickly ordered tea. He wanted something stronger, but restrained himself. A clear head would be needed to navigate through the next hour.

'I'll bring the girls in shortly.'

'Where have you brought me?' Lucy rasped as the door closed behind their hostess.

'Don't be angry,' he said, as the understanding blossomed in Lucy's eyes.

'It's a brothel, isn't it?'

'A reputable one, I'm told.'

'Is it the one you frequent?'

'I haven't been to a brothel since my university days,' Oliver said honestly. He didn't like the places, didn't like the idea of paying a woman to do something that had no feeling behind it, no real meaning.

'She seemed to know you.'

'I came by earlier to arrange this meeting,' Oliver said.

'Why are we here?'

'You wish to know how to prevent a pregnancy. I thought who better to ask than the women whose livelihoods depend upon it.'

'You want me to get marital advice from prostitutes?' Her face was incredulous.

'I thought you'd be more likely to believe it if you heard it first-hand.'

Oliver wasn't entirely happy to be here himself. He wanted to resume the physical side of their relationship, but his feelings about having children in the future were mixed. Of course he wanted a family, a brood of young children running around his estate, but he was convinced a pregnancy, especially this early on in their re-union, might make Lucy run away again. The last thing he wanted was a repeat of the situation of a year ago. One day they would be ready to be parents again, but first they needed to be comfortable with one another, to trust one another, and despite the progress they'd made the trust still wasn't entirely there on either side.

'I can't believe you'd do this,' she hissed, glancing at the door as if contemplating escape.

'You agreed for me to look into our options.'

'Last night. I didn't think we'd be sitting waiting for a horde of prostitutes the very next day.'

His eyes narrowed. 'What exactly are you protesting about, Lucy?' he asked. 'My methods or the speed at which I've come up with an answer?'

She opened her mouth, but before she could reply the door opened again and three young women came gliding in, one carrying a tray with a pot of tea and five cups.

'Lord Sedgewick,' one of the women greeted him, 'And Lady Sedgewick, we're led to under-stand?'

Oliver stood. It was true he hadn't been in a

brothel or associated with any women of the profession since his university days so he wasn't entirely sure how to act, but politeness never went amiss.

'I'm Annabelle, this is Hetty and this is Fanny,' the woman carrying the tray said as she began to pour cups of tea.

'Did Mrs Gardener tell you why we are here?' Oliver asked, taking the cup of tea that was proffered.

'Some advice about preventing a baby,' Fanny said bluntly.

'Exactly. My wife is keen not to get pregnant.'

Annabelle looked at Lucy with open curiosity, then suggested, 'Perhaps we should talk to Lady Sedgewick alone.'

Oliver shrugged. He didn't much care how they acquired the information, he was just happy Lucy hadn't run screaming from the house. He allowed himself to be escorted into a comfortable parlour where he was left to finish his tea in peace, all the while wondering exactly what the women were discussing in the next room.

'How on earth did you bag him?' Fanny asked as Annabelle re-entered the room and closed the door behind her.

'He's a handsome one,' Hetty agreed. 'Kind eyes, too. I bet he pays you well.'

'Pays me?' Lucy asked, taking a moment to catch up. 'You think I'm his mistress.'

'Well, he wouldn't really bring his wife to see us.'

'He has,' Lucy said bluntly. 'Lord Sedgewick is a singular man.'

The three women stared at her, as if still not quite believing she was Lady Sedgewick.

'And you really want to know how to stop a baby?' Hetty asked, suspicious.

'Yes.'

'Why? If that was my man, I'd get plump mothering his children,' Fanny said.

Lucy was used to the direct way of speaking these women had from her work and found it refreshing to be among people who just asked the questions that were on their minds rather than hinting they might like to know an answer.

'Our son died,' Lucy said, feeling the familiar rush of sadness. She swallowed, trying to keep the emotion from her voice. 'I can't lose another child.'

'Oh, you poor thing,' Annabelle gushed, rushing over and putting an arm around Lucy's shoulders. 'Losing a child is the worst thing in the world.' It was said with such feeling that Lucy wondered if the other woman had also lost a baby. She looked young, in her early twenties like Lucy herself, but that didn't mean she hadn't ever mothered a child. Many of their age had a brood of three or four already.

'Lord Sedgewick is keen to resume the physical side of our relationship,' Lucy said, 'so that is why we're here.'

'And do you want him?' Fanny asked, leaning forward as she waited for Lucy to answer. 'If not, send him my way and I'll keep him happy for you.'

Lucy felt a sudden rush of anxiety. When they had first reconciled she had assumed Oliver had a mistress, someone who'd kept him occupied in the bedroom during her time absent, but now she doubted it was true. The idea that he might decide to get his needs satisfied another way if she continued to refuse him was decidedly unpalatable and she felt a little swell of panic inside her abdomen.

'Hush, Fanny,' Annabelle said. 'Don't mind her. What is it you want to know?'

'Are there ways to prevent getting pregnant?'

'Oh, yes,' Annabelle said. 'Look at us, seven years we've been here between us, seeing a different man each night, and not a single baby in that time.'

'How do you do it?'

'Well, the most important thing is to never let a man finish inside you,' Annabelle said. 'I'm told it's still *possible* to get pregnant if he finishes elsewhere, but I've never seen it.'

The other two women nodded in agreement.

'Of course, persuading a man to pull back in the heat of the moment can be tricky, but I'd wager your husband is good at self-control.'

'And some of them just like to see their seed splashed on various parts of your body.'

Lucy blushed at the vivid imagery, but nodded for the women to continue. No point becoming prudish now.

'Some women also like to count the days of their monthly cycle,' Annabelle said. 'They say you are more fertile in the middle few days than at either end.'

'And there are sheaths,' Hetty piped up.

'She doesn't want to start messing around with those disgusting contraptions,' Fanny said. 'They're more faff than they're worth.'

'Of course, if you did become pregnant there are many ways to get rid of a child before your belly begins to show,' Annabelle said quietly.

Lucy shook her head. It was one thing preventing a pregnancy, but she doubted she would be able to end one when she already knew there was a life growing inside her. Especially if she didn't know if the child would be healthy or not.

'If I used these methods,' Lucy said, feeling her resolve flicker, 'how likely is it do you think that I would get pregnant?'

'Unlikely,' Annabelle said with conviction. 'Especially if you're just having sex once every few weeks.'

Thinking back to the first days of their marriage when they'd tumbled into bed multiple times a day, Lucy shook her head. They were both different now, changed by the time they had spent apart. It was unlikely that they would pick up the physical side of their relationship where they had left off over a year ago.

'If he was my husband…' Fanny started, but trailed off as Annabelle flashed her a warning look.

'I'm sure Lord Sedgewick knows of these methods, but it's up to you how much you tell him of what we've said today,' Annabelle said quietly, patting Lucy on the hand. 'We women don't have control over much in our lives, but I think your husband would honour your control over your body. Not all men are so inclined.'

'Thank you,' Lucy said.

She finished her tea, finding it surprisingly easy to talk to the three prostitutes despite the vast differences in their social statuses. When she had finished, Annabelle left momentarily to fetch Oliver and together he and Lucy thanked the women. Oliver handed over a small sum of money for their time and they dashed back outside to the waiting carriage.

'What did you learn?' Oliver asked as they settled back in the seats. He'd sat next to her, probably so they could better discuss the facts Lucy had been given, but his proximity was causing her to lose her concentration.

Lucy hesitated. She didn't know how much to tell Oliver and how much to hold back. If she admitted there were ways to drastically reduce the chance of a pregnancy then there would be no reason to stay celibate any longer. The idea both excited and scared her.

'They suggested a couple of things,' Lucy said. She should have felt uncomfortable discussing such private matters with her husband, but his matter-of-fact ways meant it was less embarrassing somehow.

'What did they suggest?'

'Apparently withdrawing before the moment of, ah…' She trailed off, wondering how to put it politely.

'Climax.'

Nodding, Lucy was grateful he'd stepped in.

'Anything else?'

'Counting days.'

'I see. So what is your verdict?'

It felt wrong discussing such an emotional issue so bluntly.

'Let me think about it,' she said, relieved when he nodded and sat back.

Chapter Thirteen

Oliver stretched, turning his face up to the warm autumn sun and tasting the salt on his lips. It was a long time since he'd visited the seaside, but immediately he was transported back to happy trips with his brothers, long sun-filled days playing on the sand while their parents strolled along the promenade.

Lucy reluctantly stepped down from the carriage, none of the joy present in his expression visible on her face.

'We could just turn around and go back,' Lucy said. 'It's not too late.' She'd been suggesting the same the whole way from London with decreasing levels of optimism in her voice.

A seagull squawked overhead and Lucy glared at it, channelling her annoyance at being forced back to her home town for the first time in two years.

'Shall we get settled into our lodgings?' Oliver asked. 'Or would you like to go directly to see your father.'

'I need to change,' Lucy said after weighing up the options for a few seconds. 'But we should see Father as soon as possible. Then we can leave again.'

'I'd have thought you'd want to have a break from travelling.'

They'd only been on the journey for two days, and today they had arrived in Brighton well before lunch. The roads from London to Brighton were relatively well maintained and it wasn't all that far a distance. Nevertheless, Oliver certainly didn't want to turn straight around and spend another two days cooped up in an uncomfortable carriage.

'I want to spend as little time as possible here,' Lucy said, then corrected herself. 'Actually I want not to be here at all, but it seems that isn't an option.'

'You might find you enjoy yourself.'

She snorted, an unladylike noise that Oliver had to suppress a smile at. She'd certainly picked up some mannerisms from the women and children at the Foundation.

'Come,' he said, offering her his arm.

Rather than upset Lucy further by suggesting

they stay with her father, he had secured a set of rooms with magnificent views over the sea. As they climbed the stairs to the first floor and waited while their host unlocked the door, Oliver felt more carefree than he had done in a long time. They might be here for a very specific reason, but it also felt like a holiday, perhaps even the honeymoon they'd never had.

Even Lucy had to gasp in pleasure as they entered the sitting room. It was light and airy, with high ceilings and two large windows with views across the promenade and out to sea.

'The bedroom is upstairs,' their host said as he handed over the key to Oliver, leaving them alone.

'Bedroom?' Lucy asked, immediately picking up on the singular.

'Bedroom,' Oliver confirmed.

She swallowed, her pupils dilating a fraction, but he noticed she didn't protest and felt a surge of hope.

'Let me show you,' he said, taking her by the hand and pulling her up the narrow set of stairs.

The bedroom was nearly as big as the sitting room below, with the same double windows and view over the seafront. A large bed occupied the centre of the room and dotted around the perimeter were various pieces of comfortable furniture.

'Only one bed,' Lucy confirmed.

'We shared a bed before,' Oliver reminded her gently.

He doubted she'd forgotten that heady month when they'd barely left the bedroom after their marriage.

'And I promise to be the perfect gentleman.' It was a promise he would find hard to keep, but he knew she had to come to him. There was no point in pushing too hard, but hopefully a few days sharing a bed and she would see the mutual benefits of renewing their intimacy.

She nodded and he was surprised at how easily she capitulated. He'd half-expected her to demand lodgings with separate bedrooms and had enquired about availability before they had journeyed down here. But it seemed sharing a bed was an acceptable next step for Lucy.

'I shall leave you to change,' he said, backing out of the room and closing the double doors behind him.

He was downstairs, staring out the window to the grey-blue expanse of sea when Lucy emerged. She'd changed into a dress she'd purchased when they'd first married—a long-sleeved cotton garment in pale blue with a white sash. It suited her, and their location, but he was glad when she wrapped a shawl around her shoulders to keep out the bite of the fresh autumn air.

'Can we go for a walk before we call on my father?' Lucy asked.

It was a delaying tactic, but Oliver readily agreed. He hoped they would have some time to enjoy each other's company while away from London and the pressures on both their time and attention, and this seemed like the perfect start to their trip.

Arm in arm they strolled along the esplanade, heads bowed slightly to the persistent wind. After only a few minutes Lucy had pink cheeks and a red tinge to the tip of her nose.

'Tell me about growing up here,' Oliver said, aware of how little he knew about Lucy's life before she had married him.

She glanced at him sharply, but after regarding him for a moment seemed to relax.

'I used to love living by the sea,' Lucy said, gazing out at the rolling waves past the pebble beach. 'My nanny was of the opinion fresh air was an important part of a young girl's development and we would go for walks along the promenade in the winter, or across the hills further afield in the summer.'

'I used to enjoy coming to the seaside as a child,' Oliver said. 'It seemed like a different world, with the beach and the tearooms and the families laughing and happy.'

Lucy grimaced. 'I couldn't ever describe my family as laughing or happy, but I did enjoy playing on the beach and dipping my toes in the sea when I was young.'

Grasping on to the little nugget of information about her family, Oliver wondered how to probe further without being too obvious.

'Did your mother take you on the beach?' he asked.

Lucy laughed wryly and shook her head. 'Never. I don't think I ever saw her set foot off the promenade once and she used to tut and reprimand my nanny if I came home sandy or with a little seawater on the bottom of my dress.'

'And your father?'

'He didn't really do much with us—me at all.' He caught the slip and saw the panic in her eyes as she quickly corrected herself, wondering who this 'us' referred to. Lucy had never mentioned a sibling and when his mother had been scouting for prospective brides for him he was sure she'd said she was an only child.

'Well, at least you had an adventurous nanny.'

He saw the relief in her eyes when he didn't pursue her slip of the tongue and felt her press a little closer to his body.

'You're shivering,' he noted, feeling the miniscule movements where her body met his.

'It is a little chilly,' she admitted. 'You forget what a sea wind feels like when you're in London.'

Quickly he led her off the promenade and into a tea shop he'd spotted earlier, making sure she was comfortable before motioning the waitress over to place their order.

Once they both had a steaming cup of tea in their hands, he decided to broach the subject of her family once again.

'Tell me, why is there such a rift between you and your father?'

'There's no rift as such—we just don't get on.'

He didn't believe her. You didn't react like Lucy had when he'd mentioned the visit to see her father if you had a mild dislike for someone.

'Is it a personality difference?'

'Perhaps. He was a distant father and I barely knew him as a child.'

'There's more,' Oliver said, 'something you're not telling me.'

She regarded him for a moment, then just when he thought she might give in and tell him she shook her head. 'You've met him. He's not exactly the most amiable of men.'

Oliver had instantly disliked the man. He

was opinionated, pompous and looked down on anyone and everyone. He had noble blood in his veins, he'd told Oliver, although hadn't bothered to elaborate where this noble blood was from. As far as Oliver could tell he was a second son of a second son of a baron. Hardly a close relative to the King.

'You can tell me,' he said softly.

'Tell you what?'

'Anything. Sometimes it helps to share.'

'There's nothing to tell,' Lucy said, taking a large gulp of tea. He didn't believe her, not one bit. Lucy had always been tight-lipped when it came to her family. Her mother had died six months after their wedding and Oliver had only met the woman once. She and Lucy didn't seem particularly close, despite Lucy being the woman's only child. Then there was her dislikeable father, of course, but Oliver had always felt there was something more to the De Pointe family, something Lucy worked very hard not to tell him. Hopefully today would be the day he unveiled a few more of Lucy's family secrets.

Twenty minutes later they were ascending the short flight of stairs to the front door of the house where Lucy had spent her unhappy childhood. Already she could feel the coil of dread deep in the pit of her stomach, but as Oliver stood back from the heavy iron door knocker he took her hand and squeezed. She found the gesture surprisingly reassuring.

'We can leave whenever you wish,' he whispered.

She began to tell him that her wish had been never to come in the first place, but the words died in her throat when the door opened and she was confronted with the sight of Jamieson, her father's ancient butler. Jamieson had been at least sixty when she was a child and must be closer to seventy now. His face was still dour and his expression unwelcoming as he looked Lucy and Oliver over.

'Miss De Pointe,' he said, not moving aside to let them in.

'Lady Sedgewick,' Oliver corrected, looming over the elderly butler.

'I shall see if your father is home.'

It would have been the accepted custom to invite them in to wait in the drawing room or even just stand in the hall while the butler made enquiries as to whether her father was at home to visitors, but instead Jamieson pushed the door closed and left them standing on the doorstep like unwanted tradesmen.

'As welcoming as ever,' Lucy muttered.

Two minutes passed, and then three. Just as Lucy was about to insist they leave, the door opened again.

'Your father will see you now,' Jamieson said.

They followed him inside to a darkened hallway and waited while he announced them before the butler stepped aside and allowed them into the drawing room.

Lucy's father lived in a modern house situated directly overlooking the sea. It had a white front, guarded by black-iron railings and beautiful round bay windows in the front rooms that gave uninterrupted views of the sea. This had always been Lucy's favourite room when she'd been growing up, but now it had been taken over by her father's oppressive presence.

'Lucy,' her father croaked from his position in his armchair by the window.

She bowed her head in acknowledgement, but did not move to embrace him. Theirs wasn't that sort of relationship.

'You found her, then.' This was addressed to Oliver, who inclined his head sharply but didn't say anything.

'How are you, Father?'

'Awful. Left to rot here on my own. No one to take care of me.'

Although he spoke the truth, Lucy found it

hard to feel sympathy for him. Her mother had died just after her marriage to Oliver, and her brother two years before that. She was the only surviving close relative and her father had never had the temperament to make friends or endear people to him. Even the turnover of servants in the De Pointe household was high due to his demanding behaviour and poor view on working conditions. Only Jamieson, the surly butler, had ever stayed for any length of time and that was because his temperament was similar to her father's.

Lucy moved forward and perched on the edge of another armchair as it became apparent her father wasn't going to invite them to sit.

'Where did you find her?' Again directed at Oliver.

'Would you like to tell your father where you've been?' Oliver asked her, standing behind the chair she'd chosen and resting a protective hand on her shoulder.

'In London.'

Her father's lip curled in disgust. He'd never liked London, allowing her a Season when she'd turned eighteen at her mother's insistence on the understanding that he would not be escorting them. Lucy didn't think she could ever remember her father travelling to the capital in her entire life, but he certainly had a poor view of the city.

'And what were you doing in London?' The tone of his voice made it clear that he suspected she'd resorted to all manner of degrading acts to support herself while she'd been missing.

'She helped to run a Foundation for women and children in the slums,' Oliver said when no answer was forthcoming from her. 'A very worthy cause.'

Snorting, Mr De Pointe grasped the glass half-filled with honey-coloured liquid and took a big gulp, closing his eyes as he did so. Lucy had known her father was a habitual drinker from a very young age, often noticing the effects of the drink on his mood: from the grouchy man who stomped around the house until he succumbed to the first drink of the day, to the more genial, relaxed midday drinker, to the cruel and sometimes even violent man he turned into in the evenings. Although now it was not yet lunchtime and it appeared he'd already imbibed a fair amount of alcohol. Perhaps in his old age and loneliness the drinking was getting worse.

'We should leave,' Lucy said, not wanting Oliver to see her father become further incapacitated.

'That's right, run away again,' her father taunted her. 'You never did care for your responsibilities.'

Feeling the anger boiling inside her, Lucy tried to suppress a response, knowing anything she said would just prolong their encounter and make things worse.

'Always happy to abandon her family, that's our Lucy.'

'Me?' she asked, unable to keep quiet. 'You talk about abandoning family and it is me you accuse.'

'Well, that's what you did. First when you got married and left me on my own after your mother's death and then when you abandoned your husband. It's a miracle he's taken you back, not knowing what filthy things you've been getting up to this past year.'

'Please do not talk to my wife in that way,' Oliver said, his voice flinty.

'Well, I learnt from the best. Abandoning William when he needed you to be his advocate, his protector,' Lucy said before she could stop herself.

Her father snorted. 'Him? You always were unnaturally fond of him.'

'He was good and kind and sweet. A hundred times the man you were.'

'He was nothing. I should have drowned him in the bath at birth.'

Lucy felt her whole body stiffen and wondered if today would be the day she would actually strike her father. She'd been tempted over the years, mainly when he'd talked about her brother in such derogatory terms, but until now she'd always feared her father just a little. It was hard not to think of herself as a little girl and him as the unforgiving head of the family, but now, after spending so much time away, she saw him for what he really was: a weak, pitiful man.

'You should have looked after him,' Lucy said, feeling the anger drain from her body. 'But you didn't. That would have been too noble.'

'God punished me with my children.'

'I think you got off lightly,' Lucy said, standing. 'Goodbye, Father. I doubt we shall see each other again.'

She didn't wait for his reply, but took Oliver by the arm and marched him to the door, not waiting for Jamieson to let them out.

Chapter Fourteen

'I need to get away from here,' Lucy said as she hurried down her father's front steps, her whole body shaking.

'Where would you like to go?'

'Somewhere quiet, somewhere private. Will the carriage be ready?'

'If we hire fresh horses.'

'Please, Oliver.'

He realised that although she'd asked many things of him in the weeks since their reunion, this was the first time she truly needed his help. Quickly he organised and paid to hire fresh horses and have them secured to the carriage and within half an hour they were on the road, weaving their way through the progressively quieter streets of Brighton and along the coast road. Lucy was deep in thought and for a while he left her to her own contemplations.

She'd revealed probably more than she'd meant to with her outburst against her father. He knew now she had a brother she'd never mentioned, a brother with some sort of handicap. Certain this was part of the reason she had reacted so mistrustingly when she'd realised their son was going to face difficulties in life, Oliver was determined to ask more about this brother, but knew he had to give her time to calm down a little first.

After a brief stop for Lucy to give directions to the coachman, they slowed as they entered a small town.

'Seaford,' Lucy explained as they stopped at one end of the promenade.

Not as upmarket or popular as Brighton, Seaford was just a small settlement, but the houses were smart and well-looked-after and the people seemed well-to-do. It had a long promenade that was above the natural beach and to one end the chalky cliffs rose away from the town.

'How long until dark?' Lucy asked.

'Three hours, maybe four.'

'Plenty of time. I don't mind if you want to stay here.'

'Where are you going?'

She indicated a small path worn into the chalky cliff, close to the edge. There was no way he was allowing her to wander off up the clifftop unaccompanied. It might be dangerous, with falling chunks of cliff, and he didn't want her going anywhere alone in the emotional state she was in.

'I'll join you.'

They walked, climbing briskly, the wind whipping around their heads and slowing their progress, but providing a welcome cooling breeze on their faces. There were stunning views in every direction, but Oliver's eyes kept being drawn out to sea, the water a deep grey with crests of white foam as the waves crashed as they broke. It was dramatic and beautiful at the same time.

'Isn't it magnificent?' Lucy said as they reached the top.

The view was more than magnificent. Rolling hills with white cliffs stretched off into the distance, and closer, down in the valley between this set of hills and the next, a snaking blue river emptied out into the sea. The sky was overcast, but the moody greys and deep purples just added to the atmosphere up on the clifftop.

'Tell me about your brother,' Oliver said as they slowed their pace, strolling now they had reached the top.

'My brother?'

'You've never mentioned him before.'

'I'm sure you don't want to know the intricacies of my family history,' Lucy said, the tension back in her voice.

'I do, Lucy. Tell me about him.'

She sighed and for a moment he wondered if she would march right back down the cliff without him. It would be in keeping with her character to avoid the conversation and easy for her to stride away from him across the grassy terrain.

Instead she looked around her, found a patch of reasonably flat, dry grass and sat down, indicating for Oliver to sit beside her. She moved in a little closer, pulling her shawl tighter around her shoulders and gently Oliver placed an arm around her in an effort to keep her warm as the wind whipped around them.

'William was four years younger than me, the much-anticipated first son after a disappointing daughter as their firstborn.'

Mr De Pointe might not have had a grand estate or title, but he was like many men—obsessed with the idea of passing on the family name and any inheritance through a son. They became caught up in the need to sire a boy, often dismissing their firstborn girls as nothing more than a nuisance. Oliver could imagine the scenario, an absent father to his daughter, but a seemingly proud father of his son.

'My mother had a straightforward birth with

me, so she was not concerned about her second pregnancy. She had her sister there for support, but no one thought there was any need to call a doctor.' Lucy paused. 'I don't know if I remember her screams, or if I imagined them at a later date, when I knew the story, but she laboured for close to twelve hours.'

Although he'd come across many ailments and injuries during his time in the army, childbirth was one thing men of fighting age were not afflicted with and so Oliver didn't know much about it. Twelve hours didn't seem unusually long, but he couldn't tell for sure.

'It became apparent that my brother was stuck about eleven hours in. My mother began bleeding heavily and that was when the doctor was called. He told my father the chances of either of them surviving were pretty poor, but with some manoeuvring he was able to deliver my brother.'

'And your mother survived.'

'Yes. She bled, a lot by her account, and was laid up for days, but eventually she recovered with no obvious long-term effects.' Childbirth was one of the most dangerous times of a woman's life and Oliver knew many families who had lost wives and mothers at the culmination of a pregnancy.

'And your brother?'

'The doctor declared it a miracle that he survived and at first my father was the image of a proud parent, doting on his first son.'

From the tone of her voice he could tell the story was about to turn sour.

'Did something happen?'

She shook her head. 'William grew and as he grew it became apparent he wasn't like other children his age. His limbs were stiff and contracted, and he did not develop as he should. By the age of five he could not speak more than a few words and he could not really walk.'

Oliver took her hand as he saw the tears in her eyes.

'My father became obsessed with what other people would think of the family and arranged for him to be looked after by a farmer's family just outside Brighton. He didn't want an *imbecile* living under his roof.' She spat out the word *imbecile* and Oliver knew immediately it would have been her father's favourite derogatory term for her brother.

'And your mother?'

'She could never stand up to my father. By this point she had realised she was unable to bear any more children, so her focus turned to me. She told me she thought my prospects of a good marriage would be harmed by William. People might think some sort of disease ran in our family.'

Oliver frowned, understanding now why she had been so reluctant to trust him when their own son had been born with problems of his own.

'It doesn't,' she said quickly. 'What David was born with and how William was are two completely different things. The doctors said William took too long to be born. He half-suffocated inside my mother, that was why he developed problems.'

'What happened to your brother? Did the family mistreat him?'

Lucy shook her head, smiling fondly for a moment. 'No, the Smiths were kind. William loved being part of their family—they would carry a bed outside for him so he could watch them all on the farm. Those were the best years of his life.'

'So what happened?'

'Mr Smith died and without him Mrs Smith couldn't continue to look after William. It was too physical a job for her alone. William was moved to another family who did not care for him in the same way.'

'They neglected him?'

'Worse, they hurt him. I never knew how badly because my father forbade me from visiting. I only managed to sneak out to see him a couple of times. But he became withdrawn, un-happy.'

Oliver could see the tension in Lucy's shoulders as she remembered that difficult period in her life and wished he could do something to wash it away.

'William lost whatever mobility he'd had and was completely bed-bound. It was a miracle a chest infection didn't claim him sooner. He died when he was thirteen.'

So two years or so before he and Lucy had married, by Oliver's calculation.

'I'm sorry,' he said, taking her hand and squeezing it gently.

'My father paid for a basic funeral, but forbade us to attend. I didn't even see my own brother buried.'

'You haven't spoken of your brother before.'

Lucy shook her head. 'I find it painful to re-member. I suppose it is guilt that I feel, that I didn't do more, that I didn't stand up to my father.'

The circumstances around her brother's ban-ishment from the family home went a long way to explaining why she had been so mistrustful when their son had been born with a similar con-dition. She'd seen her nightmare played out before, with her father as the villain and her brother as the victim.

'Lucy, you do know I would never abandon a child, no matter how they were born?' he asked softly. He found her answer mattered to him and felt the piercing pain through his heart as she looked at him searchingly.

'Who knows how they will react?' she said softly. 'If you'd asked my father before William was born what he would do, would he have admitted to not tolerating within his household anyone less than what society deems physically normal?'

'We may not have been married long, or reunited for a long time, but surely you can tell a little about a person's character even from a short acquaintance?'

Regarding him with wide brown eyes, she sighed. 'I know you are a better man than my father.'

'I would never abandon a child,' he said firmly. 'I need you to understand that and believe it.'

'Even if they were completely unable to do anything for themselves?'

'That's when they would need their parents the most.'

She stood and waited for him to rise, and Oliver felt a wave of disappointment washing over him. He might have got to the bottom of why Lucy was so mistrustful when it came to the subject of children, but if he couldn't convince her he wouldn't ever send a child away, no matter what their physical or mental problems, then he was unlikely to persuade her they were ready to start a family together again. He himself wasn't sure he was in the right place to consider a child just yet; first he had to convince himself Lucy wouldn't disappear again at the first hint of conflict, but one day he did want a family.

'I know you're a better man than my father,' Lucy said softly as they started their descent back to the long stretch of the esplanade.

It wasn't much of a compliment—one could be a poor specimen of a man and still be better than Lucy's father. For now it would have to be enough, but Oliver was determined one day she would see he would make a splendid father, no matter what challenges parenthood threw up along the way.

Chapter Fifteen

Turning over slowly, Lucy tried not to make any sudden movements. They'd spent their first night sharing a bed together since Oliver had returned to the army a short time after their wedding. All night she'd been aware of his large, masculine presence, and she'd found herself gripping on to the edge of the mattress to restrain her body from burrowing in against his.

Noiselessly she turned again, this time so she was facing Oliver. His eyelashes rested on his cheeks and sleep had smoothed some of the faint lines that were visible on his forehead during waking hours.

She'd been dreading this visit to see her father, dreading returning to all the places that held painful memories of the past, but she had to admit it had been cathartic in some ways. There was no doubt in her mind she'd seen her father for the last time and it had felt good to say a final farewell. He would never have to trouble her thoughts again.

Now Oliver knew about her brother, William, and all he had suffered and at first Lucy had been furious with herself for letting the information slip out, but the more she thought about it, the more she could see the advantages of Oliver knowing the tragic events. He would understand her reluctance to have any more children and where her mistrust came from. She truly didn't know how Oliver would react if she gave birth to another baby like David, or her brother, William. He was a far better man than her father and perhaps he would stand by his child and give him or her the best upbringing available, but Lucy couldn't take the chance that he wouldn't. She'd seen how devastating a father's abandonment could be and would never put a child of hers through the same pain.

He *was* a good man, Lucy conceded. Everything he'd done from the moment of their reunion had been considered and thoughtful. There was no denying he'd pushed her, but he'd been there to support her all the way through the difficult things he'd encouraged her to do. And he had kept all his promises. She still felt a deep, gnawing guilt for taking David away from him and

knew only time could rebuild the trust they'd
lost. It was revealing to Lucy that she wanted to
stay, wanted to spend the time rebuilding that
trust, rather than wanting to pull away any more.

Reaching out, she stopped herself before her
fingers met his face. Perhaps there was a future for them and not just a future of play-acting the lives of a married couple while doing all
the important things apart. She was beginning
to be able to imagine allowing herself to enjoy
his company fully, to spend afternoons strolling
through the park together, to discuss important
developments at the Foundation and even on occasion take his advice.

He took a deep breath in, one arm catching her
gently on the hip. Lucy froze, but there was still
no sign of him wakening. His palm was warm
on her skin, even through the double layers of
cotton of the sheet and her nightdress, and she
found herself inching towards him again. Perhaps she could even see a future where she gave
in to her suppressed desires and indulged in a full
and physical relationship with her husband again.

'Good morning,' Oliver murmured as he
opened his eyes.

Lucy made a show of rubbing her eyes as if
she hadn't been lying there staring at him for the
last ten minutes.

'Good morning.'

Now he was awake she felt self-conscious and hyperaware of the narrow space between them.

'Did you sleep well?' he asked.

'Yes, thank you,' she lied. After all, it wouldn't do for her to admit she'd spent half the night wondering how close she could move in to her husband without him noticing and the other half reprimanding herself for the unchaste thoughts that were running through her mind.

'Best sleep I've had in years,' Oliver said.

'It'll be the sea air.'

'It'll be having my wife in bed next to me,' he corrected, his voice low.

She was sorely tempted to throw caution to the wind and finally give in to the urge to move in closer, to allow herself to become lost in his kisses and start the renewal of a much more intimate part of their relationship. Still, something stopped her, and after a few moments Oliver sighed, swung his legs out of bed and padded to where he'd hung his clothes. Despite the surge of disappointment Lucy still had to suppress a smile. Her husband had never been one to lie in bed on a morning, conditioned by army life to get up and on with the day just moments after he was awake. Of course in those first few weeks of their marriage he'd found an excuse to tumble back between the sheets multiple times a day, but today she hadn't provided him with any incentive to stay horizontal.

'I'll see what can be done about breakfast,' Oliver said, dressing quickly before leaving the room.

For a moment Lucy flopped back on to her pillows, then, not wanting to be caught half-way through dressing, she rose and chose one of the dresses Oliver had hung in the wardrobe the night before. Again she smiled. Most men wouldn't lower themselves to hang their wives dresses in the wardrobe and Lucy herself had been content to leave them in her trunk, but years in the army had meant Oliver did tasks like these without thinking before retiring to bed in the evening.

Once she had fixed her hair and straightened her clothes, Lucy made her way down to the large room on the lower level that served as both a comfortable sitting room and a dining room with a small table at one end.

'How would you like to do a little sightseeing today?' Oliver asked as he slipped back through the door, followed closely by the wife of the man renting the rooms out. She was carrying one tray and Oliver a second, both piled high with almost every breakfast food you could imagine.

'Sightseeing?' Lucy asked, baffled by the suggestion.

'We *could* go directly back to London, but I don't fancy being cooped up in the carriage for another day. Why not enjoy some of the delights Brighton has to offer?'

He seemed to be in a buoyant mood, despite his obvious disappointment yesterday when she hadn't been able to tell him she believed he would act honourably if a theoretical other child of theirs was born with a physical or mental complication.

'What did you have in mind?'

'A surprise.'

She thought back to the last surprise trip he'd taken her on—the excursion to the Ranelagh Gardens—and how it had all nearly ended in seduction. With a shiver of anticipation she inclined her head.

'Excellent. Eat up—there will be some walking involved.'

Oliver felt peculiarly content walking through the streets of Brighton with Lucy on his arm. It almost felt as though they were on the honeymoon they'd never had and he was determined to utilise the holiday spirit to ensure they ended this little trip closer than they had started it.

'The Royal Pavilion has changed a little since I last lived here,' Lucy observed as they approached the grand building from the promenade, walking a few hundred feet away from the sea before the new façade came properly into view.

'What do you think of it?' Oliver asked.

'I'm not sure...' Lucy hesitated. 'It is rather ostentatious, but I suppose that is the point really.'

'Would you like to see inside?' Oliver asked casually.

She laughed. 'Of course, but without an invitation from the Prince Regent that's hardly likely to happen.'

The Royal Pavilion, previously known as the Marine Pavilion, was the palatial seaside escape favoured by the Prince Regent. He'd commissioned the architect John Nash to turn the modest palace into an impressive monument two years ago and the progress was noticeable. The façade was being transformed from neo-Classical to a fancy, elaborate design in an Indian style. When finished, it would probably look more at home next to the grand palaces of India than in among the more reserved style of the Brighton residences. According to rumour, there would be many alterations and additions to the inside of the palace, as well, making it a seaside bolthole fit for the future King.

'But if we could…' Oliver said, letting the sentence trail off into a suggestion.

'Are you suggesting we break in?'

'I never realised I had married such a criminally minded woman.'

'How else do you propose we see inside?' Lucy asked.

'I have a friend, from my days in the army. He's an architect working on the construction of the great kitchen and he's agreed to show us around.'

He didn't add that the man had been only too pleased to do Oliver this small favour after Oliver had dragged him out of a particularly nasty skirmish with a sword buried halfway through his shoulder five years ago.

'Won't he get into trouble?'

'Not if we're discreet. The Prince isn't in residence, so the only people around are men working on the construction and Wade's fellow architects.'

Seeing the gleam of excitement in Lucy's eyes, he knew he'd made the right decision when he'd contacted his old friend and asked if there was any way they could be admitted for a short tour.

They proceeded up to the grand entrance and Oliver was pleased to see Wade waiting for them.

'Good morning,' he greeted them, shaking Oliver's hand before clasping him in an embrace, then waiting for his introduction to Lucy.

'My wife, Lady Sedgewick.'

'A pleasure to meet you.'

'Are you sure we won't get you into trouble if you show us around?' Lucy asked.

'Not at all. The Prince is rather proud of the changes he's making to the palace, even when they are only half-finished. Nash, the head architect, is always showing people around and there is never any problem.'

'What are you working on?' Lucy asked as Wade led them around the side of the palace to the back entrance.

'The Great Kitchen. It is going to be a masterpiece when finished, even though it won't be a room used to entertain in, of course.'

This was where they started their tour and Lucy couldn't believe the high ceilings, the towering walls peppered with windows letting in wonderful natural light. There was easily space for dozens of kitchen staff and the room was already well stocked with hundreds of pots and pans.

'See the ventilation system?' Wade said, pointing up to the high ceiling. 'Twelve windows set high up, designed to let out the rising hot air from the kitchens.' He paused, allowing their eyes to wander for a few moments before he pointed out the next feature. 'And these columns, made of cast iron and ornamented with copper palm leaves. They actually have a structural purpose, but I've never come across something so decorative in a grand house's kitchen.'

Oliver watched as Lucy marvelled at the things Wade pointed out, feeling strangely content to be doing this with his wife.

'As you can see, the kitchen is more or less finished, just the final touches being put in. Work on the Music Room and Banqueting Room has just begun.'

They wandered through the newly built Banqueting Room, much more of a shell awaiting further design input, and into the older rooms of the palace. Here and there men bustled, carrying ladders and construction materials, but otherwise the palace was quiet.

'The Music Room will be impressive when finished,' Wade said, leading them into the room at the opposite end of the palace to the Great Kitchen.

Lucy gasped in delight as they entered the room. Four men were up a sturdy scaffold working on a huge domed ceiling. It was plain plaster at the moment, but even without any of the final decoration that would surely be added it was impressive.

'I'm told the room will have good acoustics,' Wade said.

For a moment Lucy imagined the finished room, all gilded gold with a fancy chandelier suspended from the centre. In her mind it was filled with people from the royal court and they were all entranced by the musical talents of a string quartet. It was an enthralling picture.

Lucy had just stepped away, bending her neck backwards to look up, when a shout came from above. The scaffolding, which had looked so sturdy, creaked ominously and one of the men working on the ceiling tottered precariously. Oliver leapt forward, ready to pull Lucy to safety if any danger presented itself. Just as he reached her side, the men above them laughed and it seemed as though the moment of instability had passed.

'Ready to pull me from plunging scaffolding?' Lucy murmured.

'I prefer you upright and unharmed to crushed.'

'I think I prefer me that way, too.'

She swayed towards him, affection in her eyes, and momentarily the world around them seemed to fade away. So much so that he didn't at first hear the renewed shout from above, didn't react quite as quickly as he should.

'Look out,' someone shouted.

Oliver looked up to see two planks of wood plummeting towards them. He grasped Lucy by the hand and tugged as hard as he could, swinging her round as he did so, trying to get her as far from the pieces of wood as he could.

Everything seemed to slow as he realised there was no way to prevent her from being hit. The first plank grazed her shoulder, the force of it knocking her off balance and sending her sprawling on to the floor. The second plank followed close behind, thudding down across her lower leg with a resounding thump.

Lucy whimpered in pain and immediately Oliver was by her side, kneeling close to her and gripping her hand as he began to lift the plank from her legs.

'Hush, my darling,' he whispered. 'You are going to be all right.'

He wasn't sure if it was an outright lie and he found he was holding his breath as he lifted the piece of wood clear from her body. Allowing himself a small sigh of relief that there were no obvious bone fragments sticking from her legs and no blood as yet, he carefully took one dainty ankle in his hands and began to probe for injuries. As he reached the shin Lucy winced, but did not cry out in pain. He saw her bite her lip, her teeth sinking into the soft flesh, to stop any sound from escaping her mouth.

'Just bruises, my love,' he said, moving on to the next leg.

Again Lucy grimaced as his hands pressed over her lower leg, but the ankle and knee seemed to be intact and there were no signs of any broken bones. Bruises and sprains would heal well with time.

Only when he had satisfied himself that there was no serious damage did he notice the crowd of people around them. Mainly made up of the men working on the construction, all had worried faces.

'I'm fine,' Lucy assured them, smiling through gritted teeth.

'I think perhaps I should take my wife home,' Oliver said, motioning for Wade to step closer. 'Would you be able to organise a carriage?'

'Of course.'

Not hearing her murmur of protest, Oliver scooped Lucy up into his arms, carrying her easily back the way they'd come. She wrapped her arms around his neck, pressing her body against his and burying her face in his shoulder. For once he felt like she truly needed him, but he wished the circumstances weren't so dramatic.

Chapter Sixteen

'Thank you, Dr Fisher,' Oliver said as he showed the elderly man out of the bedroom and back down the stairs.

Lucy lay back on the pillows, luxuriating in the softness as it engulfed her body.

'There really was no need to call the doctor,' she said as Oliver re-entered the room. 'I told you I was perfectly fine.'

'I don't trust your medical training,' Oliver said, sitting on the edge of the bed next to her. 'Or lack of it.'

'I was right, though. Nothing broken, just some beautiful purple bruises.'

Her legs did hurt, although not enough to even consider taking any of the laudanum Dr Fisher had left by her bed. Only once before had she injured herself severely enough to take laudanum—a tumble from her window when she was

Laura Martin   225

trying to sneak out to visit her brother. On that occasion she had twisted an ankle and bumped her head, but the laudanum her mother had insisted she swallow was the worst punishment—she had suffered days of numbness and nausea and on fully recovering had vowed never to touch the poisonous liquid ever again.

'You should rest,' Oliver said, adjusting the corner of the blanket where it had become tucked under.

'I'm not tired.'

It was only two o'clock in the afternoon and the sun was shining through the window as if taunting her about her inability to go outside and enjoy the clear autumn day.

She patted the space on the bed beside her. 'Come join me. You can keep me company.'

Not sure if she imagined the slight deepening of his breathing and darkening of his eyes, Lucy felt a surge of anticipation. Now wasn't the most romantic moment to be thinking of kisses and more, but it seemed that was the direction her thoughts were heading.

Oliver had been a perfect gentleman, she had to concede, carrying her all the way through the Royal Pavilion to the waiting coach, holding her on his lap the short journey back to their lodgings so she would not be unnecessarily jolted and racing up the stairs to deposit her gently in this comfortable bed.

'Why are you smiling?' he asked, the corners of his own mouth turning up in response to her smile.

'I was just thinking how you cannot help yourself. No matter what I do or say, you're always the perfect gentleman.'

He shrugged. 'It was the way I was raised.'

'Perhaps.'

'How would you like me to act?' Oliver asked, his voice low.

She swallowed, taking her time to ensure her voice didn't come out croaky or high pitched.

'I like you just the way you are,' she said softly.

'A few weeks ago you were pressing me for a divorce.'

'A girl can change her mind.'

'I hope you don't change it back again.'

'It was a shock, that's all. A complete change in circumstances.'

'And now you're used to the idea of being married to me?'

'I am.'

There was a heavy tension in the room as if both could see the direction their exchange was heading in, but neither could quite believe it.

'Perhaps you should remind me of some of

the advantages of being a married woman,' Lucy
said, feeling the heat rise in her cheeks, but refusing to acknowledge her embarrassment.

'Let me think. Being married gives you a constant companion at the breakfast table,' Oliver
said, keeping his tone serious despite the mirth
dancing in his eyes. He was teasing her and she
liked it.

'Very important. It is pleasant to have someone to discuss current affairs with.'

'Someone to dance with at balls and soirées,'
Oliver continued.

'And you don't even have to make idle chit-
chat if you don't want to,' Lucy added. 'You're
married, after all—no need for unnecessary conversation.'

'Good point—which leads me on to a great
advantage for you: no lecherous swine trying to
seduce you and rob you of your honour.'

Lucy couldn't help but smile. 'No one cares
about honour once you're a married woman.'

'I care,' Oliver said. 'Any man who bothers
you with his unwanted advances I will take by
the throat and sling to the kerb.'

She believed him, too.

'Any other advantages?' she asked, her voice
coming out as barely more than a whisper.

He edged closer, careful not to jolt her tender

legs, and stopped only when his face was inches from hers.

'I'm trying to think,' he said. 'I'm sure there *is* something else. Something that married men and women can enjoy without worrying about the consequences.'

'What could that be?' Lucy mused, wishing he would hurry up and kiss her. The wait was excruciating, especially when she could see they both wanted the same thing.

'Perhaps I should show you.'

'A demonstration is always better than an explanation,' she agreed.

'Close your eyes.'

Obediently she did. She waited—ten seconds passed, then twenty. Just as she was about to peek she felt his lips brush against hers ever so gently. Nothing more than a brief, sensational contact and then they were gone. Her eyes flew open and at the same moment Oliver kissed her again, this time his lips hard and insistent. Instantly all rational thought flew from her mind and she was entirely consumed by the kiss.

'You taste sweet,' he murmured as he broke away to pepper kisses along the angle of her jaw before returning to her lips once again.

As he kissed her Lucy felt herself sinking back against the pillows, subtly inviting him to join her. It wasn't what she'd planned, but the moment seemed right. Oliver had been chivalrous and attentive all day, all trip really, and every time she looked at him she felt her feelings for him grow.

Running her hands over his back, she urged him to come closer and immediately he obliged, adjusting his position until he was lying next to her.

'I don't want to hurt you,' he said, motioning towards her legs.

'You won't.'

'You don't know how long I've been wanting this,' he said quietly as he lay there, looking deep into her eyes. It seemed as though the admission came from deep inside, and he looked a little surprised at his own words.

For a moment Lucy felt as though the world beneath her had shifted. There was so much sincerity in his voice, so much depth and caring in his eyes, that for the first time she wondered why he had worked so long to find her, why he had persevered when all others would have given up.

Then all other thoughts were washed away as he kissed her again, filling her body with a wonderful warmth as gently his hands caressed her skin.

'I need to see you,' he said, his voice hoarse.

'I'm right here.'

'All of you.'

Lucy nodded, feeling a flutter in her chest. He'd seen her naked many times before, but suddenly it was important that he would still feel the same intense desire for the person she had become and the body she had acquired over the last year.

'I'll be gentle. Tell me if I hurt you.'

He helped her sit forward, then deftly began unfastening the back of her dress. Despite his obvious eagerness he moved slowly and steadily, not fumbling over the fastenings until Lucy felt her dress loosen and pool forward.

'So beautiful,' Oliver murmured, as his fingers traced a line down her back.

'Take it off,' Lucy instructed. She wanted his fingers to be able to go lower, touch more of her.

With some wriggling and shifting Oliver managed to lift the dress over her head, leaving her clad only in a thin cotton chemise.

'I remember this,' he said. 'Another damn layer.'

She giggled at the tone of his voice, but didn't protest when he lifted the cotton undergarment over her head swiftly, as well.

'Better.'

Now she was naked, her lower half covered

by the bedsheets, but her upper half completely and utterly bare under his gaze.

'This is unfair,' she pointed out. 'You're still fully clothed.'

'All in good time,' he promised.

She expected him to stand, to start shedding layers, but for a moment he sat looking at her, as if taking in every last detail. Then his lips were on hers again, kissing and nipping as she felt his body press against her now-naked skin.

Letting out an involuntary moan, Lucy felt her body tense with anticipation as his fingers danced over her skin, stimulating every inch before moving on. She felt her hips thrust towards him as his hands found her breasts and suddenly she couldn't remember why she had stayed away from this man for so long.

Just as she began to wonder if she could take much more, Oliver pulled away. Lucy's eyes flew open and she was just about to voice a protest when she saw him tearing off his own clothes. With a contented smile she watched him undress, her eyes roaming across his familiar body, working out what had changed in the past year.

'Come here,' she whispered as he shed the last piece of clothing.

Obligingly Oliver advanced towards her, taking his place on the bed beside her.

'I don't want to hurt you,' he said, his voice low and husky, 'so perhaps you had better turn over.'

He must have seen the confusion in her eyes so he gently turned her, positioning her on her side facing away from him. She trembled a little as she felt his body press in close behind her, his hardness against her buttocks. At first he hardly moved, just contented himself with kissing the back of her neck, the top of her shoulders, and draping an arm across her waist to caress her abdomen.

Lucy wanted to urge him on, but knew this was all part of the wonderful build-up of antici-pation, so instead allowed herself to get lost in the sensations he was creating. It felt like her skin was on fire, prickling under his touch, and as his fingers dipped lower and lower she knew soon the sensation would only intensify.

'Are you sure?' Oliver asked, his voice a little tense with the strain.

'Don't stop' was all Lucy could manage to say. 'Just remember not to…' She trailed off as he nodded.

His fingers touched her most sensitive place and she almost cried out, biting her lip as he cir-cled and dipped, feeling the tightness building deep inside her.

He seemed to know exactly when her climax would come, for just a second before, he thrust inside her, causing her to cry out with pleasure as she tightened around him. Wave upon wave washed over her and she felt her hands gripping the bedsheets to anchor herself as Oliver began to slowly move inside her, wondering if she could take any more of this wonderful feeling.

Faster and faster he thrust, until Lucy knew she would climax again, her muscles tightening just as she heard him groan and felt him pull out before the moment of his own release.

They lay, her body nestled against his, both breathing heavily. Lucy felt a familiar glow wash over her and realised it was contentment. She'd experienced it a lot in the first few weeks of their marriage and now it was back, embracing her like an old friend.

'I've missed you,' Oliver murmured into her neck.

'I've missed you, too.' It was true, even if she had been trying to deny the fact ever since their reunion.

Slowly she turned over, grimacing as one bruised leg knocked against the other, but determined to complete the movement all the same. Once she was facing her husband she placed a hand gently on his face, tracing his features with her fingers.

'You've been good to me,' she said quietly. 'I know that. And I've done nothing but make your life difficult.'

'I'll tell you a secret,' Oliver said with a small smile on his lips. 'You're worth it.'

Chapter Seventeen

Oliver whistled as he pulled on his boots, looking up as his valet, a smart young man by the name of Simons, entered the room with his cravat.

They'd travelled back from Brighton ten days earlier and the intimacy they'd shared on their little trip away had been continued at home. Not only were they physically closer, but he felt Lucy was truly beginning to settle into life as Lady Sedgewick and enjoying it. For his part, every day the concern that he would wake up to find Lucy gone again was a little less and slowly he felt himself letting go of some of the residual resentment he felt from her behaviour when she'd fled without a word.

'Are the boots to your satisfaction, my lord?' Simons asked, jolting Oliver away from his contented thoughts about his wife.

'The boots?' Oliver repeated, looking down at his feet for a clue as to what the valet was talking about.

'Yes, my lord.'

He looked down again. They were the same boots he'd had for nearly a year, comfortable, black and otherwise rather nondescript.

'They seem to be fine, Simons,' Oliver said warily, wondering if his valet was being unduly fussy.

'They are polished to your satisfaction?'

Again Oliver glanced down. The boots looked polished and mark-free.

'Yes, Simons.'

'Very good, my lord.'

The valet turned to leave the room and Oliver was so baffled by their exchange he almost let him go without enquiring further.

'Simons,' he called as the valet was nearly out of the door. 'Why all the questions about the boots?'

'I have a new...*assistant*, my lord. I wanted to check you were satisfied with his work.'

'An assistant?' He'd certainly not hired anyone. And he'd never heard of a valet requiring an assistant before.

'The young lad Lady Sedgewick brought to work in the household.'

'Freddy? But I thought he was going to be working in the kitchen, as an odd-jobs boy?'

'Not him. The other young lad. Charlie.'

So she'd sneaked another one of her charges from the Foundation to work in the house.

'Ah, right,' Oliver said, feeling peculiarly surplus to requirements in the running of his own household.

'Will that be all, my lord?'

'Yes, thank you.'

He finished dressing, taking time over his cravat. Most men let their valets take care of the more intricate parts of getting ready for an evening out, but the time Oliver had spent in the army had meant he was used to doing everything from polishing his shoes to shaving his face. He did let his valet do some of these tasks now, but actually getting dressed he preferred to do himself.

When he was satisfied he was presentable he made his way across the room to the door that connected his bedroom with Lucy's. The past couple of nights they had taken full advantage of this handy route to each other's bedchambers and now he barely waited for Lucy's call of *come in* to open the door.

She was sitting in front of a mirror, her maid finishing off her hair, pinning the last few strands into place. Oliver had to admit that although this young woman Lucy had brought in to be her lady's maid didn't have any prior experience, she was shaping up well already.

He waited, sitting on the edge of the bed while Lucy finished with her preparations, before sending the maid away.

'I've just been told we have another new addition to our household,' Oliver said, standing as Lucy did and walking towards her.

'Charlie, yes.'

'And he is…'

'A very nice young man.'

Oliver raised an eyebrow.

'Very well. He's been in a bit of trouble before, but he has a good heart.'

'And he is going to be…'

'Assistant to your valet,' she said quietly.

'Ah, yes, that vital position.'

'Do you mind?'

'Does it make you happy? Finding places for these waifs and strays of yours?'

She nodded.

'Then, no, I don't mind. Although I think my valet has enough assistants for now. Perhaps if you want to recruit any more we could think of who might be suitable for Sedgewick Place and a life in the country.'

Throwing her arms around his neck, she kissed him, making everything worthwhile.

'Remind me why we have to go out tonight,' Lucy murmured in his ear.

'I think you'll find it a very useful event,' Oliver replied.

'But wouldn't you rather stay here?'

He felt a surge of desire for her that he almost gave in to, but he steeled himself. Sometimes a man had to make sacrifices for his wife.

'Of course I would, but I promise you would rather go.'

'I'm not sure about that,' she said, kissing him gently on the lips.

Oliver groaned, glancing at the clock and wondering if they had time for a quick tumble into bed. The only problem was, it never was a *quick* tumble. As soon as Lucy started shedding layers he felt the need to explore every inch of her body, to make her writhe in pleasure before even thinking about himself.

'Perhaps we could just…' he heard himself saying.

'Remember, it must be quick,' Lucy said, her eyes dancing with laughter.

He watched as she hobbled towards the bed. Her legs were much improved from the accident nearly two weeks ago and it looked like there would be no lasting damage. The bruises were beginning to turn brown and yellow rather than the deep purples and blacks that had adorned her shins a few days ago, but she still limped a little when she walked. Perhaps it would be better if they stayed in.

She turned to him as she sat down on the bed, gripping the hem of her dress and beckoning him over.

Unable to stop himself Oliver crossed the room in two short strides, lifting Lucy gently and depositing her further back on to the bed.

'Mind the dress,' Lucy said, giggling underneath him.

'Damn the dress.'

She laughed, which fired him further and quickly he sought out her lips with his own. Despite his words he *was* careful not to rumple the dress too much, pushing the hem up gently as his fingers roamed up the length of her legs.

Lucy pulled him towards her, urging him to enter her, and Oliver found he couldn't resist. Together their bodies moved up and down, in perfect rhythm as if they'd been made for one another.

Faster and faster they moved, until the inevitable moment of climax, Oliver managing to pull out just in time, already longing for the day when he could stay inside her and not pull away. But for now Oliver was in agreement with Lucy; it would be best not to risk another pregnancy until they were sure of one another, sure of the fragile trust that they were beginning to build after so much had gone on between them these last few years. He was still concerned that should Lucy get pregnant she might flee again, might become distrustful and panic, and he knew he could not go through that again. Deep down he was also aware that he wasn't ready to risk the heartbreak of losing another child himself. One day…if Lucy could be convinced, but not yet.

They lay cradled against one another for five minutes, Oliver enjoying the feel of the subtle movement of Lucy's abdomen as she breathed in and out under his hand. Eventually she stirred and turned towards him.

'Do you think one day…?' Oliver said.

Lucy pressed her finger to his lips, shaking her head. 'Don't ask me that, please. Let's just enjoy what we have.'

He nodded, unsure why he'd even thought of asking the question. Neither of them was ready, not yet.

'I shouldn't have worn silk,' Lucy murmured, regarding her crumpled dress in the mirror.

'You look wonderful.'

'I look as though I've been ravished.'

'I don't mind people knowing I can't keep my hands off my wife.'

'They may not assume it is you doing the ravishing.'

'Nonsense. Everyone can see you're totally devoted to me.'

Lucy turned away from the mirror, taking a moment away from smoothing down her dress to kiss him on the cheek.

Straightening his own clothes Oliver waited for Lucy to finish, before offering her his arm.

'It's a ball,' Lucy said as they entered through the front door to the sound of musicians striking up their instruments.

'But not any old ball.'

'Delighted you could make it tonight, Lord Sedgewick... Lady Sedgewick,' an effusive middle-aged woman gushed as she rushed towards them.

'My wife is a devoted supporter of charities and good causes,' Oliver said, causing Lucy's eyes to widen in surprise. She supported the Foundation, that much was true, but she had never been involved with any other charities.

'You must tell me about the charities you support, Lady Sedgewick,' their host insisted.

'This is Lady Wentwater.' Oliver completed the introductions. 'Our hostess for the evening.'

'Gaming tables are that way, Lord Sedgewick. All proceeds go to support the Orphanage, of course.'

Lady Wentwater clutched hold of Lucy's arm and guided her off in the opposite direction. Glancing back over her shoulder, Lucy saw Oliver giving her an apologetic shrug before wandering off towards the gaming tables.

'It is wonderful you could make it this evening,' Lady Wentwater said. 'The Orphanage is always looking for new patrons and I find these annual charity events the best way to keep a cause at the forefront of everyone's minds.'

Slowly Lucy was beginning to realise why Oliver had insisted they come this evening. She had told him of some of the financial struggles the Foundation was facing and he had suggested using her new status and connections to encourage new, wealthy patrons. At first she'd thought he was joking, but now she was wondering if it might actually work. Certainly the Foundation was as worthy a cause as an orphanage.

'Tell me, Lady Wentwater, how do you put together a night like this?'

'Oh, how sweet you are, my dear. It's lovely to find someone who is interested. I started three years ago, when the Sand Street Orphanage was in dire straits. I've been a patroness for years, but many of the other supporters had drifted away, taking their interest and their money to other more fashionable causes.'

Lucy knew how fickle some of the wealthy patrons could be.

'At first I bored all my friends, begging them at every opportunity to become involved. Then I realised there was a much better way of doing things.'

'That's when you decided to have your annual ball?'

'Exactly. There are gaming tables for the gentlemen, any proceeds go directly to the orphanage and many of the men also donate any winnings. This raises a lot of money in the grand scheme of things.'

'And the rest is publicity for the cause?'

'Exactly. We have music and dancing, but everywhere there are subtle reminders of the purpose of the evening. Often I receive a few large donations on the night, but more importantly a few people are interested enough to become long-standing patrons.'

'It's all very clever.'

'I think so, my dear,' Lady Wentwater said, beaming. 'Now I must return to greeting guests, but shall I introduce you to some of the ladies first?'

'No need,' a deep voice said from over her shoulder.

Lucy smiled as she recognised Oliver's friend, Redmoor.

'Would you grant me the honour of a dance?' Redmoor asked.

Lucy inclined her head, allowing the tall man to lead her towards the dance floor.

'How was your trip to the seaside?' Redmoor asked as the dance began.

'Certainly worthwhile,' Lucy said, thinking of the closure she felt after confronting her father one final time.

'I hear you had a small accident. I hope you are recovered.'

News travelled fast to London, but she shouldn't be surprised. Someone in the Royal Pavilion would know someone else who knew someone else and soon the story would be all the way back to London, no doubt with a few embellishments.

'A minor bump, that is all. Lord Sedgewick looked after me superbly.'

'Yes, he has a habit of looking after people,' Redmoor murmured.

'He is very kind,' Lucy agreed.

'Perhaps too kind,' Redmoor said. Lucy looked at him sharply, but could see no malice in his face.

Sighing, Redmoor seemed to steel himself to say more. 'He's a good man, one of the best.'

'I know.'

'And I would hate to see him hurt. Again.'

'As would I.'

'He's strong and he puts on a good show of having an impenetrable outer shell, but he is still a man.'

'Is there something you want to say to me?' Lucy asked, trying to keep her voice calm.

'After you left he was a mess. He was frantic, didn't rest for weeks. I mean, he carried on searching for you for a whole year.'

'I understand that.'

'Do you?' He looked at her questioningly, as if he would open her head and check inside if he could.

Lucy hesitated. She had wondered at the length of time and devotion of energy Oliver had put into finding her. At first she'd assumed it was because he didn't like to be beaten in some challenge he had thought up for himself—the challenge to find her. Then she'd thought he'd wanted a wife, someone to take out into society and stop all the rumours that abounded about him. But that didn't quite fit either—he could have lessened the rumours by telling people she had died in childbirth or some such story, but, no, he'd let people gossip in the hope that one day he would find her.

'Why did he look for me for so long?' she asked eventually.

'You don't know?'

Shaking her head, Lucy felt a hollowness developing in the pit of her stomach. She had a feeling she *did* know what Redmoor's answer would be.

The music stopped and for a moment Lucy thought her dance partner was going to abandon her without revealing what he knew.

'He loves you. He's besotted with you. Surely you can see that?'

Without thinking Lucy began shaking her head. It was too much, too much responsibility to be so instrumental to another person's happiness.

Redmoor shrugged. 'Think about it. Why else would he pursue you for so long when you'd hurt him so badly?'

'But he's never said.'

'He's in denial. Won't even admit it to himself. And a few weeks ago you were pressing him for a divorce of all things. Who would reveal their innermost feelings to someone who doesn't seem to reciprocate them?'

Lucy felt a tightening in her throat and swallowed a couple of times to try to relieve it.

'You don't have to love him,' Redmoor said

softly, 'although he's certainly worthy of love. Just try not to hurt him again.'

Part of her felt embarrassed to have to be told all of this by one of Oliver's friends; part of her was still a little disbelieving.

He loved her—could it be true? They'd spent such a short time together after their marriage—surely love couldn't develop in just a few weeks. And he'd married her for such practical reasons—he'd needed a wife to produce heirs for his newly inherited estate. He hadn't even chosen her himself—had let his mother draw up a shortlist of candidates.

'How do you know all this?' Lucy asked, wondering if Oliver confided so much in his friend.

'I've known Sedgewick for a long time,' Redmoor said with a slightly sad smile. 'He's told me bits and pieces, but I know him well enough to fill in the gaps.'

'I won't hurt him,' Lucy said with more conviction than she felt. She might hurt him—having the responsibility of someone else's love was serious and it was a responsibility she wasn't sure she was ready for.

'Just don't run away again.'

Redmoor bowed, kissed her hand and stepped away, leaving Lucy to wonder exactly how she was going to deal with this new information.

Chapter Eighteen

'You're skittish,' Oliver said as they walked arm in arm through St Giles. It was a beautiful day, clear blue skies and a cool autumn breeze without a hint of the rain that had been falling on and off the last few days.

'Skittish? Like a horse?'

'Exactly. What are you scared of?'

He looked around, checking for danger, remembering when he hadn't been alert enough to keep them from being threatened with a knife.

'Nothing. I'm not skittish.'

Oliver shrugged, murmuring, 'Look pretty skittish to me.'

In truth, Lucy felt more than skittish. Her insides were roiling in turmoil and every muscle in her body felt on edge. Ever since her talk with Redmoor at the charity ball she had been unable to be in the same room as Oliver without looking at him and wondering if what his friend had said was true.

'It's a big day today,' Lucy said. It wasn't exactly a lie; it *was* a big day today, but that wasn't why she was feeling so unsettled.

'I'd like to be there for you.'

'There's no need. I've been at these meetings many times before.'

'But you just said it is a big day.'

Lucy cursed, trying to think quickly, but her brain refused to co-operate.

'I'll be more nervous with you there.'

He smiled at her with affection in his eyes and once again it set Lucy off to wondering if there were deeper feelings hidden inside Oliver.

'It's your choice,' he said with a shrug. 'I'd just like to see what you do.'

'Perhaps another time.'

They reached the Foundation and went through the passageway to the courtyard beyond, where Mary was bustling about, dressed in a severe black dress, her normally wild curls pulled into a tight bun.

'You're here!' Mary exclaimed, striding over to Lucy and clasping her tightly to her. 'It's a complete disaster. Lord Pennywater sent a note saying he would not be attending today and that unfortunately he cannot continue to support the Foundation.'

'He didn't even bother to tell you in person?' Lucy asked.

'No. Just a scribbled note. And you know what half the rest of the patrons are like. Once the first one leaves the rest follow, thinking it is fashionable to support only the causes that have a lord or lady attached to them.'

'Surely they won't all go, Mary,' Lucy said soothingly. 'Mrs Hunter seems keen and generous and only joined us a month ago and Mr and Mrs Felixstone have been supporters for years.'

'But the rest. We can't survive if the donations fall and I'm afraid this might be the beginning of the end for us.'

'Lucy,' Oliver said quietly, 'a word please.'

She patted Mary on the arm once again and crossed the courtyard to join him.

'What is the problem?' he asked.

'Mary is worried that now Lord Pennywater has decided to stop supporting us the rest of the patrons might follow.'

'Is that likely?'

Lucy shrugged. 'I've never seen Mary in such a state so she must believe it to be true.'

'Perhaps I could help.'

She looked at him blankly.

'I am a viscount,' he reminded her. 'And one who has a definite interest in seeing this place succeed.'

'You'd become one of our patrons just for me?'

'Of course.'

'Really?'

'Yes, Lucy. If it makes your life easier and stops you from worrying.'

He saw the tears in her eyes the moment before she flung her arms around his neck and embraced him deeply.

'It's true, isn't it?' she murmured so quietly he barely heard her.

'What's true?'

'It doesn't matter. Let's tell Mary.'

Pulling him by the hand, Lucy rushed back over to where Mary was still pacing and murmuring under her breath as if trying to find the solution to an impossible puzzle.

'All is not lost,' Lucy said firmly. 'Oliver— Lord Sedgewick will step in as one of our patrons. Surely the others will not abandon us because a baron is replaced by a viscount?'

Mary turned to him with hope in her eyes. 'You will?'

'Of course. This is important.'

He wasn't ready for the shower of gratitude from both women, thanks and praise which lasted for well over two minutes, and by the end he felt a little embarrassed. He'd only hoped to banish the worry and desolation from Lucy's eyes. The Foundation was a good cause, of course, but he wouldn't be doing this if it didn't mean so much to his wife.

'We'll announce it at the governor's meeting today,' Mary said excitedly. 'It will be the first item on the agenda—a change in our patrons.'

'Let me take you upstairs,' Lucy said, taking him by the hand to the office she and Mary usually shared. Today it had been cleared of the mountains of papers and the two desks had been pushed together to make one long table in the middle of the room. Twelve chairs were arranged around the table and Lucy indicated he should choose one.

'Do I have to do anything?' Oliver asked, realising he had never volunteered to become a patron of a charity before. Of course he'd donated money to various good causes, but usually never got more involved than that.

'You can say a few words once we introduce you if you wish, but otherwise this is more of a business meeting. A few of our patrons like to attend to keep abreast of what is happening at the Foundation, but this is more about the governors going over our accounts and checking we are doing what we say we are with the money.'

'I see.'

He took a chair and Lucy did, too, sitting sideways so she faced him.

'This means the world to me, Oliver. I'm so grateful.'

'I would do anything to make you happy,' he said, feeling a little exposed with the admission, but seeing the nervous smile on her lips made it all worthwhile.

'You would, wouldn't you?' she said and it was as much a statement as a question.

'I just want you to be safe and happy. It's all I've ever wanted.'

'I can't believe I didn't see it.'

'See what?'

'How much you care. When you first found me I wondered why you had spent so much time and effort tracking me down when you could have been building a new life for yourself.'

'I couldn't,' he said quietly. It was true. Despite everything he'd told himself, all the lies about wanting to have his wife home because that was what society expected, he was coming to realise there had always been more to his search than that. He'd missed Lucy, yearned for her, and despite her betrayal, despite how she'd shattered his heart when she'd taken their son away, it was *her* he'd wanted, not just a wife back home.

'I thought perhaps you had an issue with ownership, like some men do with their wives. They want to possess them completely, to rule their lives.'

'I *do* want to possess you completely.'

'But not in that way,' she said softly.

He shook his head.

'I never thought ours could be anything more than a convenient union,' she said. 'After the way it was arranged and the reasons behind both of us wanting to marry.'

'Nor did I. But I know I would be devastated if you decided to leave again.'

Watching her closely, he saw her swallow, saw the tension creep back into her face.

'Hush,' he said. 'One day, this past year will be nothing more than a distant memory. We'll have the rest of our lives ahead of us.'

'I want to stay,' she whispered, leaning forward and kissing him.

Oliver believed her. Over the last few weeks their relationship had blossomed from an awkward arrangement where they barely spoke to a comfortable companionship to a marriage filled with passion. It was reassuring to hear the words, but he still felt a little bubble of concern deep inside him. Even though she told him she wanted to stay, even though he could see the growing affection in her eyes, he still worried one day she would just be gone without a trace.

Lucy barely registered when one of the governors criticised the way they recorded new residents, or when Mrs Hunter, one of their newest patrons, twittered on about putting more stringent measures in place to record what happened to their residents when they left the Foundation. Lucy delivered her piece on the accounts succinctly, but only because she was well practised.

Oliver sat quietly at the other end of the table with the patrons and governors, giving her encouraging smiles whenever she looked his way. All she could think was *He loves me*. The words were tumbling around in her head, repeating themselves over and over again. She'd never thought she would experience love, never expected it. When agreeing to marry Oliver she'd had her own selfish reasons, just as he'd had his. She'd hoped for mutual respect and perhaps even companionship, but from a young age she had resigned herself to a life without experiencing love.

He hadn't said the words, not out loud, but she was beginning to realise that Redmoor was right. Oliver did love her—it was the only explanation for how he had never given up his search for her and why he was so patient with her now.

Considering carefully, she examined her own feelings for him. She cared for him, deeply, more than any other living person. She enjoyed spending time with him and couldn't imagine being married to anyone else. But was that love? It wasn't that instant gush she had felt for David, that overwhelming tenderness she'd experienced the first time she'd held her baby.

'Thank you, everyone, for your time,' Mary was saying and people were starting to rise.

Lucy smiled absently as the governors and patrons left the room, ushered out by Mary who would no doubt escort them safely out of St Giles.

'I hope you didn't mind my input on the record keeping,' Mrs Hunter said as she paused next to Lucy. 'The last thing I wish is to be interfering. You do such a wonderful job here.'

'Not at all, Mrs Hunter,' Lucy said with a smile. 'It is always helpful to have someone else's opinion on these matters, especially someone invested in the success of the Foundation.'

'I do think it is the most worthwhile cause.'

Lucy had to agree with her.

'Thank you for coming to the meeting,' Lucy said. 'And we should arrange to have tea together some time soon.'

Mrs Hunter's face lit up at the prospect and Lucy, who had issued the invitation out of politeness, realised that she wouldn't mind spending an hour talking over a nice cup of tea with her.

'That's very kind, Lady Sedgewick.'

'You'd be very welcome at Sedgewick House any time.'

Mrs Hunter clasped her hand and squeezed it, before hurrying out after the other patrons. She was a relatively new supporter, joining the small group of patrons a little over a month ago, but she seemed keen and intelligent and willing to be an active member of the board.

'Well done,' Oliver said, coming to her side. 'You did splendidly.'

'Thank you for stepping in.'

'My pleasure. Are you staying here for the rest of the afternoon?'

Lucy hesitated. There were a few administration bits and bobs she needed to get done, registering a couple of the new arrivals properly and seeing if she could match them to any work, but none of it was pressing.

'I'll return home with you. The paperwork can wait until tomorrow.'

'You've been very quiet,' Oliver observed as they sat in the small library together. The maids had lit a fire and the room was illuminated in a soft orange glow. With the curtains pulled and the door closed, it was cosy and intimate.

She smiled at him, trying to think of some little white lie, not wanting to tell him she was still mulling over the realisation that her husband loved her.

'Come sit with me,' he said.

'There's hardly room for you in that chair.'

He was seated in an upright armchair, with huge leather arms that took up most of the space, leaving just enough for one man to sit in.

'Is that a challenge?' Oliver asked.

Lucy rose and crossed the small room, stopping in front of him. Looping an arm around her waist, he pulled her towards him, tugging until she tumbled into his lap.

With a giggle, she shuffled her bottom until she was comfortable.

'Plenty of room for two,' Oliver declared.

'Only if you like your companion close.'

'I do.'

He leaned in and kissed her neck, just at the base where it met her shoulder, sending a shiver of anticipation down her spine.

'I can't think of a better way to spend a cold evening,' Oliver murmured. 'Seated by the fire with my wife close by.'

'Very close by.'

'Maybe not close enough,' he said, pulling her back a little more so her body rested against his.

'A servant could walk in at any moment,' Lucy whispered, looking at the door.

'They should know better than to disturb a man and his wife in such a romantic spot.'

He kissed her again, tracing his lips over the nape of her neck, the light touch tickling and making her squirm in his lap.

'If only the chair was bigger,' Lucy mused thoughtfully.

'Why?'

'Then I could turn around and face you.'

'Why would you want to do that?' he asked.

'It would make certain things a little easier.'

Understanding dawned in his eyes and within a second he had risen from the chair, Lucy cradled in his arms, crossed to the door and flicked the lock, then seated them on the much larger sofa in front of the fire.

Wriggling, Lucy managed to turn around so she was facing him, her legs straddling his.

'I like this position,' Oliver murmured, his hands resting just above her hips.

'I thought you might.'

Dipping her head, Lucy kissed him gently, sighing as he ran his hands over her waist and on to the top of her thighs before rustling the material of her dress to get to her skin. Once under the multiple layers of dress, petticoat and chemise, he began caressing her thighs, making her rock in his lap.

'Lucy,' Oliver groaned and she felt a smile blossom on her lips. She liked that she could make him almost delirious in just a few short minutes. Reaching down, she found the fastening to his breeches and began to slowly work it undone. He was hard and ready for her and without any hesitation Lucy moved her hips to position herself over him. Gently she sank lower, loving how he moaned as she took him inside her and only pausing when he filled her completely.

Slowly, trying to draw out the pleasure, she rose again, working out a rhythm to her movements as his hands guided her hips, urging her faster and faster. She held out for a few minutes, keeping the slow steady pace, but gradually she felt her resolve slipping and her movements become more frantic. Her head dropped back and she felt the tension building deep inside her.

Wave upon wave of pleasure crashed through her body, every muscle tightened and beneath her she felt Oliver stiffen. She was too deep in her own pleasure to understand what his frantic movements meant, resisting when he tried to push her off him, wanting to draw out her climax for a few moments longer.

'Lucy…' he cried, panic in his eyes.

It was twenty seconds before she had recovered enough to understand what he had been trying to tell her.

'No,' she gasped, pushing herself off him so quickly she stumbled backwards, arms reeling as she tried to regain her balance.

Oliver was scrambling to his feet, tucking himself away as he did so, but she just kept backing away.

'What have we done?'

'Just keep calm, Lucy,' Oliver said, his voice soothing. 'It was just the once.'

It was true; all the other times they had been intimate Oliver had spilled himself on the sheets. This time, when she was in control, she'd just completely forgotten in the midst of her desire.

'Think about it, Lucy, people try for months to get pregnant without any success. How likely is it we succeed with just one slip?'

She knew he was right, but still she felt a deep-seated panic taking hold of her.

'We can't…' she stuttered.

'Hush,' he said, crossing the room and taking her in his arms. 'There's nothing to be done now.'

'But we…' She trailed off again, unable to finish a thought let alone a sentence.

'Come, sit. Take a few deep breaths.'

With small steps he led her back to the sofa and sat her down, rubbing her back as he encouraged her to breathe. Slowly Lucy felt some of the panic lifting as she calmed.

'I can't get pregnant again. I can't do it.'

'Just try to relax,' Oliver said, his voice low and reassuring. 'As I said, it is unlikely that this one slip will lead to anything. We've been so careful.'

'But we conceived easily last time.'

He hesitated for a moment and Lucy could see he had to concede her point. 'We did, but we hardly left the bedroom for a month and we certainly were not taking precautions like we have been.'

'You think it will be all right?' she asked, needing him to reassure her one more time.

'I think it will.'

Breathing deeply, she managed to nod. He was probably right—what were the chances they would conceive with just one slip?

'Would it really be so terrible?' Oliver asked as she sank back into him, her heart finally slowing to a normal pace. Lucy knew her husband has misgivings about starting a family again soon.

She suspected he was wary of how she would react to a pregnancy and worried she might flee again if there was something wrong with their next child. However, whenever children were brought up she saw the longing in his eyes and knew one day he would want a family.

'Yes,' she said firmly.

'Tell me again why.'

'David's death nearly killed me. I barely functioned for a very long time. I don't think I could go through that again.'

'The grief I understand,' Oliver said, 'but what makes you think we would lose another child?'

'People do, don't they? Even if they're born healthy there's all the childhood illnesses and fevers, the chance of pneumonia and the perils of other maladies.'

'But every parent goes through that worry.'

'And I'm sure some can cope perfectly well with losing more than one child, but I couldn't.'

She closed her eyes, hoping it would signal an end to the topic, but Oliver pushed on.

'Do you think we have a higher chance of having another child with health issues like David?' he asked.

She shrugged, not able to look at him.

'I don't think it's true, Lucy. As I've told you before, when I spoke to the doctor he said there was no reason our next child couldn't be completely healthy.'

The doctor had told her the same thing only moments after David's birth, his voice commiserating as he looked over the newborn in her arms.

Over the year she'd considered many times whether she might one day want more children, but always it had seemed too dangerous to her already fragile heart. Even wishing for another child made Lucy feel guilty, as if she was dismissing David and his short life as not worthwhile.

'It would be better if we didn't have to have any more children,' Lucy said firmly. 'We have each other. You have your estate to run. I have the Foundation. We both lead very full lives.'

She didn't tell him about the yearning she felt when a mother brought her young baby to the Foundation, or when a child lifted its arms for a hug. Every time she told herself it was an inbuilt instinct all women had, that desire to be a mother, but she was determined to suppress it to protect herself from further heartbreak.

Chapter Nineteen

A bright October ran into a cold and rainy November and every day Lucy got up in the morning, hoping for a sign that she was not pregnant. Normally her cycle was regular, but it could vary from month to month by a couple of days, so when she was four days overdue she told herself not to panic and to be patient. Five days and then six came and went, and only when she was a week late did she start to feel flustered.

Feeling ridiculous, but unable to stop herself, Lucy made an appointment to see a doctor when she was eight days overdue. He was a kindly man in his late fifties who volunteered some of his time for free to treat the women and children at the Foundation when they first arrived. Lucy had initially enquired about seeing someone else, someone she didn't know, but if she were going to keep the appointment secret from

Oliver she knew she would have to make it seem like a meeting that was to discuss Foundation matters, not something private.

She arrived at Dr White's office ten minutes early and entered to find a middle-aged woman behind a desk in the hall.

'Lady Sedgewick to see Dr White,' Lucy said quietly, although the hall was deserted.

'Please take a seat. He will be with you in a few minutes.'

As she sat Lucy wondered if the woman was the doctor's wife. She looked about the right age and she had a confidence about her that suited a relation rather than an employee.

With great effort Lucy tried not to fidget. She was petrified of what Dr White might tell her and felt sick and tremulous. As she sat she realised her hands were shaking and it took some serious concentration to still them as she laid them in her lap. Trying to distract herself, she looked around, but found nothing could take her mind off the worries that were circling inside her head.

'Lady Sedgewick,' Dr White said as he came out of his office a few minutes later. 'Do come in. Can I offer you some tea?'

Lucy thought she might vomit if she consumed anything, so declined politely.

'It is a pleasure to see you here, but I do hope you're not unwell.'

'Not unwell as such, I'm just looking for a little advice.'

'Please ask anything. I shall endeavour to help.'

'It is a little sensitive.' She hesitated and glanced up at the reassuring older man. He sat quietly, waiting for her to proceed. 'I am overdue my monthly courses, not by very long, but I wanted to know how early one could be sure of a pregnancy.'

'You and your husband are eager for a child?' the doctor asked.

Lucy felt the heat rising in her cheeks and a lump forming in her throat.

'Not exactly,' she said. 'I would prefer *not* to be pregnant, but more importantly I need to know.'

'Might I enquire as to the reasons behind your reluctance?' Dr White said. From anyone else it might seem like an impertinent question, but Dr White made it sound like a routine medical enquiry. He had a soft and reassuring voice, and Lucy knew over the years many of his patients would have been induced to tell him their darkest secrets by that calming tone.

'We had a child—a son. He was born with certain difficulties and he died at a very young age.'

'I see,' Dr White said. 'And you worry another child might be the same.'

She nodded. Despite what the doctor had told her after the birth of David she had always wondered if she could give birth to a child again without any problems. Her brother and her son had seemed to have different conditions, but what if something *did* run in her family?

'I couldn't cope with losing another child.'

'And your husband?'

'He would like us to try for another baby, at some point in the future, but I don't think he truly understands the risks involved.'

He might say he would love a child with difficulties, but would he really if he was presented with a child that looked or acted differently? So many people couldn't see beneath that initial impression to the wonderful, unique child. Oliver was a good man, but she couldn't be sure how he would react.

'Have you discussed your differing opinions with your husband?'

Lucy sighed, looking down and picking absently at the hem of her dress.

'He knows how I feel.'

Deep down Lucy knew Oliver didn't accept her decision as final. She could see the hope in his eyes, the belief that one day she might change her mind and decide that starting a family with him was a good idea. Right now he wasn't pressing the subject, but one day, when he was confident the trust between them had been rebuilt, she knew it would become an issue.

'I see.'

'I need to know if I am pregnant and, if I am, I can plan accordingly.'

'You don't mean…' The doctor trailed off, his eyes wide with shock. It seemed the man who had seen all manner of maladies and injuries was still shockable.

'No, I don't mean abortion,' Lucy said quickly. 'I just need to know.'

'Right, well, let's see what we can find out.' Doctor White sat up straighter now they had left the emotional issues behind them and were talking purely of the practical.

'When was your last menstrual bleed?'

'Five weeks ago.'

Doctor White's eyes widened and he stroked his smooth chin.

'Not very long ago, then.'

'I understand that. I just wasn't sure if there was any way of finding out this early.'

'Unfortunately not. I wish there was—I would be a rich man if I could tell women one way or another this early on.'

'And there can be other reasons for my monthly courses to be delayed?'

'Indeed. Stress, a change in diet, a change in circumstances—a myriad of things. Many times we do not know why one way or another.'

'So the only way of knowing is waiting for my belly to grow and to miss more courses.'

Doctor White nodded. 'Of course some women experience certain symptoms in the early weeks of their pregnancy. Nausea and sickness, bloating, tenderness in the breasts, extreme fatigue.'

Lucy felt herself relax a little; she hadn't felt any of these things so far.

'I'm sorry, Lady Sedgewick. There is nothing more I can tell you at present, but perhaps you should discuss your concerns further with your husband.'

'I'm sure he's aware of them.' He had to be— she still cringed at the violent way she'd reacted when she had realised how their lovemaking in the library had ended. And it was all her fault; he'd tried to warn her, tried to push her off.

'Go home, rest, try not to worry yourself too much. Perhaps come back and see me next month and we can see what the circumstances are then.'

'Thank you,' Lucy said, reluctant to leave without a more definitive answer, even though she'd known all along it was unlikely she would get one.

'Take care of yourself, Lady Sedgewick.'

She rose and he escorted her to the door. Once back in the street she began walking, needing to clear her head before heading back home. She didn't think Oliver had noticed anything was amiss with her yet, but she was having to work hard to keep up the pretence. It wouldn't do for her to arrive home flustered and out of sorts, he was far too astute to miss that.

She didn't want to tell him, not yet, not until she was sure one way or another. Their fragile relationship was just beginning to recover and the stress of a pregnancy wouldn't help it. She knew one day Oliver would want children again, but at present he was content with trying to rebuild the trust and intimacy between them. Lucy agreed, they needed time to get to know one another, as well as deal with their grief over losing David, before they even thought of children. She wasn't sure she would ever be ready to try again and right now she wished they could focus on their fledgling marriage without the added stress of a possible pregnancy.

'How was your day?' Oliver asked, trying to make the question sound nonchalant.

'Fine, thank you,' Lucy said, not looking up from her dressing table.

He glanced at her surreptitiously, trying not to alert her to his concern. She'd been acting strangely for weeks—ever since their *accident* in the library—becoming quiet and a little withdrawn. Oliver had expected her to perhaps worry for a short while and then bounce back. It wasn't as though there was much chance of them conceiving after just one little slip. But as the days had passed she had got worse rather than better, withdrawing into herself, lost in her own thoughts and barely registering his presence.

'I was thinking of visiting Sedgewick Place in a couple of weeks. There is some business I want to go over with my steward and I thought you could select any clothes you wanted to bring to London for the rest of the Season.'

'Mmm-hmm,' Lucy murmured as she brushed out her hair.

'We could spend a few days there, enjoy the countryside before the really cold weather sets in.'

'Mmm-hmm.'

Oliver frowned. She was completely preoccupied and he doubted she was taking in a word he was saying.

He tried to catch her eye in the mirror, but although she was staring at the glass he could tell she wasn't seeing anything in front of her.

'We could go crocodile-hunting, track a pride of lions, join some eagles on a flight over the estate.'

'Whatever you think best, dear.'

He stood, striding over to the mirror and placing his hands gently on Lucy's shoulders, feeling her jump beneath his palms.

'You're preoccupied with something. Talk to me.'

'I'm just tired.'

'Don't lie to me, Lucy,' he said quietly.

She swivelled slightly so she was looking up at him and he saw a mixture of fear and despair in her eyes.

'Whatever it is, we can work it out together.'

There was a moment of hesitation, as if she might be considering telling him exactly what was troubling her, but then she shook her head.

'There's nothing, Oliver. I'm fine, just a little tired.'

With a smile that was nowhere near genuine she set down her hairbrush and stood, taking his hand and leading him to bed. Over the past month they had found themselves sharing a bed more and more, and now he felt bereft if he spent a night without Lucy in his arms. Since the episode in the library when he had climaxed inside of her, their lovemaking had become a little less frequent, but it was still at least a few times a week.

Climbing into bed behind her, Oliver looped an arm around his wife and pulled her a little closer. He felt her tense under his touch and a sharp stab of pain shot through his body. He didn't know exactly what Lucy was thinking or feeling, but never before had she reacted in this way to his touch.

'Let me in,' he whispered in her ear. 'I might be able to help.'

Wordlessly she shook her head. Oliver couldn't see her face, but he fancied he felt her take a few shuddering breaths and wondered if she was crying.

'I'm here for you, Lucy.'

Despite his reassurances, she still didn't say a word and twenty minutes later, when he felt her body relax into sleep, he felt more distant from his wife than he had in a long time.

Chapter Twenty

'He's trailing mud all over my clean floors, eating enough to feed three grown men and he dawdles every time I send him out to pick up an order,' Mrs Finch reeled off a list of Freddy's less desirable attributes.

'It is still early in his employment, Mrs Finch,' Lucy said soothingly. 'And Freddy is just a child. I am sorry if he is inconveniencing you, but if we invest the time in him now he will grow up to be a valuable part of this household.'

They'd had the same discussion four times over the last few weeks since Freddy's arrival at Sedgewick House. He was a lively child, maybe not suited to life as a kitchen boy, but nowhere else would take him so it would have to be here.

'Have you seen any improvement?' Lucy asked.

'I suppose he's starting to follow orders a bit better,' Mrs Finch admitted reluctantly.

'He needs us perhaps more than we need him at the moment. He needs someone to believe in him, to give him the start in life he's never had before. That might mean a little inconvenience here and there, but I'm sure we can cope with that to give a young boy a better chance in life.'

Mrs Finch grumbled, as she always did, but Lucy could see she'd got her point across.

'Lady Sedgewick, your visitors have arrived,' Parker said as he descended the stairs into the kitchen.

'Visitors?' She wasn't expecting anyone. Since resuming her place as Lady Sedgewick and Oliver's wife she had contrived not to be at home to most visitors, mainly by not actually being in the house at popular visiting hours, but a few persistent people had slipped through.

'She said you had invited them to come calling. It is Mrs Hunter and her three children.'

Cursing silently, Lucy stood and straightened her skirts. She'd half-forgotten about the invitation, but there was no way she could turn the woman away now.

'I've shown them into the drawing room.'

'Thank you, Parker,' Lucy said.

Steeling herself for an hour of swapping social niceties, Lucy ascended the stairs and made her way to the drawing room. Just as she was about to push open the door she heard a giggle of laughter, too young and innocent to be Mrs Hunter—it would be one of the children.

'Annabelle, put that down,' Mrs Hunter rasped as Lucy opened the door.

'Good morning,' Lucy greeted the woman and her children. Mrs Hunter stood as Lucy entered the room and Lucy caught a glimpse of the almost bald head of a small baby. She'd known Mrs Hunter had been pregnant—the woman had first shown some interest in the Foundation nearly a year ago, but had delayed her involvement due to the pregnancy—but the sight of the small baby in her arms was enough to send Lucy's heart fluttering.

'It's so kind of you to receive us,' Mrs Hunter said. 'I normally would leave the children at home when out visiting, but their governess left us unexpectedly and they've run the maids ragged ever since. I'm sure you know how it is.'

Lucy murmured in agreement, even though she had no clue as to how it was. Her stint at being a mother had lasted for less than a month and during that time David had been in her arms almost constantly.

'This is Annabelle, my eldest, and this is Alexandra.' Two pretty girls bobbed curtsies. They looked angelic, but from their mother's tired visage Lucy suspected they were more difficult than their sweet faces would suggest. 'And this is Arthur. He's five months old now.'

Feeling her heart thump inside her chest, Lucy smiled as Mrs Hunter manoeuvred the baby so she could see his peaceful face. Lips pouted under chubby cheeks and as they watched he let out a contented sigh.

'Please, have a seat. I'll ring for some tea. And perhaps some lemonade for the girls?'

'Thank you, that's most kind.'

Despite being married to a viscount, Lucy was not confident at entertaining visitors. She'd hardly received any visitors during the first month of their marriage at Sedgewick Place. There they'd had no close neighbours and Lucy hadn't ventured out into the village much or attended the popular local events to meet people.

Even before marriage, when in London for the Season or at home in Brighton, her mother had done most of the entertaining. Not that they'd ever had many visitors. Her father hadn't encouraged interlopers into his domain at the family home and when in London they were hardly influential enough for many people to call on them.

Ringing the bell, Lucy waited for a maid to appear and ordered tea and lemonade, then returned to sit opposite Mrs Hunter and her children.

'I have to say I wasn't aware of your marriage to Lord Sedgewick,' Mrs Hunter said as they waited for the tea to arrive. 'Did you marry in the country?'

'It was a quiet ceremony. Lord Sedgewick is a private person so we had no announcements,' Lucy lied, not wanting to explain that the marriage had occurred two years earlier—not recently, as Mrs Hunter was assuming.

'It is very good of Lord Sedgewick to step in and become one of the primary benefactors of the Foundation.'

'Indeed, he is a generous man.'

'I've tried to get my husband interested in the work we do many times. He indulges me, but I don't think he would ever agree to take an active role.'

Most men wouldn't. They were often of the opinion that charity work was women's work, something to keep their wives occupied while they did the important job of making money.

The baby in her arm snuffled and shifted and Lucy felt a tug in her chest. She remembered that sound, that beautifully contented sound only a very young baby could make.

'...Lady Sedgewick?'

Lucy's head snapped up. Mrs Hunter had asked her a question and she'd completely missed it, being too preoccupied with the little bundle in the other woman's arms.

'Would you like to give Arthur a cuddle?' Mrs Hunter said kindly, her voice full of understanding.

She began to say no, but found her body responding instinctively to the offer, rising from her seat and holding out her arms.

'Do you have children?' Mrs Hunter asked as she passed the small baby over for Lucy to hold.

'We had a son,' Lucy said, her voice catching in her throat. 'He passed away when he was very young.'

Despite finding it difficult to talk about David to people she didn't know well, Lucy never denied the existence of her son. Even if it led to questions she found hard to answer or platitudes she didn't wish to accept.

'Oh, I'm so sorry. What a terrible thing to happen.'

Lucy nodded, trying not to shed the tears that were forming in her eyes and instead looking down at the sleeping boy in her arms. It seemed it would always be painful to talk about David.

'You'd be a wonderful mother,' Mrs Hunter

said quietly. 'One can see that by the way you are with the children at the Foundation.'

'I'm not sure…' Lucy said, choking on the few words. She didn't want to be discussing this, not with Mrs Hunter, not with anyone.

'I'm sorry, it's none of my business.'

They fell silent as Arthur shifted, letting out another contented little sigh. Lucy felt a deep yearning, one that she had no conscious control over. This last year, ever since David had died, she had been very hands-on with the older children at the Foundation, but had found it too painful to do too much with the mothers with very young babies. Seeing them reminded her too much of David.

Looking down at the little baby in her arms, she had a moment's hesitation. Would it really be so bad if she was pregnant? She might get to experience all this for herself, the joy of waking up every day as a mother again, of quiet cuddles in the early morning with a baby that was wholly dependent on her.

The warm glow she was feeling was suddenly replaced by a vivid memory of the pain. She recalled the debilitating numbness she'd felt after David's death, the horrific thoughts she'd been plagued with about ending her own life. Even now she sometimes woke with a feeling of overwhelming sadness, a deep-seated ache for the baby she'd loved more than life itself.

Lucy was just trying to regain some of her composure when the door opened.

'Lucy…' Oliver said before pausing as he saw Mrs Hunter and her children. 'Forgive me—I did not realise you had company.'

His eyes flitted to the baby in her arms and as she glanced quickly at him she could see the pain behind them. It was selfish, the way she acted sometimes, she knew that, and often she forgot that she wasn't the only one who had lost a child. Just because Oliver had never got to hold their son in his arms, never got to listen to his steady breathing or contented snuffles, it didn't mean that losing David had hurt him any less.

She knew he grieved for their son, knew he had visited the grave on numerous occasions in the past few weeks, and sometimes she caught him staring off into the distance and she was sure he was thinking about the child he'd never got to hold.

'I'm sure you remember Mrs Hunter, from the Foundation,' Lucy said, her voice cracking slightly as she spoke. 'And these are her three children.'

'Delighted to see you again,' Oliver said, his eyes still not moving from the baby in Lucy's arms. He was looking at Lucy warily, as if unable to believe what he was seeing.

'I was just saying to Lady Sedgewick how wonderful it is you stepped in to become a patron.'

'It is a cause that means a lot to my wife,' Oliver said, 'and so it means a lot to me.'

'I think the work they do there is just wonderful,' Mrs Hunter gushed, her words coming out fast as if she wasn't used to speaking to a viscount, which Lucy supposed she probably wasn't. Oliver wasn't an intimidating man when you got to know him, but his upbringing and social polish meant he must seem daunting to converse with to most people.

'Indeed,' Oliver murmured, but Lucy could tell only a fraction of his attention was on Mrs Hunter. 'Anyway, ladies, I will leave you. It is a pleasure to have properly made your acquaintance, Mrs Hunter.'

He was gone before Lucy could utter another word, closing the door quietly behind him.

Wondering what she could do to speed up Mrs Hunter's visit, Lucy jumped when the door opened again and a maid came in with a tray of tea and two tall glasses of lemonade. Reluctantly she passed baby Arthur back to his mother while she prepared the tea. Her arms felt empty without the warm little bundle snuggling into her chest and she had to keep her hands busy to stop them from shaking.

'He keeps me up half the night,' Mrs Hunter was saying. 'I have a nursemaid, of course, but he doesn't seem to quieten for anyone but me. By the time he's been crying for an hour or two the whole house is awake and it just seems kinder for me to take him.'

Lucy knew most women of higher social status employed wet nurses, nursemaids or even nannies for their young babies. They would do all the hard work, the washing and dressing, the getting up in the middle of the night, while the mothers would see their children when they were properly presented for a limited amount of time every day. It had been similar to her own upbringing—she'd always felt much closer to her nannies than she had her own parents.

Despite it being the norm, Lucy couldn't quite understand why anyone would want to hand their precious baby over for long periods of the day, only to see them during the quiet times. Of course all mothers got tired and having an extra pair of hands to assist was nothing to turn your nose up at, but she couldn't imagine ever having wanted to hand David over to someone else.

'He's lovely,' Lucy said, finding her voice at last.

'Looks nothing like me, of course, none of

them do, but I find I rather like having three miniature variations on my husband.'

Mrs Hunter was small with dark hair and a fair complexion. All three children had blonde curls, blue eyes and dimples when they smiled. Lucy had never met Mr Hunter, but she was now imagining a rather ridiculous-looking man with swathes of curly blond hair and deep-set dimples not suited to anyone over the age of ten.

They finished their tea, talking about the Foundation and Mary's plans for expansion for the future, which Mrs Hunter supported wholeheartedly. As the time ticked by Lucy found she was focusing less on her grief and more on what Mrs Hunter was saying, as well as the antics of the two older girls. They had dug a pack of playing cards out from somewhere and were currently squabbling quietly over a complicated-looking game.

Mrs Hunter reprimanded them wearily every time it looked like the quarrel would get violent, but Lucy could still hear the affection in her voice.

'Thank you very much for receiving us,' Mrs Hunter said as she finished her cup of tea. 'Especially with all the children in tow.'

'Not at all, it has been a lovely morning. We must do this again some time,' Lucy said, sur-

prising herself with the invitation and the fact
that it wasn't just issued out of politeness.

'That's most kind, Lady Sedgewick.'

Lucy watched out of the window as the woman
and her children traipsed off down the street. It
seemed petty to feel jealous of what Mrs Hunter
had and it wasn't exactly jealousy that Lucy was
feeling. More a vague sense of wanting to experience someone else's life for a few days, just to
try it out.

'You received a visitor,' Oliver said a few minutes later when he walked back into the room.
He must have been listening for Parker to show
Mrs Hunter out before making a reappearance
as it was remarkable timing.

'I have received one or two,' Lucy said, more
defensively than she meant to.

'It is good for you to socialise,' Oliver said,
his smile just a little too bright and his tone just
a little too breezy.

'Indeed.'

'Especially with someone you have so much in
common with,' he said. Lucy must have looked
blank as he continued after a few seconds, 'The
Foundation, of course.'

'Of course.'

'Adorable baby,' he said when it was clear she
wasn't going to fill the silence.

'I'm not going to change my mind about a family just because I held a delightful baby for five minutes,' Lucy ground out, even though her heart had melted when baby Arthur was in her arms.

'I didn't say anything.'

'It was what you were implying. Baby Arthur was indeed delightful, but Mrs Hunter's circumstances are very different to mine.'

'Indeed.' It was his turn to resort to single-word contributions to the conversation.

They stared at one another in silence for a while before Oliver continued.

'So there is no consequence from our mishap in the library?'

'No.'

Lucy wasn't sure why she lied. The word was out of her mouth before she even had chance to consider it. She should have told him that she didn't know, but it was too early to tell one way or another. All that would have been simple to explain, but instead she took the coward's way and lied. She supposed it was so he wouldn't be asking every few days, so she wouldn't have to see that hope in his eyes when it would contrast so sharply with her own feelings on the matter.

'We leave for Sedgewick Place first thing tomorrow morning,' he said. Although his voice was strong and unwavering, Lucy could see the disappointment behind his eyes. Perhaps he was more ready to try for a family than she had suspected.

'I will tell Florence to pack. How long will we be away for?'

'A week, maybe two.'

Lucy bit her tongue and said nothing about being needed in St Giles. She could take the most pressing of paperwork with her, and would use the travelling time to jot down some ideas about how to help Mary in her planned expansion of the charity. Her classes were being more than ably covered by an enthusiastic young man whom Mary had found and persuaded to join them for a few months.

'I will be ready to leave straight after breakfast.'

Chapter Twenty-One

They had stopped for lunch at a coaching inn on the very outskirts of London. Oliver had hoped to be further into their journey by now, but it had taken them so long to navigate through the crush of London that they still had a fair distance to cover. He had almost suggested pushing on for another hour, but one look at Lucy's pale, drawn face and he had instructed the coachman to stop at the next reputable inn.

'You look unwell,' Oliver said as he helped Lucy from the carriage.

'Just a little nausea from the motion of the carriage,' she said, giving him a weak smile.

Admittedly he hadn't travelled many long distances with his wife in a carriage before, just their trip to Brighton a few weeks previously, but he hadn't known her to be affected by the

motion of the carriage then. It seemed to him
to be something he should know about his wife.

'Come and sit down. I'll get you a drink.'

'I think I need some fresh air,' Lucy said, resisting his movement in the direction of the inn.
'Could we take a short stroll?'

'Of course.'

Quickly he instructed Robertson, the coach
driver, to see to the horses and then get some
lunch himself, before returning to Lucy's side.
She still looked pale and was taking deep breaths
as if trying to quell a persistent nausea.

Gently he took her arm and led her away from
the overpowering smells of the coaching inn's
yard and out on to the road, in the direction
they had just travelled. The road was rutted and
muddy, but there was a grass verge running along
the side which allowed them to walk side by side
without getting too dirty. Lucy clutched his arm
as they walked and was bent a little at the waist
as if really struggling to keep from being sick.

'I didn't know you suffered from motion sickness,' Oliver said. 'There's so many things I still
don't know about you.'

She glanced at him, but didn't reply, and he
reasoned she was battling the urge to vomit, although there was a hint of suspicion in her eyes.

'We can rest here as long as you need. There is no rush to get to Sedgewick Place.'

'Thank you,' Lucy murmured. 'I'm sure I'll be quite recovered in a few minutes.'

'I believe food can also help. We'll make sure you have a good meal before we set off again.'

Nodding, she quietly agreed, although she didn't look overly keen at the prospect of food.

'I'm very much looking forward to showing you around Sedgewick Place again,' Oliver said, thinking a distraction from her nausea might be just what she needed. 'It has probably changed a little since you were last there.'

Sedgewick Place was his ancestral home and as such the interior was made up of mismatching designs as the different generations over the years had tried to put their stamp on the old house. When he was growing up Oliver hadn't taken too much of an interest in the function and decoration of various rooms—after all, he'd never expected the grand Elizabethan house to be his—but once his mother had passed away, he had started to get the urge to make the place into *his* home.

'No major changes, but a little building work on the east wing and some landscaping of the gardens. Of course I'd be very happy for you to change any of the rooms—the place could do with a feminine touch.'

'I barely know anything about curtains and soft furnishings,' Lucy said, trying to summon a smile.

'Well, perhaps we could start with our bedroom, make it a little less dingy.'

The master bedroom at Sedgewick Place was a huge, high-ceilinged room, especially for an Elizabethan house. It had large windows which should have let in plenty of light, but heavy curtains and dark furnishings made the room seem dark and unwelcoming. It still retained a very masculine feel, which he supposed was unsurprising since he'd been the sole occupant for so long.

Lucy nodded, then clutched his arm, bending forward at the waist and sucking in great lungfuls of air.

'Lucy,' Oliver cried, seeing the blood drain from her face.

She flapped her free hand at him, in what he supposed was meant to be a reassuring gesture, and he bit back his next question. If she was concentrating on not throwing up over her shoes, she didn't need him talking.

After a minute she straightened back up, but her skin still had an unhealthy green tinge to it.

'Perhaps we should return to the inn,' Lucy said with a weak smile. 'I might need some water.'

Slowly they retraced their steps. They'd only made it a couple of hundred yards from the inn so within a few minutes he'd settled Lucy at a table and was asking the serving girl for a cold glass of water.

With concern, he watched as his wife sipped from the glass, some of the colour slowly returning to her face as the water settled in her stomach. She closed her eyes for a long moment, her hands holding on to the edge of the table as if using the solid oak surface to steady herself.

'Would you like something to eat?' he asked once she was looking more like her normal self.

'Perhaps just some bread,' Lucy said.

'I'll order a few things from what they have available and you can choose what is most appetising.'

'Thank you.' She grimaced as another bout of nausea must have overcome her.

Once again Oliver jumped up to find the serving girl and put in their order for lunch, glad when he was able to focus on doing something practical rather than just sitting there watching his wife suffer.

'I didn't know motion sickness could persist

so long after you stopped moving,' Oliver said as he returned to the table. 'Does it normally happen like this for you?'

She shook her head. 'Perhaps I'm sickening for something.' Once again she smiled weakly, but the smile didn't reach her eyes.

'Once we get to Sedgewick Place we can call the doctor out to see you.'

'I'm sure there's no need,' she said quickly.

The serving girl brought a plate of crusty bread to start before the rest of the food arrived and Lucy gingerly took a bite. She chewed slowly, her brow furrowed as she must have been fighting the waves of nausea.

'Is that any better?' Oliver asked and was pleased when she nodded, taking another small bite.

'I'm sure I just need something to settle my stomach,' she said, sipping at her water in between bites of bread.

By the time the rest of the food appeared Lucy had returned to a normal colour.

Once they'd eaten, Lucy excused herself and made her way into the courtyard to get some air. She was no longer feeling sick, but a deep knot of worry had formed in her stomach and she couldn't bear to be in the same room as Oliver any longer. It felt like every time he looked at her he saw a little deeper into her soul.

In the twenty-one years she'd been alive she'd never once suffered from motion sickness. Even when winding through the snaking roads of the South Downs she didn't suffer from even a hint of nausea. It just wasn't something she'd ever had to deal with.

There's always a first time, the optimistic part of her said, but Lucy knew it wasn't true. What was it Dr White had told her to look out for? Tender breasts, fatigue, nausea. All things she'd been experiencing the past couple of days.

Realising she was worrying the skin around her thumbnails with her fingers she made a conscious effort to stop all movement. Making her hands bleed wouldn't solve the problem; she was pregnant and she could no longer deny it.

Expecting to feel overwhelmed or petrified by the realisation, Lucy was surprised to realise all she felt was numb. She couldn't process all the emotions. It was as if her body had shut down on her. Every time she contemplated the future her mind blanked out the pictures and the possibilities and she found herself thinking about nothing at all.

'How are you?' Oliver asked as she re-entered

the dining room, the concern etched upon his face. 'We can stay here tonight if need be.'

'It isn't yet much past two o'clock, plenty of time to reach Sussex yet.'

'I don't want you travelling if you feel unwell. It might harm…you.'

She noticed his slight hesitation and felt her eyes narrow, but didn't want to open up the conversation, so tried to ignore the feeling Oliver knew her secret.

'I'd rather push on. It'll be much better sleeping in our own bed.'

'True.'

He fell silent and Lucy picked up a small piece of bread, pulling it apart with her hands to keep herself occupied and so Oliver wouldn't notice they were shaking.

'So did you suffer from motion sickness as a child?' Oliver asked after a few minutes.

She hesitated, not wanting to lie outright, but not able to see any other way. 'A little. Not often but sometimes. We didn't do much travelling.' That much was true at least.

'I always thought people got it or they didn't.'

'Evidently not,' she murmured, not able to meet her husband's eye.

'And you were absolutely fine on the trip to

Brighton—you even had your head buried in the accounts for half the journey.'

'Perhaps it was a bumpier road today,' Lucy said, clutching at any possible explanation.

'Perhaps, but the road to Brighton is notoriously overused. You would have thought it more liable to wear and tear.'

'I don't know, Oliver,' she said wearily. All she wanted now was to put her head down on a soft pillow and sleep for the rest of the afternoon. 'Can we get on with the journey soon?'

He went to pay, whistling as he exited the room, far too jolly a tune for Lucy to deal with.

The approach to Sedgewick Place was grand and drawn out, like many important country estates. The drive went on for over a mile, curving this way and that through the rolling hills until a wonderful view of the house was afforded a good five minutes before any carriage actually reached the front entrance.

If Oliver was honest he still thought of Sedgewick Place as his parents' house, even though they were both long deceased. He'd never expected to inherit it, so when he did it had taken a lot of getting used to—not only the title and new responsibilities, but the piece of family heritage that had suddenly been entrusted to his care.

Lucy had fallen asleep over an hour ago, after their fourth stop for her to jump from the carriage to be sick. Each time she'd returned, quiet and subdued, but insisted they carry on with their journey. Now they were approaching the house he didn't want to wake her; she looked so peaceful with her eyelashes resting against her cheeks. She needed the rest and he wasn't going to be the one to stop her from getting it.

As the carriage drew to a stop he saw the staff assembled in front of the huge front door, lined up for the master and mistress of the house despite the late hour. Parker had travelled on ahead to ensure everything was ready for their arrival and always liked to have the staff well turned out for when Oliver stepped out of the carriage. Despite all their efforts tonight the staff would only be greeting him, for he wasn't about to disturb Lucy's slumber.

Stepping down, he twisted and lifted Lucy out in his arms, having to suppress a smile as she mumbled something incomprehensible and snuggled into his chest. She was light, still thinner than she had been when they'd first married two years ago due to a long time of lean living, but he could feel the curve of her bottom under his arms and the swell of her breasts pressed against his chest.

'Would you like me to take Lady Sedgewick, my lord?' Parker asked quietly.

'No need. I'll carry her upstairs to the bedroom myself. Is everything prepared?'

The butler confirmed it was and Oliver nodded in greeting to all the other assembled staff before entering the house. Quickly he climbed the stairs, ducking his head under a low beam and striding along to the master bedroom. It was the same chamber they had shared in the first heady few weeks of their marriage and Oliver hoped it would contain more good memories than bad for Lucy.

'Where are we?' she murmured as he pushed open the door.

'Home, my love. You rest.'

Gently he laid her down on the bed, smiling as she rolled immediately to one side, curling up into her usual sleeping position. With a frown he tried to remove her shoes, failing completely with the intricate little buckles and resorting to pulling them off without undoing them.

He wasn't sure how comfortable all the layers of clothing Lucy was wearing were, but he couldn't see a good way to undress her without waking her completely. Instead he shed his own clothing, stoked the fire that was beginning to dwindle in the fireplace and got into bed beside his wife. With a contented sigh she nestled into him and as he blew out the candle he wondered how he could make her so content during her waking hours.

Oliver knew she was unhappy and it pained him. She was still grieving for their son, which was entirely understandable, but he knew it was hurting her. It was stopping her from enjoying their renewed relationship, stopping her from wanting more children. She was scared, understandably so, but that fear was just adding to her unhappiness.

As he drifted off to sleep Oliver wondered what more he could do. He'd hoped showing her love and affection would be enough, but now he wasn't so sure. She needed something more, something he had a horrible feeling she was going to have to work out herself.

Kissing the nape of her neck softly, he allowed himself to succumb to sleep, hoping tomorrow he would be able to see things clearer.

Chapter Twenty-Two

Although she'd only lived there a short time before fleeing to London, Lucy had always loved early mornings at Sedgewick Place. The master bedroom looked out over the sweeping deer park and the first rays of sun that filtered through the trees and over the hills always made the land look almost magical. Even more so on a day like today when there were wisps of mist lying in the shallow valleys.

Despite the beautiful view, Lucy only managed to stay at the window for thirty seconds before collapsing back into bed. The awful nausea that had plagued the journey from London was back and this time she had hardly moved. She certainly couldn't blame it on motion sickness when she'd only taken a few steps from the bed to the window.

Oliver was still sleeping, that deep, undisturbed slumber he fell into nearly as soon as his eyes closed and remained in for the rest of the night. She sometimes envied him his sleep, being a restless sleeper herself, and wondered if the ease at which he switched off from the day had something to do with being satisfied with the person he was.

Closing her eyes and gently resting her head back on her pillow, Lucy tried to focus on quelling the roll of nausea that seemed to want to take over her body. Now she knew she'd been right; the sickness was a sign of the life growing inside her. She'd experienced the same with David, that unmistakable sign that a little baby was taking nest inside her womb.

I don't want this, she told herself.

For so long she'd been adamant she would never get pregnant again, never risk bringing another child into the world to suffer like David had. She felt guilty for the spark of pleasure and anticipation she could feel whenever she thought that she might get to be a mother again.

That's not what I want, she told herself more firmly.

Opening her eyes for a few seconds as the sickness subsided a little, she focused on Oliver. She wondered how he would take the news. He wanted more children, that much she knew,

but she wasn't sure he was ready for them yet.
Despite how their relationship had evolved over
the past few weeks she could tell he still didn't
quite trust her, wasn't convinced she wouldn't
run away again. A pregnancy would only complicate things. One day he would probably want to
be surrounded by a brood of children, but not yet.

Lucy knew that in Oliver's eyes everything
had a set order. First he had to learn to trust her
again, which she knew he was slowly beginning
to do as they allowed themselves to get to know
one another better, to enjoy each other's company. Then he might be ready to consider more
children. They weren't there yet, but one day...

In Lucy's mind the major factor holding her
back was her grief. Grief over what had happened
to David, concern that it might happen again.
She knew Oliver mourned their son deeply, too,
and before they could even consider having any
more children they would both have to deal with
that grief and the fear that they might lose another child, too.

For a moment she allowed herself to picture a
happy scenario, her and Oliver, smiling and content, with four or five healthy, boisterous children. It was seductive and she could feel herself
being pulled towards the idea. If life was that
simple and good, then of course she'd choose a

large and happy family, but she *knew* it couldn't be like that.

'How will you react?' she whispered, confident that Oliver was fast asleep and wouldn't ever hear her question. 'When you see our child for the first time and he looks different.'

That was her main fear, despite all his assurances, all his protestations, that Oliver would be unable to love a child like David, or like William. He was a good man, one of the best, but when it came to their firstborn, men could be very particular. She'd seen it with her own father and society was full of children who had been more or less disowned by their families.

'You look very serious,' Oliver said, opening his eyes and studying her face.

She should tell him. Soon he would guess and it would be better if she was the one to break the news.

'I feel a little nauseous,' she said, giving a weak smile.

Immediately he was wide awake, sitting up in bed. She couldn't deny he would look after her. Attentive and considerate, that was her husband—why then did she find it so hard to believe that he would be the same to their children?

Perhaps the problem was hers: a lack of trust.

She'd always suffered from it, never having had a close confidant growing up.

'I think there's something we should talk about,' Lucy said, feeling his eyes on hers as if he were reading her very soul.

'You look worried.'

'I've been feeling sick for a few days and tired.'

Oliver remained silent, looking at her expectantly, and she wondered if he had already guessed. He was an intelligent man and, although he'd been absent when she'd had the worst of her symptoms with David, most people knew unexplained nausea and fatigue in a young woman often hinted at a pregnancy.

'I think…' She trailed off before taking a deep breath. 'I think I might be pregnant.'

She watched his face, saw the range of emotions flicker across it until he managed to get himself under control and nodded silently. For a moment she felt sad that neither of their first reactions was that pure pleasure, that limitless excitement, she'd felt when realising she was going to be a mother for the first time. Instead they were both plagued by worry.

'We will get through this, together,' he said, pulling her into a deep embrace. The words were reassuring, but his body felt stiff and unfamiliar.

Desperately she wanted to believe him, she wanted that perfect family of her imagination, one filled with love and happiness.

'I'm scared,' she whispered, surprising herself with the show of vulnerability.

She expected him to offer words of comfort, but he just nodded, as if he were too preoccupied with his own thoughts to be able to reassure her. Slowly she backed out of his arms, saw his eyes searching her face and realised for the first time in a long time that he was wary of her and how she was going to act.

'Tell me we can get through this,' Lucy whispered.

He hesitated, just a second, but it was enough to break her heart. 'We can get through this,' he said, but there was no conviction behind his words. After a moment he seemed to rally a little. 'There's no reason to suspect anything will go wrong,' he said, as if trying to reassure himself.

Lucy felt a stab of pain through her heart.

'Whenever you feel uncertain, I need you to come to me,' Oliver said, gripping her by the arms and waiting until she met his eye.

She nodded. It wasn't a promise she was sure she could keep, but right now she was determined to try. For their child, their baby. She knew that the best way to face the challenges of this pregnancy, all the fears and worries, would be together, but already she had a deeply ingrained desire to run, to hide somewhere and withdraw into herself until her baby arrived into the world.

With a small nod of his own Oliver released her. Feeling a pang of disappointment, Lucy busied herself with rearranging the bedclothes. She'd hoped for something more, for a positive reaction to her news. Deep down she knew Oliver wouldn't abandon a child, he wasn't like her father, but his reaction hadn't exactly been reassuring.

He'd left Lucy in bed, battling the nausea. She had reassured him she would rather he got up and started his day and she would join him in her own time. Normally Oliver wouldn't hesitate to spend the morning in bed with Lucy, but he'd felt an overwhelming need to escape the house, go somewhere deserted and try to make sense of all the emotions fighting for supremacy inside him.

Once again he was going to be a father and he wasn't quite sure how he felt about it. On the one hand, he felt like shouting a prayer of thanks to the heavens. The loss of David still affected him every day and he knew another child would never heal the hole in his heart, but perhaps it would allow him to move forward with his life. He'd never hoped for a child again so soon, knowing his heart was still fragile from the loss of his son, but he knew he did want to have another child *one day*. Ideally first he and Lucy would work through some of their residual issues with trust, get to know one another properly and build a solid foundation to start a family on, but he knew not everything could be planned so precisely.

On the other hand, his first reaction had been one of fear. Fear of history repeating itself. Lucy didn't want to have another child, not yet, and that could only mean a difficult road ahead of them. Oliver had remained strong for over a year, but if Lucy were to disappear again, if she were to take another child away from him, he didn't think he could cope. She had assured him time and time again that she wouldn't run, wouldn't abandon him, but what if something were to go wrong? What if they were to lose another child, or the pregnancy never reached that far—could he really be sure she wouldn't flee again because of it?

'You need to forgive her,' he murmured to himself.

It was true, despite all the progress they'd made over the last few weeks, he still hadn't really forgiven Lucy for everything she'd put him through. It was hard to. She'd apologised and

Oliver believed she was truly sorry for hurting him so badly, but when she'd left without a word Lucy had ripped his trust to pieces and he wasn't sure if anything could ever mend that. And now they were bringing a child into the mix.

Striding out over the lawns at the back of the house, he revelled in the crisp crunch of the frosty grass under his feet and had to suppress the urge to break out into a run. He was still Lord Sedgewick, master of Sedgewick Place, and certain standards of behaviour had to be adhered to even when he felt like running as fast as he could and never stopping.

Only when he had circled behind a small copse of trees and was completely hidden by the house did he allow himself to slump on to a fallen tree trunk and rest his head in his hands.

This time will be different, he tried to reassure himself.

He wasn't going to spend the majority of Lucy's pregnancy away from her as he had before. Every day he would work on building their relationship, ensuring that when their child was born they were a strong family, ready to face any adversity.

But she might still leave.

And that was the crux of the matter. He couldn't allow himself to be excited about impending fatherhood because he didn't know what his wife would do, how she would react, if something were to go wrong with the pregnancy.

Forcing himself to appreciate the calm morning sunshine, despite the cold bite of the air, Oliver strolled back through the gardens at a leisurely pace. He felt agitated and uncertain, but knew he had to give himself time to work out the best way to tackle his fears.

'Parker,' he called as he entered the house through a side door. His butler was there almost immediately. 'Ready for some practice?'

The butler grinned and strode off to collect the fencing foils. Oliver needed to work off some pent-up energy.

At Sedgewick Place there was no need to clear a room for their practice. There was a long, flat terrace that ran the entire length of the back of the house and it made the perfect location to fence. Even on a day like today when frost covered the grass, the sunshine struck the terrace early meaning it was rarely too icy for them to fence.

Oliver shrugged off his jacket, despite the cool temperatures, and stretched out his arms, swinging them from side to side as Parker reappeared with the foils. They fenced without the protective outfits that were popular among those who practised seriously, with an unspoken agreement that both men would avoid blows to the other's face or neck. The foils were not sharp and tipped with a smooth metal ball so no real injury could be sustained from that either. Both men had experienced enough violence and injury in the army to be careful about not hurting the other and both were talented enough to be able to control their movements with fine precision.

'Fine day for it, my lord,' Parker observed as he stretched out his shoulders in much the same manner Oliver had.

'Indeed,' Oliver agreed grimly.

Without any further conversation they began. Each man advancing forward in attack before having to retreat under the other's onslaught. Foil clashed against foil, with satisfying metallic clinks and swishes and today Oliver scored point after point after point.

'You're very fast today, my lord,' Parker observed as they took a few minutes to catch their breath.

Oliver knew it was the effect of his agitation from Lucy's news, but he forced a grin at his butler and slapped him on the back.

'Or maybe you're getting slow.'

'I blame a life of domesticity,' Parker observed.

'Better than another decade camping in muddy fields and being hated by at least half the local population,' Oliver said.

'Very true, my lord, even with that menace of a child Mrs Finch has in her kitchen now.'

Freddy had still not settled into the life of a servant. He caused mischief and extra work for almost everyone in the house, but Oliver had noticed Parker take him under his wing. The young butler treated the scallywag of a child like a younger brother and hopefully soon Freddy's behaviour would benefit from the calming influence.

'I came to see if you were ready for breakfast,' Lucy said, her pale face peeking out from the warmth of the house. 'And I find you fighting our butler once again.'

'Thrashing the butler,' Oliver corrected her.

'Only this once,' Parker remarked. 'Shall I let Mrs Finch know you're ready for breakfast, my lady?'

Oliver's household was a little unusual in that he transported many of the more senior members of servants between his two residences. He put it down to being a creature of habit, preferring one cook and one butler to run the households rather than two competitive sets. Here at Sedgewick Place he also had the indomitable Mrs

Hardcastle as housekeeper, to keep everything running like a military operation.

'Yes, please, Parker—although no kipper this morning.'

'Very well, my lady. I shall inform Mrs Finch.'

Lucy stepped outside and immediately Oliver was by her side. 'It's too cold for you,' he said. She smiled at him warily.

'Don't fuss,' she said, although her expression told him she didn't mind really.

Placing an arm around her shoulders, he led her back inside, trying to act as normal as possible, but knowing Lucy would sense his tension.

Chapter Twenty-Three

It was mid-morning by the time Lucy's nausea had properly subsided. Up until then she'd been hiding out in the vast library, curled on a sofa in front of the fire with a book in her hands but barely turning the pages. Now she was feeling a little better, she thought she would seek out her husband to have a serious talk about what this baby would mean for them.

Sedgewick Place was large, but not enormous by ancestral-seat standards. It was originally an Elizabethan mansion, with various wings and rooms added over the years giving it a maze-like interior structure, but still retaining its original charm. The warren of corridors was the reason Lucy was still searching for Oliver ten minutes after she'd left the library.

She'd checked his study, the drawing room, the master bedroom and even stepped out on to the terrace to see if he had decided to continue fencing with the butler.

Just as she was about to give up and retreat to the warmth of the library again she heard a few creaks above her head. The old building was prone to making strange noises, but it definitely sounded as though someone was walking about in the far reaches of the west wing.

Ascending the main staircase, Lucy proceeded along to the west wing, the rather grand name for a collection of six rooms that led off the main upstairs corridor. They hadn't been used in years and Lucy wasn't sure what their original purpose had been. The rooms weren't small, but lacked the fancy design features of some of the grander bedrooms in the house. She supposed they could have been servants' bedrooms at one time, before the roof space had been renovated to accommodate most of the house's serving staff.

As she reached the door of the first room in the west wing she paused, hearing Oliver's voice and wondering who exactly he was talking to up here.

'We don't know what sort of challenges they might face,' Oliver was saying, 'so we need a dedicated space.'

'And this is the room?'

'I think so, but I was wondering if it was possible to add a door, with a lock of course, in here.'

Lucy felt her blood run cold in her veins. Why was Oliver talking about converting a room only to put a lock on the door? He could only be talking about their child, mentioning the challenges they might face, and already he was thinking about locking them in.

'That would be possible. This wall isn't load-bearing. It would be simple to add a door through here.'

'Privacy is of the utmost importance,' Oliver stressed.

And with those words Lucy's heart broke. She'd been almost convinced he was speaking the truth when he'd said nothing would induce him to abandon a child, but here he was thinking about how to shut their unborn baby away from the world and she wasn't even two months pregnant yet.

'We may not need it,' Oliver said quietly, 'but I'd rather be prepared.'

Unable to listen to any more, she crept back along the corridor, trying to process the words she'd heard. There was no other possible meaning; he had to be talking about their child, and the plans he was making weren't those of a proud father, more that he was thinking how to hide their son or daughter away.

She reached their bedroom before the tears came, great heavy sobs that racked her body, the sorrow making her legs buckle underneath her.

'I'll look after you,' she whispered to the unborn child inside her.

And she would. That was what being a mother was about. It appeared she couldn't trust Oliver to be the perfect father to their son or daughter, so she would have to trust her instincts and strike out on her own once again.

A small voice of doubt niggled inside her head, telling her not to be so hasty. Oliver was good and true and had never lied to her before. Surely she could give him the benefit of the doubt this once and, instead of fleeing without an explanation, she could confront him about the conversation she had overheard.

Slumping down on the bed, Lucy tried to think rationally, but panic seized her, and the urge to get away was strong. She couldn't think while she was under the same roof as her husband. His kind gestures and soft words blinded her to what was really going on underneath and she couldn't afford to be blind. She needed some space, some time to think and plan.

Quickly she rummaged around in the wardrobe for a small bag, nothing that would be too obvious so someone might see and work out her purpose, but big enough to hold a change of clothes and a little money. Before she could stop herself she had packed the bag, snapped it shut and was peering out the door into the hall.

She hesitated before leaving the bedroom, then placed her bag back down on the bed and slumped down next to it. She couldn't leave, couldn't just run away again. That was the coward's way out. Oliver might not have seemed happy about the pregnancy and had been acting strangely all morning, but she couldn't just run without giving him a chance to explain himself.

Five minutes later she was still sitting on the bed, lost in her own thoughts when the door opened and Oliver entered the room. Steeling herself to confront him over what he had been discussing with his steward, she saw his eyes flick immediately to the small bag that was beside her on the bed.

Without a word he crossed the room and opened the bag, peering inside.

The blood drained from Lucy's face and she felt her head spinning.

'It's not what you think,' she said quietly.

'You've packed a bag. You're leaving.' His voice was flat and devoid of any emotion.

'No...' She hesitated. 'Well, yes, I packed a bag. But then I reconsidered.'

'Oh, how wonderful—you *reconsidered*,' Oliver said.

'You don't understand.'

'I understand perfectly well. You tell me you're pregnant again, decide you don't trust me and run away *again*, without a thought for me.'

'No,' she protested, trying to keep as calm as possible. 'It's not like that.'

'Then what is it like, Lucy? Because it certainly seems that way to me.'

'What were you talking about in the west wing?' she asked, hating the accusing tone of her voice.

'You were up there?' Oliver asked. 'Listening?'

He made it sound as though she'd been spying on him.

'What were you talking about?' she persisted.

'I was making plans with my steward. He has a brother who did some work on the house before.' Oliver frowned, as if he couldn't see why talking about converting the rooms into a *locked* nursery would make Lucy flee.

'You were talking about turning them into a

nursery, a nursery where you could lock our child away if necessary.' He looked puzzled so Lucy pushed on. 'You stressed the importance of a lock on the door and you said we didn't know what our child would be like, but it was better to be prepared.'

'And you thought I meant to lock them away, hide them where no one would see them?'

'What else could you mean?'

'I wanted to convert the rooms into a nursery, with the option of a master bedroom in the largest of the rooms so we would be on hand if our child did need us. The lock was to be on *our* door for privacy.'

Lucy closed her eyes. She'd assumed the worst from the snippet of conversation she'd heard and rather than asking her husband about it she'd reacted rashly.

'You think so little of me?' Oliver asked. His tone was impassive, but Lucy could see the hurt behind his eyes.

'I misunderstood,' she said, reaching out and trying to take her husband's hand.

Pulling away, he crossed over to the window, leaning against the windowsill in what seemed like an attempt to get as far away from her as possible.

'And your solution was to run away?'

'No,' Lucy protested, even though it had been her first reaction.

He motioned to the packed bag on the bed. 'Don't lie, Lucy. You were going to leave without a word again.'

'I thought about it,' she admitted. 'I got as far as packing my bag, but I couldn't go through with it.'

Oliver shook his head. He didn't believe her, that much was clear.

'We can't do this,' he said after a long minute's silence. '*I* can't do this, not again.'

'What do you mean?' Lucy asked, feeling an emptiness in the pit of her stomach.

'I can't do this,' he repeated.

She waited for him to elaborate, at the same time hoping he wouldn't say any more.

'You don't trust me,' he said finally. 'And I don't trust you. That's no way for a relationship to be.'

'I do…' Lucy trailed off as she saw the expression on her husband's face.

He was right, she didn't trust him. It wasn't anything he'd done, or anything he'd said, just her own inability to trust.

'Maybe it would be better if we spent some time apart,' he said.

Lucy felt her mouth drop open in surprise.

Whatever she'd expected she hadn't ever thought he would suggest that. Over the last few weeks Oliver had been working to keep them close, to build their relationship and break down the barriers between them. Now he was suggesting they cut their ties and spend time apart.

'Perhaps it would,' Lucy said, trying to keep the catch of emotion from her voice. Despite the packed bag by her side she didn't really want to leave. She wanted Oliver to hold her in his arms and reassure her that everything would work out in the end.

'I will make arrangements,' he said, pushing himself away from the windowsill and striding across the room.

He left without a backwards glance and before the door had closed, Lucy felt the tears beginning to roll down her cheeks.

Trying to keep her pace slow, as if she were in no hurry, Lucy descended the stairs, forcing a smile when she passed Parker in the hall. The smile must have been more of a grimace than anything else for the butler started forward, but Lucy waved him away with a dismissive hand.

'Please inform my husband I have done as he wished,' she said, trying to stop her voice from breaking.

'Do you need some assistance, Lady Sedge-wick?' The butler's voice was full of concern and Lucy couldn't look at him in case she burst into tears.

'No, thank you, Parker.'

And with that Lucy fled Sedgewick Place less than twenty-four hours after arriving.

With a growl of frustration Oliver threw down the papers he'd been trying to read for the last hour. He'd told himself he needed a distraction, anything to stop him thinking about the disaster that was his marriage, but in truth not even a stampeding herd of cattle through his study could distract him from his thoughts.

Standing, he stalked over to the window and stared out over the garden. The grass was wet from the melting frost and it glistened in the sunlight, although in the distance he thought he could see dark clouds gathering. All in all it was a beautiful day. It was as though even the weather was mocking his foul mood.

She'd been ready to run away again, that was what he couldn't believe. So early on, at the very first sign of controversy. Perhaps she had mis-understood him about his plans for the nursery, but any normal person would have spoken to him about it, asked him to explain his words, not packed a bag and been ready to flee.

He would never be able to trust her, that was the problem. Every day he would wake and wonder if today was the day his wife disappeared without a trace.

'What can I do?' he murmured to himself. They were married, they were expecting a child together, in so many ways they were tied together for the rest of their lives. Perhaps he needed to lower his expectations. If he was honest with himself, Lucy's behaviour hurt so much because he cared so much. He wanted to have a full and loving relationship with his wife, but perhaps that was too much to ask for. The only way to protect himself, to stop her from hurting him again, was to pull back. They would have a child together, but that didn't mean they had to live in the same house. He owned a total of four properties, they never had to see one another if they didn't wish to.

Feeling a squeeze on his heart, Oliver tried to steel himself. It had to be done. He couldn't live every day not knowing when his wife would abandon him and take their child, too. He would make arrangements for Lucy to travel back to London later today. She could stay at Sedgewick House, continue her precious work at the Foundation, while he spent time in the country trying to work out exactly how their future would look.

Before he could change his mind he turned

and strode from his study, ready to make the arrangements that would separate him from his wife, at least in the short term.

'Have you seen Lady Sedgewick?' he asked Parker as he descended the stairs.

'She's walked into the village, my lord. Left rather abruptly.'

'In this weather?' It was bitterly cold outside and the clouds were gathering faster than Oliver liked. He could understand her desire to clear her head, but it was the start of winter and in her condition she shouldn't be out on her own.

'Shall I ask the grooms to ready your horse?'

'Yes, please.' Oliver paused, thinking of Lucy's safety when he caught up with her. 'And perhaps get the carriage sent on behind to transport Lady Sedgewick home.' He didn't want her riding in her condition.

'Very good.'

Just as he left the warmth of the house, he wondered for a moment what she'd been thinking, but then quickly dismissed the thought. He was giving up trying to understand his wife.

An hour later, Oliver was beginning to get worried. It was only a short distance into the village, barely fifteen minutes by foot and less than half that on horseback. He'd expected to see Lucy ambling down the High Street, perhaps browsing a few shop windows. When he hadn't spotted her in the street he'd wondered if she'd entered one of the few shops that were dotted throughout the village. He'd dismounted, leading his horse so he could peer into the shops as he passed, but still there was no sign of Lucy.

After two laps of the village Oliver felt the panic start to take over him. Perhaps he'd missed her on the ride in. She could be lying in a road-side ditch, injured and alone, and he'd ridden straight past her. Before deciding to retrace his steps he headed for the village inn, an ancient establishment frequented by most of the villagers on the colder winter evenings. Even today it was busy with the lunchtime trade, mainly older men setting the world to rights over a glass of ale and whatever was on the menu for lunch.

Oliver pushed his way inside, the villagers making a path from him, the men doffing their hats as they caught his eye.

'I'm looking for my wife,' Oliver said as he reached the bar.

The landlord, a man by the name of Black, stopped what he was doing and looked at Oliver with concern. There had been rumours throughout the village when Lucy had disappeared a year ago—the servants from Sedgewick Place were mainly local and they'd talked to family members and friends. The result of which was the entire village knowing at least the bare bones of the story of Lucy's disappearance. The news that she was back would have circulated among the locals already, but Oliver couldn't worry about adding fuel to the rumours. The villagers could think anything they liked as long as he found Lucy safe and unharmed.

'Lady Sedgewick?' Mr Black asked, frowning. He stopped polishing the glass in his hands, giving Oliver his full attention.

'We arrived yesterday. She came into the village to do a little shopping and I can't seem to find her.'

'I haven't seen her in here, my lord,' Mr Black said, lowering his voice deferentially.

Oliver nodded his thanks. It had always been unlikely for Lucy to have entered the Green Man unaccompanied, but at least now he knew for sure and could look elsewhere.

Just as he was winding his way back through the crowds, one of the older men of the village caught him by the arm.

'Sorry to accost you, my lord, but I overheard your question about your wife.'

'Have you seen her?' Oliver asked.

'Pretty young thing with blonde hair and a blue dress?'

Oliver nodded. It was a good description of Lucy from someone who didn't know her well.

'There was a young lady getting on the coach to London half an hour ago. She looked too well dressed to be one of the normal customers.'

'You're sure she got on the coach?' Oliver asked, his heart sinking.

'Watched it leave and she was by the window.'

'Thank you,' Oliver said, shaking the man by the hand, then quickly exiting the inn. Once outside, he took deep gulps of air, trying to still the spinning of his head.

Surely the old man had been wrong. He'd said they should spend some time apart, but he hadn't meant for her to take the public coach not an hour later. His plan had been to safely transport her back to his London house; had he not made that clear? A wave of panic overtook him. She'd disappeared again. Right now she would be halfway back to London and once there she could go anywhere. He'd wanted space, wanted time apart, but he'd never meant for her to disappear completely.

Vaulting on to his horse, he galloped out of the village at top speed, only to rein the animal in once they were a few hundred feet down the road.

'Enough,' he said to himself. 'You can't keep doing this.'

Slowly, hating the sinking feeling inside his gut, he turned his horse around and slackened his grip on the reins, allowing the stallion to pick his own speed as they worked their way back towards the village.

He wasn't going to chase her again. He told himself he knew where she was headed. In the first instance she would retreat to St Giles and surround herself with people she knew and felt comfortable with. In a couple of days he would have worked out how best to suggest they move forward with their lives, but right now he needed to work out what he wanted and what he was willing to compromise on.

Chapter Twenty-Four

'Stupid, stupid girl,' she murmured as she alighted the coach at Charing Cross, chilled to her very core and feeling decidedly foolish.

The long coach ride to London had given her time to think and time to dwell on her actions and now she was regretting them with every passing minute. Why hadn't she unpacked the bag when she had decided to stay? Why hadn't she tried harder to convince Oliver that she wasn't going to run again? Foolish, that was what she'd been, and now she was wishing she could be back in their bedroom in Sedgewick Place, finding the words to convince Oliver she wouldn't run away with their child again.

Lucy was stunned he'd sent her away. Perhaps he hadn't meant for her to catch the public coach back to London, but the end result was the same. He wanted time away from her, time to work out how they would move on from the mess that was their marriage.

Walking briskly up Charing Cross Road, she headed for St Giles. It was the first place Oliver might think to come looking for her and she didn't want to make it hard for him to find her.

'Lucy?' Mary called, leaning out of one of the upstairs windows as Lucy entered the inner courtyard of the Foundation.

It was late and most of the residents were in their rooms, so Lucy was able to make her way upstairs without anyone else seeing her. Once on the landing, Mary's door opened and the older woman ushered her inside.

'What on earth are you doing back here?' Mary asked. 'I thought you went to Sussex yesterday.'

'I did, we did,' Lucy said, fighting the urge to burst into tears.

'Come, sit down. I'll make us a nice cup of tea and you can tell me all about it.'

Sitting in her usual fireside chair, Lucy edged closer to the flames to warm her frozen fingers by the fire. She'd left in such haste that she hadn't been appropriately clothed for the chilly November weather and the coach to London had been draughty and uncomfortable. As the warmth slowly seeped back into her body she began to feel the muscle aches in her shoulders and back from holding herself so tense over the last few hours.

'Tell me what happened,' Mary instructed as she placed the cup of tea in Lucy's hands.

'It's over, Mary. My marriage is over.'

'Come now,' Mary said, 'surely it can't be as bad as all that.'

Morosely Lucy nodded—it was as bad as all that. The more she thought about her relationship with Oliver, the more she couldn't see a way out of their current predicament.

'Start at the beginning,' Mary instructed, her voice soft but firm, and Lucy found herself obeying.

'I'm pregnant,' Lucy said. 'At least I'm reasonably sure I am.'

'And I take it congratulations would be a little premature,' Mary said cautiously.

'I never thought I'd have another child, not after David. I'm not sure my heart can take any more heartbreak.'

'This child will likely be healthy,' Mary said, echoing the words Oliver had spoken to her on so many occasions.

'But what if he's not?'

'You can't go through life thinking like that, Lucy dear. Bad things don't always happen.

Many, many children are born healthy and happy every single day and there is no reason to believe that you would have another child who did not thrive.'

'I'm so scared,' Lucy said, not able to meet the other woman's eye as she admitted her innermost feelings. 'I feel panicked every time I think about this baby—I worry they might suffer and I'll be the one who's brought them into this world.'

'Of course you're scared. It's natural after everything you've been through, but we can't let ourselves be governed by our fears. You have a baby growing inside you and there is nothing that can be done about it. Now you have to be strong—you have to be that child's mother even though it hasn't been born yet.'

'I am its mother,' Lucy murmured, as if only just realising it.

Mary was right, there was nothing to be done now. In seven to eight months she would give birth to a baby who would need love and care, but the love and care didn't start when she gave birth—it started now. Looking down and placing a gentle hand on her abdomen, she tried to picture the baby that was growing inside her, but found it impossible.

'I feel so guilty,' she whispered.

'Worrying you might love another child as much as you did David?'

Wordlessly Lucy nodded. It was one of her greatest fears. She had promised her young son no one would ever replace him in her heart.

'You will love it as much as you did David,' Mary said, reaching across and squeezing Lucy's hand. 'Of course you will. This baby will be as much your child as David was. You can't feel guilty for loving another.' She paused, as if thinking. 'Just think, if David were still alive and you were pregnant again, would you worry about giving the second child as much of your heart?'

Lucy shook her head.

'Then you can't worry now.'

'I've been so foolish, Mary.'

'Sometimes we act in ways we regret when our hearts and our heads are all in a muddle.'

'I told Oliver about the baby.'

'How did he react?'

'Not well.' Lucy thought back to the forced smile and the way he'd quickly left the room after she'd told him the news. She'd expected him to be wary, but not as reticent as he had been.

'You have to remember he lost a child, too.'

'I know,' Lucy said, running a hand through her hair. It was a fact she did sometimes lose sight of. Oliver might not have been there in those first weeks of David's life, but he had been the young boy's father.

'Every uncertainty you have, every worry, he will have, too.'

Nodding, Lucy realised she had never tried to see things from Oliver's perspective. She'd apologised for her behaviour, for running and never contacting him to let him know what had happened, but she hadn't ever really considered how it might have affected him.

'He wants us to spend some time apart,' Lucy said quietly.

She couldn't tell Mary that when he'd uttered those words it had felt as though her heart was breaking. Despite her fears and her worries, she'd wanted him to fold her in his arms and tell her everything would work out.

'And you don't want that?'

'Yes, no… I don't know.'

'Lucy dearest, you need to work out what you want. No wonder your husband is on edge all the time. You tell him you want to be independent, a life of your own, and then you get upset when he suggests time apart. You need to start admitting to yourself how you truly feel about this marriage.'

Mary had never held back on her opinion, it was one of the things Lucy loved best about her dearest friend, but right now she didn't know what to say to her.

'I'm scared,' she admitted.

'About the baby?'

'Not just the baby. I'm scared about losing myself.'

'You think if you fight to be Lord Sedgewick's wife, you'll have to give up the other parts of you?'

Lucy nodded.

'Our characters and needs are always evolving, dear. Next year you will be a different person to who you are today. The key is to be satisfied with the decisions you make today and not worry too much about the future.'

'It probably is out of my hands anyway,' Lucy said. She remembered Oliver's face when he'd seen the bag on the bed beside her. The trust between them had been fragile before that; now it was shattered into a million pieces. She doubted any decisions about her future were hers to make.

Lucy slept fitfully, missing her husband's presence next to her and almost falling out of the narrow single bed in her room at the Foundation, so used to the larger four-poster she shared at Sedgewick House with Oliver.

The morning dawned, dull and grey, and still

Lucy was plagued with regret and anger. She half-hoped Oliver would come crashing through her door, demanding she return home, much like he had when he'd first found her months ago as she was walking to St Giles from Russell Square. Of course the door remained firmly shut and there was no pounding of feet on the stairs. This couldn't be that easy.

Rising, Lucy washed her face with the cold water from the night before and dressed quickly. She was unsure what to do with herself. Too distracted to take up her normal activities, too proud to find a coach straight back to Sussex. She wouldn't beg her husband not to send her away. Even though it felt like a dagger through her heart every time, she wondered if she'd ruined things between them for good. She had been so focused on this pregnancy, so worried about what might happen if they had another child, she hadn't allowed herself time to realise how happy she'd been. Her relationship with Oliver was more than she'd ever hoped for—he cared for her deeply, probably had loved her before she'd ruined everything. And she was beginning to wonder if she might love him.

It would explain why everything was so painful now. Why she felt like her heart was breaking every time she pictured her husband's face.

After spending fifteen minutes pacing round her small room, she flung open her door and marched into the corridor, determined to find some task to keep her busy.

Downstairs in the courtyard there was a commotion and she could hear the children chattering excitedly. Most were on their way to their morning lessons, but had obviously got waylaid by something novel happening in the open space. For a moment hope soared in Lucy's heart and she half-expected to see Oliver's tall, lean form striding across the cobbles towards her. In that instant she was ready to promise him the world, to promise him that she would give up everything but being his wife and the mother to his child. Then fear gripped her and she slowed.

Of course it wasn't her husband. Instead of Oliver was a man dressed in black, holding on to his reins with an air of detachment as the children gathered round his horse, some bolder than others, reaching out to touch the placid animal. The side gate was open, the double panels of wood thrown back to allow the messenger to enter, and Lucy couldn't remember the last time there had been a horse admitted to the courtyard. No wonder the children seemed frantic with excitement.

'Lady Sedgewick,' the messenger called,

catching Lucy's eye. 'I have a message for Lady Sedgewick.'

'I am Lady Sedgewick.'

The man reached into his breast pocket and withdrew a small envelope, closed with a waxen seal that Lucy immediately recognised as the Sedgewick coat of arms. It was a letter from Oliver. Her heart sinking, she realised he wasn't coming himself to see her, instead he'd sent a messenger with a letter.

'Thank you.'

After giving the messenger a coin for his troubles, although no doubt he'd already been paid handsomely by Oliver to ride through the night, Lucy shooed the children on their way and watched as the man remounted his horse and led him out of the side-gated entrance. Only when he had disappeared completely and she'd secured the gate again did she turn on her heel and quickly hurry back up the stairs.

Once in her bedroom, the door firmly locked so there would be no interruptions, Lucy turned the letter over a few times in her hands. The outside was addressed formally to *'Lady Sedgewick'* and Lucy wondered if the contents of the letter itself would be so formal.

With shaking hands she broke the seal and opened the thick, folded paper.

Dear Lucy,
I do not expect anything of you, but for the
sake of our unborn child I will be await-
ing you a week today at Sedgewick House.
    Please do not disappoint me.
Yours,
Oliver

Tears flooded her eyes and spilled out over her
cheeks. She'd done this, by breaking his trust.
Oliver loved her, she was sure of it. She could see
it in the way he looked at her, from everything he
did for her, and now she'd turned that love into
something cold and unfeeling.

The tears lasted for well over ten minutes and
it was only by conscious effort that she managed
to stop her shoulders from heaving and the salty
water spilling down her cheeks. Right now she
needed to decide what she wanted and then she
needed to act.

Mary was right—she needed to work out what
she wanted from her life. For so long she had
been someone's daughter, someone's wife. It was
only the past year she'd felt free. But was that
really a good enough reason to throw away the
love of a good man? A man she thought perhaps
she might love in return.

Then there was their unborn child to think of.

She was pregnant now; there was no going back. In a few months she would be a mother again and Oliver a father. Either they could reconcile with the idea of having a child, no matter what difficulties they might face, or they could try to deny it was happening, but a baby would arrive all the same.

Shaking her head, she fought back another bout of tears. It wasn't just about the pregnancy—there was their marriage to consider. Her husband, the man who had refused to let her go even after a year of searching, was a good man. She knew that, just as she knew she *couldn't* lose him, not now. Not now she was realising the depth of her feelings for Oliver.

He made her smile every time she thought of him and deep inside there was a warm glow when she pictured their future together. After all her protestations, all her awkwardness, she wanted to be Lady Sedgewick, wife of Lord Sedgewick, in every way possible. She loved him and she had never once told him, had always been intent on pushing him away.

'I *can't* do this without you,' she said, running her fingers over the dried ink of the note. Despite her doubts and her insecurities, she realised she didn't want to do any of this without Oliver, not the pregnancy or parenthood, or indeed the rest of her life.

'Will you forgive me?' she murmured, picturing Oliver sitting at his desk penning the note.

Despite Mary's assurances that Oliver would eventually forgive her for abandoning him again, Lucy was afraid he might not. Love was wonderful, but it couldn't paste over such a terrible breakdown of trust. She knew, deep down, that Oliver had still not forgiven her for running away a year ago and she wasn't sure if he would ever be able to. If he couldn't, their relationship could never flourish and they would be doomed to spend their lives apart. Lucy knew this, but she was determined to do everything she could to reconcile—even if it meant spending the next ten years proving she was worthy of his trust again.

Chapter Twenty-Five

'You're going to give her another chance?' Red-moor asked, looking at Oliver with incredulity in his eyes over his glass of whisky. They were sitting in comfortable armchairs by a roaring fire, with a bevy of staff to see to their every need. Oliver wasn't a frequent attendee at Boo-dle's, where he was a member, but on an evening like tonight he appreciated the fine alcohol and friendly company.

He shook his head. 'I just want to talk to her about the future of our child.'

He'd ridden up to London the day before to ready for his meeting with his wife. Ever since her departure he'd been in a black mood, swing-ing between incredulity that she would even think about fleeing again and concern about her safety. Of course he'd made discreet enquiries and made sure she was ensconced safely back at the Foundation with the indomitable Mary looking after her, but he was still worried she might decide to disappear completely again, take off into the night leaving no trace.

'Not just about the child,' Redmoor said. 'You need to secure your own future, too.'

'There isn't much to discuss,' Oliver said with a shrug. 'We will lead separate lives. Our only connection will be our child.'

'And that will make you happy?' Redmoor asked.

Oliver sighed. He couldn't really imagine being happy ever again. Right now his mood was black and his optimism at an all-time low. Of course he wanted a normal marriage—in fact, he wanted more than that. He wanted a union where he and his wife completely trusted one another, were open and honest and had no fear of betrayal.

No, he wanted even more than *that*. He loved Lucy; he'd loved her for a long time. Despite not wanting to admit it before, he knew he'd started to fall in love with his wife soon after their marriage, and that love had never diminished. Even now, even when he was so despairing of the future, he still loved her deeply. He wished they could be together, wished for nothing more than the woman he loved to be back in his arms planning their future together, but right now he couldn't see how that could ever happen.

'What happened?' Redmoor asked softly.

Oliver ran a hand through his hair. He'd been over it so many times in his own mind and still couldn't separate the facts from his own fears and worries.

'I found her with a packed bag, after she told me she was expecting.'

'She meant to run away again?'

'She says not, but the evidence disagrees with her.'

'And did you want her to stay?'

Opening his mouth to answer, Oliver paused and considered for a moment longer. He was afraid, he realised, and it was not a familiar sensation. Ever since Lucy had told him they were expecting another child he had begun to worry whether they would survive. The grief of losing one child was hard enough to bear; he wasn't sure what he would do if they lost another.

Added to that were the feelings of betrayal. Once again Lucy had disregarded how it would affect him and set to flee. How could he ever trust her, not knowing if she would be there when he woke up every morning?

'I love her,' he admitted for the first time aloud. 'But that's not enough.'

'It's a good foundation,' Redmoor said.

'A good foundation would be trust.'

'There can't be any trust between you until you forgive her. Completely and utterly with no reservations. You need a fresh start, if you ever want this to work.'

Redmoor rose and patted Oliver on the shoulder, leaving him to his glass of whisky and his thoughts.

A fresh start; Oliver shook his head. Impossible. He knew what Redmoor meant—if he did want their relationship to thrive he had to let go of the residual resentment and feelings of betrayal that had developed when Lucy had left a year ago. Nothing good could be built on a foundation of mistrust. But given her recent attempt to run away he didn't know if he could ever truly trust her.

He hadn't slept, not a single wink, a mixture of worry about how the day would go and early morning insomnia from one too many fortifying whiskies at the club the night before. The result was a pounding head and a dry mouth, along with a foul temper to start the day off with.

He hadn't specified a time when he'd sent the note to Lucy, but didn't try to pretend he would be able to do anything else until he had confronted her. Instead he prowled around the house, snapping at anyone who got in his way, waiting for Lucy to show up, convinced she had fled London already. Nine o'clock came and went, then ten. He'd resolved to give her until midday and then, if she still hadn't shown her face, he would take a trip to St Giles and escort her home. If she was still there, of course.

Just before eleven, there was a knock at the door. Oliver knew it was she as he was pacing up and down the hallway at the time and saw the dark blonde of her hair through the glass panel. Resisting the urge to go and throw open the door and pull her into his arms, he stepped into his study and took a seat, waiting for Parker to show her in. He steeled his face into an unreadable expression and forced himself to relax back into the chair. It wouldn't do for Lucy to see how tense and miserable he was from the very beginning.

'Lady Sedgewick, my lord,' Parker said two minutes later as he opened the door.

It was rude not to get up and it went against every deeply ingrained instinct, but he forced himself to remain seated. Lucy was left hovering, looking decidedly uncomfortable.

'Sit,' he instructed.

She did, without protest, despite it being a direct order.

'We have things to discuss.'

'Oliver…' Lucy said, his name coming out in a big gush.

He held up his hand, stopping whatever words would come next. Suddenly he didn't want to hear any apologies, he just wanted to sort out exactly what was to happen between them and then send her on her way. He knew if he faltered in the slightest he would crack. He could barely look at her without wanting to pull her into his arms and declare his love for her, but he needed to protect himself, his heart, from further heartbreak.

'We need to decide what will happen to our child.'

'What about us?' Lucy asked quietly.

'You've made it perfectly clear what you think of our relationship. I have no desire to trap you any longer in a marriage you do not wish to be in.' He took a deep breath, steeling himself for the dagger of pain that shot through his heart at his next words. 'I shall apply to Parliament to grant the divorce you're so eager for, with certain conditions, of course. I'm sure you know it will be the talk of London, but that seems a minor issue compared to everything else.'

He looked down, unable to keep up the pretence any longer. If he looked into her eyes again he would crack, break down and show her just how much she'd hurt him. He wondered if she knew that he loved her, that he would do anything for her if only he thought she would not flee and break his heart again.

'No,' she gasped, springing out of her chair and rushing over to him.

Again he held up a hand, halting her progress.

'I was wrong to try to force feelings that were never there. I understand now that you do not wish to remain married to me—you do not wish to be my wife. I will release you from that obligation.'

Divorce would involve a lot of scandal and no doubt mar the early life of their son or daughter, but he would not continue to force a relationship with someone who clearly did not want to stay. It would also involve a lot of money and a private act of Parliament. Oliver wasn't sure, but he thought you had to prove adultery before they would grant the divorce, but as heartbreaking as it was he was willing to pay some desperate chap to pretend he'd had a relationship with Lucy.

For him, he couldn't care less about the scandal. Divorcing Lucy would break him, his heart would never recover, but if it was what she wanted, he was willing to destroy himself to give her that.

'Stop,' Lucy said, finally finding her voice. 'Just stop this.'

He looked up to see the tears streaming down her cheeks and his first instinct was to reach out and try to comfort her. His arms were already outstretched before he caught himself, but Lucy didn't miss the gesture.

Ignoring his shaking head and stiff posture, she advanced towards him, only stopping when she was close enough to lean forward and kiss him softly on the lips. At first Oliver resisted, almost pushing her away, but Lucy was relentless, inviting him in with her warm lips until he felt something give in deep inside him.

'Stop this,' Lucy repeated as she pulled away. 'Let me talk.'

'I can't listen…' he said, stopping when he heard the choke in his voice.

'I've hurt you, badly and that is unforgivable,' Lucy said, perching on the arm of the chair so her body was pressed up against his. 'But this…' she motioned to his stiff posture and dark expression '…isn't helping either of us.'

A voice inside his head screamed at him to keep pushing her away, that only further heartbreak could come of allowing her to explain, but eventually he quietened it and a small flicker of hope won through. He nodded for her to continue.

'I'm sorry,' she said quietly, looking into his eyes. 'I'm sorry for so much.'

He'd never expected her to apologise quite so sincerely, but still a part of him remained suspicious. She'd apologised for running away after David was born, but that didn't stop her from ever running away again.

'I'm sorry,' she repeated. 'I'm sorry for hurting you. I'm sorry for destroying your trust. I know it will be difficult for you to ever forgive me for what I did a year ago, but I want you to know I am truly sorry.'

'We have more immediate concerns——' he said.

But Lucy interrupted. 'We don't,' she said. 'Our whole relationship, our whole future, depends on your ability to forgive me. I understand if you can't, I do…' her voice broke and she took a deep breath to compose herself '…but I am asking you to try.'

'To forgive you?'

'For running away, for taking your son away from you, for not allowing you to grieve for our boy.'

He saw the tears in her eyes and reached out slowly to take her hand. It was an instinctive gesture, a need to comfort his wife when she was so upset.

'I haven't made it easy for us to reconcile,' she continued. 'I was so worried about losing myself, losing the freedom I'd grown used to over the last year, that I didn't realise something much more important was at stake.'

'More important?'

She nodded. 'Our future. Our happiness. Together.'

He felt a surge of hope. It was the first time she had ever initiated a conversation about their future.

'But we can't move forward if you are always going to doubt me,' Lucy said. 'I know I haven't given you much reason to trust me, but I promise you I will never leave again, not unless you want me to.'

Oliver found her eyes with his own and saw the sincerity there. She truly believed she wouldn't ever run again, wouldn't ever deal with adversity by fleeing from him.

'I don't know if I can believe that,' he said quietly.

Lucy nodded, her face a picture of pain. 'I understand,' she said. 'Then perhaps we should discuss how best to move forward with our lives.'

Oliver had a sudden unwelcome image of

Lucy living independently from him, waking up in her own bed, going about her life without him by her side. It was painful and uncomfortable. He wanted his wife—it was all he'd wanted this past year—and the only thing holding him back was his own inability to forgive.

'Wait,' he said, reaching out for her hand once again.

'I love you,' Lucy said so quietly he barely heard the words. 'I want to be your wife, I want to raise this child with you, whatever challenges we might face.'

'You love me?'

She nodded. 'And I know you love me.'

It was hard to deny, despite him trying for the past year. He'd fallen in love with his wife and loved her all the time he'd searched for her. Oliver knew that now, but he'd never expected Lucy to love him in return. His heart soared and he wondered if this could truly work.

'All I have to do is forgive you,' Oliver said, more to himself than Lucy.

'If you can.'

He thought about the year of pain, the worry, the suffering of not knowing what had become of his son. It would never go away and the grief he felt was still acute, but what was the point in holding on to the feelings of betrayal and mistrust? If he forgave Lucy, they could have a fresh start; they could build a life together with no underlying resentment or fear.

'I forgive you,' he said softly.

'Truly?'

'Truly.'

Bending down, she kissed him again and this time he pulled her on to his lap for a longer embrace.

'And if this child is born the same way as David?' Oliver asked.

'We will love the child with our whole hearts and we will be stronger together,' Lucy said.

Oliver closed his eyes, wondering if all the heartache was truly over. All he'd wanted this past year was his wife back in his arms, and of course their son. Nothing would bring David back, but at least he had Lucy.

'What do we do now?' Lucy asked.

'Let's not get a divorce,' he said with a grin on his face. 'Too much bother.'

She shook her head. 'Let's never say that word again.'

'Perhaps we could travel back to Sedgewick Place and start making plans for the future together.'

'I'd like that very much.'

He held her tightly on his lap, wondering if he

was being foolish. Could it all really be as simple as deciding he was going to forgive her and moving on? Love meant he couldn't bear to be apart from her, but he knew it wouldn't necessarily be a straightforward path.

'I'll never hurt you again,' she whispered as he pulled her closer. 'I never want to cause you any more pain.'

Oliver found that he believed her.

'I can't ever lose you,' he said, nuzzling into her neck.

'You never will.'

Epilogue

The day was bright and sunny, the streets bathed in the warm glow of autumn. It was nearly a year to the day since Oliver had first found her walking south of Russell Square, heading back to St Giles, and dragged her home to start their life again together and Lucy couldn't believe now how much she'd resisted at the time.

'This way,' she said, grabbing Oliver carefully by the arm and pulling him along a narrow alleyway. 'We don't want to be late.'

'Your mother is getting impatient with our slow and steady speed,' Oliver whispered to the little bundle cradled in his arms, loud enough to be sure Lucy could hear him.

'Your father is dawdling again, Georgina. He spends all his time staring into your eyes.'

She had to admit it was hard not to get lost in the huge dark eyes of their baby daughter. Lucy thought she was the most beautiful child in the world, although she probably was a little biased. Oliver seemed to agree with her, though. The little girl had Oliver's dark hair and huge brown eyes that were beginning to resemble Lucy's. Her skin was soft and smooth and when she looked into Lucy's eyes the new mother found her heart melting.

They rounded the corner and Lucy marched up to the smartly painted black door that looked a little out of place in The Mint. A highly deprived area of Southwark, it had seemed the perfect place for Mary to open her second location for the newly renamed London Women and Children's Foundation. Lucy suspected Mary had plans to expand throughout all the largest slums of London; this was just the first step in the grand master plan.

'Come in, my dears,' Mary said as they pushed open the door, revealing a wide hallway with rickety stairs rising to the upper floors. The building had been in an awful state when Mary had bought it a few months ago, but hard work and some generous donations from their benefactors had meant she was able to fix the worst of the structural damage and spend a little on getting the new location equipped.

As yet there were no residents—Mary would

open the doors to the women and children of Southwark from tomorrow—so for now the hallways and bedrooms were silent and empty. Lucy had no doubt they would fill up soon after word got around about the new charity. There were plenty of women in Southwark who would be relieved to find someone to help them in their darkest hours.

'The guests will all start to arrive in a few minutes, but first let me have a cuddle with my goddaughter.'

Oliver handed her over and Lucy watched with affection as her closest friend cooed over the little baby. Georgina's lips twitched into what passed for a smile in a two-month-old baby. Mary had travelled down to Sussex for the christening a couple of weeks ago. It was the first time she'd left London or the Foundation in the years Lucy had known her, but nothing was too much bother for her beautiful goddaughter.

'I need you to be all lordly today,' Mary said to Oliver as she led them into what would be a communal dining room, but today was serving as a place for all the invited benefactors and governors to mingle.

'I'll try my best,' Oliver said.

'It is amazing how people are swayed into sup-

porting a cause when someone titled and important is attached to it.'

For the past nine months Oliver had given support to the Foundation whenever he could, often
just needing to lend his name to inspire others to
do the same. He'd done this willingly, but at the
same time had asked for something from Lucy in
return. She'd agreed not to go traipsing through
St Giles after the eighth month of her pregnancy,
and had happily retired to Sussex to give birth to
Georgina shortly after. They'd spent two blissful
months in the countryside, ensconced in Sedgewick Place, falling more and more in love with
their little girl every single day. Today was their
first day back in London and, although she was
nowhere near ready to step up to her previous
levels of commitment, Lucy was eager to start
getting involved with the Foundation again.

'I've brought the accounts back to London
with me,' she said to Mary as they entered the
empty dining room.

'She was doing them while in labour,' Oliver
muttered.

'You exaggerate,' Lucy said, shaking her head.
Although he wasn't, not really. She *had* insisted
on finalising the accounts for the last quarter
while getting the first few twinges that had indicated Georgina was on her way, but it had been a

good distraction, and as soon as the contractions had started properly she'd put the books away.

'What would I do without you?' Mary said affectionately.

Handing the little baby to Lucy as there was a knock on the door, Mary rushed out to greet the first of her guests.

'Now I'm going to have two slums to choose from when searching for my wife,' Oliver murmured as he looked around the room.

'I promise to leave you a note,' Lucy said, smiling down at Georgina as she wriggled in her arms.

'Perhaps I'll just have to accompany you everywhere.'

'Now that would be a hardship.' Lucy smiled, glancing at the door just as her husband leaned in to kiss her. There was no one there yet, so she allowed herself ten seconds of bliss before pulling away. 'Someone will catch us.'

'I know it's not *fashionable* to be seen to be so in love with one's wife,' Oliver whispered in her ear as Mary led the first of the guests in to the room. 'But I just can't seem to help myself.'

Before she could stop him he captured her for another quick kiss, despite the two women bustling across the room to greet them.

Her cheeks pink, Lucy didn't bother reprimanding him again. In truth, she loved it that he still couldn't keep his hands off her—even if it did lead to one or two embarrassing situations.

* * * * *

COMING SOON!

We really hope you enjoyed reading this book. If you're looking for more romance, be sure to head to the shops when new books are available on

Thursday 29th November

To see which titles are coming soon, please visit
millsandboon.co.uk

MILLS & BOON

Coming next month

A SCANDALOUS WINTER WEDDING
Marguerite Kaye

'Kirstin.'

He blinked, but she was still there, not a ghost from his past but a real woman, flesh and blood and even more beautiful than he remembered.

'Kirstin,' Cameron repeated, his shock apparent in his voice. 'What on earth are you doing here?'

'I wondered if you'd recognise me after all this time. May I come in?'

Her tone was cool. She was not at all surprised to see him. As she stepped past him into the room, and a servant appeared behind her with a tea tray, he realised that *she* must be the woman sent to him by The Procurer. Stunned, Cameron watched in silence as the tea tray was set down, reaching automatically into his pocket to tip the servant as Kirstin busied herself, warming the pot and setting out the cups. He tried to reconcile the dazzling vision before him with Mrs Collins, but the vicar's wife of his imagination had already vanished, never to be seen again.

Still quite dazed, he sat down opposite her. She had opened the tea caddy, was taking a delicate sniff of the leaves, her finely arched brows rising in what seemed to be surprised approval. Her face, framed by her bonnet, was breathtaking in its flawlessness. Alabaster skin.

Blue-black hair. Heavy-lidded eyes that were a smoky, blue-grey. A generous mouth with a full bottom lip, the colour of almost ripe raspberries.

Yet, he remembered, it had not been the perfection of her face which had drawn him to her all those years ago, it had been the intelligence slumbering beneath those heavy lids, the ironic twist to her smile when their eyes met in that crowded carriage, and that air she still exuded, of aloofness, almost haughtiness, that was both intimidating and alluring. He had suspected fire lay beneath that cool exterior, and he hadn't been disappointed.

A vision of that extraordinary night over six years ago flooded his mind. There had been other women since, though none of late, and never another night like that one. He had come to think of it as a half-remembered dream, a fantasy, the product of extreme circumstances that he would never experience again.

Continue reading
A SCANDALOUS WINTER WEDDING
Marguerite Kaye

www.millsandboon.co.uk

LET'S TALK
Romance

For exclusive extracts, competitions
and special offers, find us online: